CONTAGION THEORY

RICH RESTUCCI

SEVERED PRESS

CONTAGION THEORY

ISBN: 978-1-922551-37-5

This book is for those who can't speak for themselves. Your voice is as strong as anyone's. Unless you're Ship.

"And in those days people will seek death and will not find it. They will long to die, but death will flee from them." — Revelation 9:6 ESV

"A zombie film is not fun without a bunch of stupid people running around and observing how they fail to handle the situation." — George A. Romero

NEW BEGINNINGS
JOURNAL ENTRY 1

I popped the chili-mac bag from my MRE into the ration heater and balanced it against a broken piece of concrete. I dumped a bit of water from my water bladder into the bag as well. I glanced at my buddy, Ship. He was pointing toward one of the small packets from my MRE. He wanted the chewing gum. I hated gum in general, but the shit they packed in these MREs was astoundingly horrible. Reminded me of Chicklets, those rock-hard pieces of gum you used to get when there was a world. Chicklets mixed with cement.

I smiled, tossing him the small clear bag with a raised brow. I pointed to the drink mix bag from his MRE. Grape. Ship hated grape drink as much as I hated gum. He smiled back leaning his rifle against his shotgun and passed the drink mix to me. Ship also had two sidearms and a gigantic machete on his person.

We were both sitting with our backs against the structure edge, on the roof of a big building in the Fisherman's Wharf section of San Francisco. The building housed the Ripley's Believe it or Not Museum and an Applebee's restaurant. If I stood up, I would see the sign For Madam Tussaud's two doors down.

My entrée was ready, and I picked it up by the edges with my tactical glove so as not to burn myself. Chili-mac was alright. It was certainly better than the nothing I would have eaten instead. I dumped it into the small plastic bowl I used for all my meals, while I marveled at how hot the flameless heater had made my chili-mac. I didn't know how the heater worked, but knew it had something to do with the water.

If I had asked Ship, he would have launched into a fifteen-minute narration on the chemical properties of the heater, the exact BTUs produced, and chemical energy, and science, and science, and blah blah blah. He would have done all of that in silence, using his pen, notebook, and sign language to communicate because Ship is mute as fuck.

Twenty feet of muscle and genius packed into a seven-foot frame, this guy knew everything. Not just about MRE heaters, but also about M4 battle rifles, unit tactics, proxy servers, stealth, theoretical physics, and history. If you can think of it Ship knows more about it than you. If you can't think of it, he still knows about it. Ship is extremely handy to have around. He's huge too, and he's also my best friend.

As the chili-mac cooled (I didn't want to burn my tongue, I don't like next-day tongue-zits), I adjusted my position and dared a slow, furtive glance over the side of the building with my inspection mirror. I looked left, then right, then sighed.

The street was packed curb to curb with the living dead.

The dead are wicked killjoys and time wreckers, so I busted out this brand-new notebook and began to write.

If you're reading this, I'm probably dead. That sucks. It might be that I gave you this journal to read, but more likely you killed me and took it, or you re-killed me and took it because I was already dead, and I was trying to eat you. You're a dick if it's the first option, and thanks oodles if it's the second.

This is the beginning of a new journal, so I should probably clear a few things up for you. We're about two years into a zombie apocalypse, this you know. You also know that the apocalypse happened because these particular zombies don't bring you cookies, they eat you. There are two varieties of infected: fast and slow. You know about the slow ones; they're dead, they stink, and they're extremely durable. You know that the fast ones are alive but infected with whatever shit caused the aforementioned apocalypse. They want to eviscerate you and play jump-rope with your small intestine. You may or may not know that certain people can stand in a group of the dead ones and they won't get eaten. Nobody can figure out why this is, although there are theories. The fast ones will tear into those fortunate souls, and then they turn just like anyone else. Infected can be silent as the grave or they can make horrible sounds.

What you certainly don't know is that I've travelled the length and breadth of this infected country since the beginning of the plague. I've met some great people and some superior assholes along the way.

I was in prison before the outbreak. A convicted felon, but not of anything heinous. I didn't steal from the church, or con old folks out of their life savings. I didn't rape or kill anybody pre-plague. Post-outbreak is where I found my murder switch.

I've slain plenty of assholes who've deserved it since dead people started walking. Every one of those whom I've killed was either trying to kill me or someone I love or was trying to make killing us easier by taking our stuff.

Fuck 'em. No regrets.

I've seen a lot of the United States in the past two years. Way more than I did before the damn apocalypse. I started my journey in Boston then traveled to New Hampshire where I lived in an Airstream trailer, an A frame survivalist's house, and a church. The wilds of New Hampshire is also where I began my new family. I flew to Tennessee, flew to Mississippi, then took a boat into the Gulf where I lived on an oil rig for a while. I was kidnapped from the rig by one of those assholes I mentioned above and carted off to a secret government lab in Montana. They ran experiments on me for a while. That was fun. When that place fell to the dead, I escaped and got all the way back to the oil rig before yet another group of assholes blew it up. From there I trekked through the infected Texas scrubland to a horse ranch and stayed there for a bit. It seemed that is where my family and I were going to make a home, but more assholes came knocking, then the dead showed up, and we were forced to leave.

We appropriated a plane and flew to my current location: San Francisco. Alcatraz Island, actually. That's where I keep my stuff now.

I was never really in the habit of picking up strays, but it seems I am a magnet for great people. It must be because I'm so cool. The giant smarty-pants who is currently chewing ridiculously loudly for a man who can move so quietly, (I just showed that last line to Ship, and he gave me the stink eye) is my best pal. I know I wrote that up above, but it bears reiteration.

Kat, a 19-year-old woman who I consider a sister, and Ship are my oldest friends. Going on two years. Kat is one of our snipers, and you really don't want to piss her off.

Speaking of people you don't want to piss off; Donna is my apocalypse-wife. I met her on the oil rig, and now she can't get rid of me. She keeps me in my place and emasculates me in front of the boys as every good woman should. She's also an extremely capable medic and has stitched up pretty much everybody I know at least once.

I was fortunate enough to find two little brats during a sojourn in Utah and they have proven more than just useful. Richy and Chloe, now about fifteen years old, are my kids. They can do anything, and they never complain. I was lucky to come across them.

I met Alvarez, a skilled army guy, in Tennessee. He's one of the three guys I always want to be on mission with. He and Kat are an item now, and she keeps him alive.

Then there's Remo. Remo is MARSOC, which loosely translated means: Don't Fuck With Me. MARSOC sounds better than DFWM, which is probably why Marine Special Operations Command chose it as their acronym. Remo is a killer. A dyed-in-the-wool badass who has proven time and again that no situation is impossible. He is both tactical and taciturn.

In our group of adults:

Donna is the medic.

Kat shoots stuff half a mile off.

Ship is the genius.

Alvarez is the cool-headed one.

Remo is the badass.

I am the dumbass.

But I have other qualities. Good ones. Most important of which is: I'm immune.

As you know, whenever a human being is bitten, or sometimes scratched by an infected, they become infected and will die within a day. Everyone, absolutely everyone who is bitten by an undead, dies and turns into one of them. If you get scratched or bitten by one of the Runners, you'll suffer the same fate. Everyone dies.

Except me.

I've been bitten a few times now and have yet to shuffle loose the old mortal coil as it were. I contract the disease, I get sick, and then my body tells it to fuck off. I'm right as rain in a couple of days at most. There have been certain... side-effects, but they've been mostly beneficial up to now.

I did a stint in an underground lab where doctors and military scientists studied me, and they couldn't find anything different between me and anyone else. Not only that, but they couldn't find any type of virus or fungus or bacteria in any of the infected or their fluids. The reason they can't find any diseases is because this zombie plague isn't your garden-variety sickness. It's a damn computer virus that has affected human hosts. Now, I gotta tell you: that last sentence looks as stupid to me as it does to you. Seriously, this is what I've been told. It makes sense too, considering the amount of tests done on me and other infected and the fact that the smartest doctors on the planet are stumped.

Whatever. Old news.

So, you're more-or-less caught up on the apocalypse, my friends, my immunity, and where I hang my hat.

I finished the chili-mac (which was delicious) and took another peek over the edge of the building again. I sighed and shrugged at Ship. The rest of our merry band was in the building below us, securing it from both the dead and the living. Ship and I were the lookouts. Probably should have led with that, but I didn't.

Remo and Alvarez were clearing the building along with four other people I had just met. Normally, I wouldn't have agreed to go on a mission with strangers, but these were tough times. More importantly, a guy named Dallas who I met in Montana has vetted everyone in my fire-team that I didn't know. I trust Dallas with my life, ergo, I trust these other guys. Well, three guys and a girl. We substituted our medic for one of theirs. A girl named Anna, and she's super smart and nice. Seyfert; a Navy SEAL, Sergeant Dan (Lieutenant Dan would have been way better); I dunno if he's army or Marines, and Kevin Murphy, who everybody calls Kev; a cop formerly of SFPD and from what I hear a full time fucking legend, are the other three guys, and they seem capable. Seyfert traveled with Dallas across the country to aid in the search for a cure. I also traveled across the country and know how difficult that is. If this guy did it too, then he's aces in my book. I trust them. The coolest thing is that I'm part of *fire-team*. That is undeniably fucking awesome. Have you ever been part of a fire-team? No?

I win.

I just realized that this is the first time I've ever sought out murder. The first time I've gone on a mission looking to kill human beings. There was a side mission back in a little town in Montana where my MARSOC buddies killed a bunch of evil bikers, but I was basically just along for the ride on that one. Truth be told, I rode a jail cell bench and had to have my ass saved, but let's move on.

This mission is a search and destroy for a group of douches that are killing living people in San Francisco. Another type of gang. They've launched several unsuccessful attacks on Alcatraz, but there have still been friendly casualties. The military leader of Alcatraz, a guy named McInerney, has had enough, and he wants heads. McInerney is the captain of the submarine that's parked off Alcatraz.

Both Remo and Alvarez called him Captain, so he's gotta be the captain of the sub, right? Come to think of it, I don't know the name of the sub, but I will find out in a few minutes.

Anyway, the reason the street is full of infected is that they must have either heard or seen us come ashore in our Zodiac inflatable boats. The boat motors are really quiet, but the dead have nothing else to listen to. The dumb things know they heard a noise, but they don't know what it means, and anything that is outside the normal ambient sounds of the city bears investigation from the dead. The things tend to flock together as well, so there's a shit-ton of them right outside the door.

It was dark when we got here, but the sun has since come up. That was how I was able to see both the dead in the street, and that the handle on the door thirty feet away had begun to turn slowly. Ship and I glanced at each other, then trained our rifles at the door. Alvarez and one of the Alcatraz guys, Seyfert, stepped onto the gravel of the roof, and we moved from seated to crouched, lowering our weapons. We kept low as we moved over to our friends to get a SITREP. That means Situation Report, or in layman's terms, a quick discussion on what the hell is happening.

"Building is clear," Seyfert told us, "but we've attracted a shit-ton of limas."

Lima-Deltas are the Alcatraz term for living dead. I just call 'em pus bags.

"Gotta be sixty of them out there," Alvarez added.

Ship scribbled something in his book and passed it to Alvarez, who read it softly.

"Sixty-eight of the dead are outside the front door. More could have come or some could have left since my last count."

"Right," continued Seyfert. "That's a few too many to contend with if we want to save our ammo for breathers. We'll set up here and wait for them to fuck off, then we'll head into the city."

We all put the middle and ring fingers of our right hands to our ears. A call was coming in from Alcatraz. *Sabre, this is Rock, how copy, over?*

Seyfert spoke softly into his microphone, "Rock, Sabre Actual. Five by five, over."

Sabre, be advised, Reaper One has a large group of limas near your position, over.

"Roger that, Rock. Sabre is aware. We counted sixty-eight."

Negative, Sabre. Reaper One counts over two hundred inbound from your east.

Dear Reader, one of the things I always mention in my journals is that every time any type of military guys are on any type of communication device, they always say *over* when they're done talking. I'm done writing it, so I hope you've caught on.

"Sabre copies all. We'll be on our toes."

Seyfert indicated we should follow him, and we shifted our position to the northeast corner of the building. We couldn't see shit other than some abandoned vehicles and a few unmoving skeletons dressed in rags on the street behind us.

The SEAL brought the mic back to his face, "Rock, that's a negative sight picture on the horde from our position."

I shook my head and leaned toward Ship so only he could hear me. "He sounds like Remo. Why couldn't he just say, 'We can't fuk'n see them.'"

Stink eye from Ship, so I shut up. Seyfert went back and forth with the radio guy from Alcatraz a few more times before we heard the swarm coming. I don't know if it's the same for everybody else, but for me, when I hear the sounds of those things, I experience an instant feeling of dread. Two years into this little apocalypse thingy, and you would think I'd be used to the sounds the dead make, but nope. They still creep me out.

Ship pointed down the road and handed me the binoculars. I sighed. "Here they come."

The first ranks of the gray things shuffled into view down Jefferson St. They came around the corner with the CVS on it and streamed right at us. It was a wall of gray in a sea of rot.

Now, two hundred may not sound like a lot to you if you've seen some of the swarms out there, but when you're on a roof with nowhere to really escape to, two hundred is two hundred too many.

The good thing is that we were positively bursting with ammo, and everybody knew how to shoot.

The noises the things make were way louder now that they were closer, and our mini-swarm of seventy moved toward their bigger swarm. It was funny to watch because both groups thought the other was food and they picked up a little speed until they realized that everybody was already dead. What wasn't at all funny was when the merged groups both headed back in our direction.

"You seeing this?" came through our radios. It was Kev from inside the building. He must have been looking out a window at the oncoming swarm.

It was me. It was always me. If I hadn't been there, those damn infected would have either turned around and headed to parts unknown, or they would have been carrying boxes of cookies to share.

I looked up at the sky wondering if God really did have it out for me. I noticed something pass by very high in the air and remembered the Reaper. The Reaper is a drone launched from a crude runway the sub dudes had built somewhere they wouldn't tell me. It had a shit-ton of armament for such a little aircraft, and it could give accurate camera readings on the ridges of a dime a mile away. There was a control room for the Reaper on the sub, but that was all I knew. Something else I knew was that zombies chase anything they see or hear.

"Seyfert," I whispered. "Can we have the Reaper fly low?"

The SEAL shook his head. "The swarm is too close. The bombs could damage this building or even kill us outright."

"Yeah, but what if it didn't drop any?" He looked at me funny, so I continued. "What if we used the Reaper as a distraction? Have it fly low and away from us, and maybe the pus bags will follow it?" I shrugged and searched the faces of the others up on the roof with me, looking for agreement. They all shrugged too.

Seyfert made a call, and soon enough the little plane was buzzing past us fifty feet over the heads of the infected in the street. Like a flock of birds, they all turned and gave a pathetic chase after something they couldn't possibly catch in the vain hope that they could eat it.

Fucking idiots.

The most important thing was that they were all stumbling away from us. I felt pretty proud of myself right then and I smiled a giant face-splitter.

"Not bad," Seyfert said and nodded.

In twenty minutes, the horde had moved off to the east, the last of them rounding the corner by the CVS. We moved as a group down into the building, meeting up with our other team members. Standing in front of the glass windows of the Applebee's restaurant, I was immediately filled with dread. I usually liked a bit more than a quarter inch of glass between me and a continent full of insatiable, carnivorous undead. Remo offered me a toothpick and I accepted it, opening the cellophane immediately and popping the fang-splinter in my yap.

I felt a little pain in my arm and rubbed the bandage there. Although mostly healed, the last bite I had received from an infected had been bad and it still bothered me on occasion. Remo noticed me rubbing the injury and raised his eyebrows in question.

"I'm good," I told him. "This place was totally clear?"

"More or less." He pointed behind me. Half under one of the tables was the desiccated corpse of a woman. The disposition of her body, and the headwound she possessed indicated she had taken her own life a long time ago, probably at the start of the outbreak. With all the death and carnage I had seen since the world fell apart, you would think I was used to seeing such horrors, but they still plagued me. If I had seen this poor woman in such a state five years ago, my chili-mac would have threatened to come back up. Now I just felt sad for her. I hope I never lose that sadness, I think it makes me a better man.

"There's one in the walk-in freezer," Danny told me. "We can hear it banging around in there, but it can't get out." He jostled a fat shotgun-looking weapon slung on his back to get more comfortable. I didn't know what it was. I would have to ask one of my guys, so I wouldn't look like an idiot to the new folks.

Seyfert spread a picture out on one of the tables, and we gathered around it. The photo was incredibly detailed and was actually a map. "Intel puts the hostile breathers in this area." The SEAL indicated an area of the city, drawing a circle around it with his finger. It was an area north of Rincon Park, near the old Ferry Building Marketplace. It was a little less than a mile and a half from where we stood.

Seyfert drew his finger down a red line already on the map. "The Captain wants this shit done most ricky-tick, so I think we should follow this route." He looked up, his eyes darting to each of us questioningly. "Anybody got a better idea?"

The route looked as good to me as any other, so I kept my teeth together.

He rolled his map up and stuck it in his pack. "Let's move out."

LESSONS LEARNED
ALCATRAZ

"If you step here instead," Chloe told Kyle, "you'll be able to untwist and deliver a much stronger strike. Don't forget to use your hips."

The young girl demonstrated her technique by moving the boy's foot to a different spot on the floor. She took up the same position copying his stance, then unwound with her hips, giving a vicious palm heel strike to the air. The boy copied her and smiled.

"That's awesome!"

Richy nodded, pointing to Kyle's feet. "Great positioning. See where your knee is now? If you've done the first part of the technique right, you're primed to raise it into your attacker's face." Richy smiled and looked around the room. "Light's out. Your attacker should be all done."

A group of eight children ranging from seven to seventeen years old all nodded.

"But," he added, lifting his index finger skyward, "you may not want to finish this technique when confronting the undead." He put his hands on his hips and asked the room, "Why?"

A nine-year old girl raised her hand.

Chloe pointed at the girl, "Sam?"

Sam hesitated only slightly, "Cuz you might hit the rotter in the mouth with your knee."

Richy and Chloe both bowed to her. "Correct," rewarded Chloe. "All of the techniques we teach you in this class will have two variations; one for human targets, and one for the dead. You never want to hit the dead in the mouth or present a target for their teeth. You need to tailor your strikes and your position recognition to the attacker. Got it?"

All the kids nodded.

"Line up!" Chloe shouted.

All the kids lined up in facing Richy and Chloe. Richy held up his right fist. "This is for the what?"

"The Warrior," all the kids chimed in unison.

Chloe had mimicked her brother's hand motion and raised her left hand such that the palm was six inches from the knuckles of her right fist. "And this is for the what?"

10

The children answered together again, "The Scholar."

Everybody bowed their heads, placing the fist and the palm together, closing the fingers over the top of the fist. They all remained silent for a few seconds.

"Get out of here!" Richy growled and two smaller boys giggled. All the kids milled off as a few parents and some other adults clapped.

Chloe, Richy, Kyle, and Vanessa remained behind to talk. They had become fast friends as all four of them were new to Alcatraz. The zone they had created for their training was in a corner of the former inmate recreation yard.

Sam approached the four kids with her father, Rick. "That was some neat stuff you guys were teaching," he told them. "I wish I had taken karate when I was a kid.

Richy cut a wry smile, "Did someone tell you that you couldn't train now?"

Rick was confused, "Huh?"

"Why don't you join us for the next class? We can teach you some stuff, but you could really learn a lot from Remo when he gets back."

"I saw him kill a guy with a toothpick," Chloe said absentmindedly. She looked around at everyone, embarrassed that she had divulged that information.

"Umm...yeah, well I might just come in for a class. You guys wouldn't mind?"

Chloe smiled too. "We'd love to have you."

Sam beamed. She and her dad talked as they trod across the dust of the yard.

When the four of them were alone, the teenagers began to talk about Alcatraz. For a kid with no true guardians, the island was a virtual paradise of places to discover and now that the adults had left, they focused on the next area to explore.

"This place was a fort before it was a prison," Chloe told them.

"And how in the nine hells do you know that?" Richy asked.

"Books, dumbass. The first thing I did when we got out of quarantine was hit the giftshop. Almost nobody had been in there yet, and there are tons of books."

Vanessa giggled and punched Richy in the arm. The boy held up one fist, "I vil keel you. So, what if this was a fort?" he added.

She cocked an eyebrow and gave him a sideways glance. "Forts mean tunnels."

"Oooh!" Vanessa exclaimed. "We going on an adventure?"

The exercise yard wasn't exactly full of people, but it certainly wasn't empty. A small group of adults was using a few tools to assess some possible farmland. The kids talked as they moved toward the far wall. A white-haired man entered the yard through a rusty doorway. He noticed the group of four youngsters and altered his course to intercept. Richy gave the guy a casual glance, but he didn't recognize the man. There were plenty of people he hadn't met yet, so he didn't give it a second thought. The old timer was probably going to lecture them on how they shouldn't be alone.

"We should try under the power house," Chloe told her friends. "I bet there's some cool stuff down there."

Kyle crinkled his brow in thought. "Yeah, but won't everybody tell us that area is off-limits? I mean we could get a skinned knee or something."

The other three kids scoffed. Since they had arrived, the adults on the island, including the ones the kids had come in with, had become annoyingly overprotective. *Can't do this, can't go here, don't go to the bathroom without an adult.* The teenagers thought that the end of the world would mean more freedom, not less. They had only been allowed to be in the yard right now because there were already adults here and the self-defense class had adults watching.

The man was about forty feet away when Richy leaned in to the group, speaking in a low voice, "This guy is probably gonna tell us we should have an adult with us." The kids snickered, except Vanessa, who stopped in her tracks.

"Wait."

The other three turned to regard her and she pointed at the man coming at them.

She squinted, then pointed. "He looks wrong."

The others faced the older man. He shuffled like one of the dead, but he didn't appear to have a scratch on him. All four kids drew their knives simultaneously.

"Get behind me," Richy told them and Chloe laughed out loud.

"Yeah, like that's gonna happen. Vanessa, run over and tell them we got a dead guy in here." Chloe pointed at the farming group of six men and women to the left. Vanessa took off at full speed, the man altering his course for a moment, then refocusing on the three left behind.

Vanessa began to shout and wave her arms, the adults immediately searching for the problem.

As he closed, the kids could tell that the man was indeed dead. His eyes were the blood-red color of one of the infected and he had begun the all-too familiar rasping hack.

Kyle was the tallest of the three and the thing focused on him. The adults sprinted toward the kids shouting and telling them to run, but they stood their ground.

"I'm the bait, you two take it out," Kyle said. Richy moved left and Chloe right. The thing's eyes switched from kid to kid for a moment before returning focus on Kyle, who began to back up slowly. The dead man reached out one arm and drooled as he opened his mouth to growl. Chloe darted in, giving a vicious side kick to the creature's knee. There was an audible snap, but before it could fall, Richy dropped to his hands and swept the thing's remaining leg out from under it with a sweeping kick. The dead thing hit the ground hard, Chloe stabbing it through the left eye with her combat dagger.

The two kids stood as the adults and Vanessa rushed up to them. One of the smaller men put his hand down hard on Richy's shoulder and spun him around. He wagged his finger In Richy's face and began to yell at the boy, "The next time you're told to—"

In one motion Richy, who was half the weight of this man, twisted the guy's hand off his shoulder and brought the man's arm up high in a wrist-lock.

"Ow!" the man shouted, completely helpless.

Richy let him go. "Yeah, why don't you try touching me again? See what happens."

"What the hell is going on here?" Donna, one of the newcomers to Alcatraz asked. She had run up to the group with Juanita, one of the teachers on the island. They both looked at the re-killed zombie, then back at the kids.

"We killed that," Chloe pointed at the thing on the ground, "Then Richy almost killed him."

"Mr. Martingale, are you ok?" Donna reached down to help the man up, but he brushed her off in anger. "I'm fine!" he spat. He stood and stormed away rubbing his wrist.

Donna stood at the forefront of the small group of adults. She pointed her finger at the twins, "Explain!"

Both Richy and Chloe had been through hell. They had lost their family, hid out in an attic for a year while infected roamed inside and outside their home, been scooped up by a group of military, and carted halfway across the country. They had been attacked by mercenaries and countless undead. While all that was some scary stuff, it paled in comparison to a pissed-off Donna. She was their apocalypse mom and brooked no bullshit.

Richy shrugged, "He put his hand on me."

Her eyebrows shot skyward. "So, you tried to rip it off?"

"No, I just put him in a wrist-lock that Remo showed me. He was never in any danger."

"Did it work?"

The kids didn't know what she was asking, and she could tell. She rolled her eyes. "The wrist-lock, did it work?"

"Well, yeah."

She strained her chin high to look over the group of kids and adults. Martingale had just exited using the entryway on the far side of the yard.

"Good. He's a prick." She immediately covered her mouth in embarrassment. She grew stern again re-pointing her finger at the kids. "And don't say 'prick'! Ever!"

"He is a prick, though," Juanita added. Several of the group of men nodded in agreement.

"How did it get in?" Captain McInerney asked. He didn't lift his eyes from a report he had been reading.

He was sitting at a round table in the guard's lounge at the head of the cell blocks. McInerney was flanked by Commander Pitt, the island's military liaison, while his civilian counterparts, Detective Captain Mike Meara, Alcatraz's leader and Mr. Martingale, the civilian liaison, sat in two other rickety metal chairs. Dallas and his friend Rick Barnes also sat in ancient chairs. Mismatched ceramic and plastic mugs sat on the edge of the table, some with the contents still steaming.

Richy, Chloe, Vanessa, and Kyle stood with Donna and Juanita Del Carmen, the six of them waiting patiently.

"It didn't, sir," answered Pitt. "The Lima was already on the island. It was Mr. McLeod. He must have died of natural causes."

McInerney nodded, letting loose a sigh. He opened his mouth to say something, but Martingale cut him off by standing quickly, his chair falling over behind him. "That kid is dangerous!" he almost shouted, pointing at Richy. "I came to help, and he threw me to the ground. He could have been killed! There's no place for such violence on this island."

Dallas made a face as he swallowed his coffee. He was clearly displeased with the taste. "Way I heard it, the kid did fine. It was *you* almost got killed."

There were several snickers and Martingale's face burned.

McInerney was full of sighs, and he let loose with another, "Alright, enough. Richy?"

For the first time in a long time, Richy looked scared.

"Please apologize to Mr. Martingale."

"I'm sorry, sir," Richy said without hesitation. Martingale folded his arms and scowled.

McInerney nodded and addressed the kids. "If anybody lays a hand on you again, you have my permission to tear it off."

Chloe looked away, a huge smile on her face.

"Can we get our guns back?" the boy asked. He and his sister had carried a handgun each during their travels and had been trained in their use and safety, but they weren't allowed to carry firearms on Alcatraz. "I wouldn't have wasted a bullet on one of them, but it still couldn't hurt to have our guns."

Both McInerney and Pitt smiled, "Not yet." the captain told them. "You can go," he added, nodding toward the door. They filed out. Pitt nodded in approval to the boy and the kid saw it. McInerney addressed the rest of the group, How the hell did we not know the health of Mr. McLeod?"

Commander Pitt opened his steepled hands, "We don't have the resources to watch everyone on the island at all times, sir. Mr. McLeod must have died while he was outside his cell."

Meara flipped up a page on a clipboard, "The cell block patrol report has all cell doors closed last night during lights out."

"Those kids are disrespectful and rude," Martingale blurted with a glower. "They could have been killed."

Dallas didn't look up from his cup when he asked, "Are ya pissed 'cause ya got yer butt kicked by a kid, or 'cause that kid didn't listen to you?"

McInerney pinched the bridge of his nose. "Dallas, please."

"Sorry, Kevin, but I kinda wanna know. I know the guy them kids came in with, an' he tole me that between the two of 'em, them kids killed more'n twenty of the dead ones." Dallas swiveled his head toward Martingale. "How many have you killed?"

Martingale tried to brush off the question, but now everyone was interested, "How is that important? Not listening to an adult could get those kids or all of us killed."

"I only ask because I think I'd rather have the kids backin' me up than you."

"Then I guess it's a good thing that—"

Pitt slammed his fist on the table. "Alright, stop it! Both of you! This doesn't help." He glanced sheepishly at McInerney. "Sorry, sir. Please continue."

The captain nodded. "It's fine, Commander. Now, about the lower defenses, can we shore them up with what we have on the island, or do we need to schedule another foray?"

RUN!
JOURNAL ENTRY 2

"There's six of them," Seyfert told us. He had a pair of binoculars up to his eyes, staring down the street from the second story window of a corner bodega.

He tried to pass the binoculars to Remo, but I intercepted them, flipping my buddy the bird. There were indeed six men at the end of the road. Four were loading boxes into a red pickup, with two covering them.

"That's them," Danny told us through teeth gritted in anger. "They killed my friend."

I gave Remo the binocs. "Then let's just shoot 'em." I aimed my rifle at one of the pricks guarding the others. I flicked off the safety, but Anna put her hand on my shoulder. I glanced at her, and she was smiling.

She pointed up another street, perpendicular to where the assholes were, "Look there."

A group of fifty or so dead shambled in the direction of the pickup. The dead would be on the living in a minute or so. I copied her smile.

"Good," Danny effused. "I wouldn't mind—"

He was cut off as the radio attached to Seyfert's tactical vest screeched to life. The voice was close to panic as it yelled over the airwaves, "*Saber, Rock. Danger close! Get out now! Now! Exfil to the southwest of the building! Large force of hostiles is on you!*"

Seyfert turned the knob on his radio and it shut off. We didn't have much shit to pack up, but it was done in less than fifteen seconds. We rushed to the back door and peered through the glass of the small window. Two hundred feet away was a force of undead the likes of which I hadn't seen in a long time. Thousands of the things plodded toward us, and I have no idea how we hadn't heard them until now. They filled the street from side to side, some scraping rotting bits of themselves off on the brick facades of several of the abandoned shops.

"We have twenty seconds to figure out what to do," Alvarez told us.

"Can we just stay here?" Anna asked. "Maybe they'll just move on like the last group."

"Yeah, but maybe they won't," I countered. "Then what?"

Seyfert was done hypothesizing. "We move, now!" He was out the door and on the stairs in an instant. We all followed him, taking careful consideration of how close the massive horde was. They also noticed us, and this shit was on.

We were down the rickety stairs as a group quickly. I turned to gauge the proximity of our imminent demise and was shocked to see they were way too damn close. A single form fought to get to the front of the crowd of dead. I could see its blood-red eyes from a hundred feet away. They burned twin holes into my soul and I knew what the thing wanted. It tore its way through the mob. Legs pumping, it came for us.

"Runner," I said a bit too unconcernedly.

Way too casually, veritably putting my nonconcern to shame, the extended barrel of Remo's suppressed handgun came up and he fired a single shot. The round took the sprinting horror center mass, the thing stumbling and scraping its infected face off on the asphalt. It looked up at me before I turned to run. I could see bone where it had landed on its cheek, but it didn't give a shit. The only emotions on its ruined face were a mix of hatred and rage.

Bleeding out, with a facial injury that would have debilitated a living person, this thing clawed its way toward us with a single-minded intention. It would never stop coming, even after it died. It would rise as a pus bag and start to rot, but it would still hunt the living.

As I ran after my friends, I couldn't help but feel bad for the person the Runner had been. A young man who had prospects and friends. Someone who had loved and had been loved back. This damn plague had not only taken everything from him, it had added some of its own vile shit to him, changing this twenty-five-year-old into something out of a nightmare.

Except now nightmares were a better place than real life.

Remo waited up a bit for me. He still had a bad wheel from a few months ago in Texas when he had twisted his ankle. He wouldn't say shit about it though no matter how much it hurt. It would be easier to get blood from a stone than a complaint out of this guy.

The suppressed shot echoed through the empty street we were running down, bouncing off the buildings and abandoned vehicles. Something you should know about silencers: they don't exist. They're a Hollywood invention to make movies cooler. A suppressor does just that; it suppresses the sound, but that shit is not silent. The suppressor also makes the shot seem to come from everywhere, making the action of identifying the shooter's position difficult. It's also not supposed to echo, but I was hearing it right then.

The things behind had sight of us, and once they saw you, you needed to run. Hiding would work sometimes, but with so many of them, sometimes wasn't good enough, so we ran. They began coming from two other sides in numbers that would wreck our day, so Seyfert altered course forcing us to run right toward the living bad guys.

We moved quickly, but not at a sprint. It didn't take long for the pricks with the pickup to notice us and I saw one of them tap another on the shoulder. The second guy called out, the other four looking at where he was pointing. They began to laugh, one guy even slapping his knee. Two of them raised rifles and that would not do.

Clearly these assholes had no idea who they were fucking with.

One shot came from them and eight shots came from us. Two of the pricks dropped where they stood, another two clutching at themselves and diving for cover a bit late. The remaining two ducked behind the pickup.

They had cover and we had an open street. Not very tactically sound of us, but we were running from a huge horde of infected. I saw one of the guys take up a firing position from behind the truck, but he suddenly turned to his right, bringing his rifle barrel with him. All it did was smack the side of the head of the vanguard of the fifty or so infected we had seen sneaking up on these dickheads from the window.

The dead washed over them, biting and gouging. The screams were brief, but we didn't really care. We had been about to murder them anyway. What we all cared very much about was that we had a few thousand dead behind us, some coming from the left by the water, the city with its tall buildings was off to the right, and fifty more dead knelt in front dining on the dickheads.

So, three directions of zombies or into the city. Which way to go?

We fled past the feeding infected, some of whom opted to follow us but most of whom continued their smorgasbord. We never even fired a round at them. I juked around an outstretched hand missing a finger and we were clear in front.

And then we weren't. They came from every direction. Out of doorways, from the back of an abandoned Fed-Ex truck, out of alleys. I even saw one stand up in a green dumpster. A big park with beautiful unmown green grass was between us and downtown. Several of the dead dotted the pretty green park, but they were spread out, so we opted to dash across the common.

Ship used his giant machete to end the suffering of one of the things that reached for him, but other than that we made it through the green without incident. Then it all went to shit, as it usually does. Tens of thousands of the things were now in front of us. They packed the streets from side to side a thousand deep on every road. These ones made the horde behind us look small.

We were trapped. Totally surrounded. Shrieks from the runners in the crowds carried across the park and through my ear canals making my nuts shrink. I would never get used to that sound.

Ship pointed to the glass-front of a tall building in front of us. It looked clear, although we couldn't see too far in. We had nothing else, so I shouted to Seyfert, pointing as had my colossal buddy. The SEAL didn't say anything, he just took off, sprinting toward the glass walls. We tailed him across a pretty, mosaic tiled courtyard, dodging big planters and the occasional hand grab, and soon we were staring at the locked door of a shop called Loft. The door was chained with a heavy chain and an enormous lock

We had twenty seconds to live.

"Fuck it!" Seyfert shouted, and fired three times point blank, from top to bottom at the big plate glass next to the door. *That* was loud. Anything in the area not completely deaf would have heard that. Not that we didn't have zombies a-plenty about anyway.

The glass dropped out of the frame and shattered, spewing shards every which-way. Seyfert went first, climbing through, and we all followed him into the building. We moved through the abandoned women's clothing store, which looked to be untouched and more importantly, free of infected. That didn't last long as we heard the first of the throngs of dead assholes crunch across the broken glass.

"Oooh, that's nice!" I heard and saw Anna holding out the arm of a gray sweater admiring it. "Feel this material," she told me.

I ripped the garment off the rack and gave it to her. "It's on sale!" she told me, holding out the yellow tag. How the fuck was she not shitting herself?

Seyfert had found the door from the shop into the office building, but it was also locked. This entrance was also glass, but it didn't have a giant chain on it as had the exterior door. What it did have was a steel roll-down shutter that was trundled up in its housing. Seyfert kicked the door and the lock broke instantly. The glass door flew open and thumped into the wall on the other side with the breaking of glass. We filed through, weapons ready and the SEAL pulled down the steel door. There was no way to lock it from this side though, so we would have to deal.

We stood on the second floor of the massive two-floor lobby of the building. A giant white banner with multicolored letters stretched across the walkways in front of us. FOUR EMBARCADERO CENTER WELCOMES LOCAL 6 IBEW, it silently announced.

Two other banners that I couldn't read from this angle made other proclamations, but I didn't give a shit what they said, only what they meant.

We were smack dab in the lobby of a fucking convention center in the middle of a city. We panned our weapons around and I realized it was not an empty convention center. Silent escalators descended into the lower area, where dozens of infected milled around below us. One shuffled toward us from our left and Kev ran to it, jamming his knife into the side of the thing's head. The creature collapsed immediately.

I heard the noises of the dead behind us in the store; that hacking rasp, the moans, and the sounds of them breaking shit as they traipsed about. Nothing attempted a beat-down on the metal roll-down barrier though. They must not have been able to figure out where we had gone. That was good news at least. The potential for five thousand conventioneers was the total opposite of good news though.

But, where were they? There were a bunch of infected below us, and they were on the way up the powerless escalators, but they were so spread out they wouldn't be difficult to deal with.

We moved quietly down these elevated walkway thingies with glass sides about hip height. They were windy and intertwined, and I couldn't help but dig the architecture. It was dust-free and pretty after a couple of years of plague. I could see shadows dancing on the floor below us by the base of the escalators. It was the horde moving past the floor-to-ceiling glass windows a floor down. That floor was lower than this one and must open-up on a street a bit below the one we had just escaped. I told the group to hold on and got down on my belly. I could just see the bottoms of the windows on that portion of ground floor. These too had big metal shutters and they were closed. All except one, but that one was fifteen feet wide at least. If the things figured out where we were and pressed against that glass, it would give. No plate-glass wall would stop a hundred thousand pounds of dead former human pressing against it, at least not for more than a few minutes.

I relayed this information to my team, and we moved on. There were six escalators and eight of us. Two each at the top of each of the metal stairways should be enough to deal with what comes up. Kev and Anna would cover our backs as we dealt with the small groups of infected as they ascended toward dinner. And before you get all pissy and think our group is sexist for having the girl watch our backs: she's the medic. She *should* be in the back. Also, while I'm not an operator like the rest of these guys, I'm fairly decent at sizing people up. I'm giving it to you straight: Anna is tough as nails.

Seyfert gave us our assignments, telling us to use our blades until we deemed it unsafe. Danny and I got the second escalator, and we waited for our first infected. It was a kid and I sighed. There's nothing worse than zombie kids. It just isn't fair.

"Aww shit," Danny said, and I had to agree. I picked up one of those plastic poles used for separating queues of people and pulled the little separator bands off. I hefted it like a club, but then had a better idea. I took two steps down, my boots clanking on the toothed-steel steps. The boy, probably about twelve when he died, made it to within five feet of me and stretched his arms toward me in frustration. I used the pole to stop him in his tracks as he hissed and growled. Danny moved past me and sunk his blade into the top of the kid's noggin. This kid couldn't have cared any less, increasing his growls. Danny's blade came out of the boy with a sucking sound and he plunged the knife in a second time. The thing's legs gave out and it fell backwards down the stairs into the others behind it. They wasted no time in crawling over the boy, their disgusting and filthy figures headed for a feeding.

A dead man in a Lakers jersey and a huge dude in what was left of a postal carrier's uniform squeezed over the dead kid at the same time. They both did that super-fast cheetah thing the undead do when they get close and lunged. Normally we would have been prepared and would have been able to juke, but there was nowhere to juke to. The Lakers fan wasn't ready for the thrust of my plastic pole, and I thumped him hard. The skin on the left side of his face sloughed off, the wide plastic base making a rasping sound as it scraped across the bone. He didn't really care about the free exfoliation and continued to struggle toward me, several of the things behind him attempting the same thing.

The big postal guy, who looked exactly like a dead version of my buddy, Levon from prison, was able to skirt past my polearm and snag Danny's pantleg. I whipped the pole sideways, the base impacting the dead guy's arm, but he held fast. Danny tried to poke a hole in the head of the dead man, but his leg was pulled forward and he fell on his ass on the escalator. The thing crawled up him, trying to bite as it moved forward, but Danny pushed it's head up with his hands. Danny began to make panicked sounds, and I realized we might be in trouble when a suppressed pistol shot came from behind me. The postal worker's head snapped back, the shit flying out of the back of its noggin coating the dead faces behind it. It fell on Danny, and the ones in back began to crawl up and over, pinning my new friend.

I abandoned the pole and grabbed my rifle. I began firing, the sound of the suppressed rounds echoing all over the lobby. Seyfert showed up a moment later and boogied down the stairs to help Danny. An emaciated woman in the rags of a blue dress reached her claws toward the SEAL, so I shifted my aim and put a hole in her head. Seyfert tried to pull Danny by one arm, but he was stuck on something and wouldn't budge.

Seyfert, Kev, and I fired into the dwindling crowd while Danny struggled to extricate himself. Ship was suddenly there, and I had to wonder who was covering all the other escalators.

We rinsed and repeated for a while, the bodies stacking up. The last one, a rotten woman in an apron, reached over the pile of destroyed creatures toward us as I slapped a fresh mag into my rifle. I gave her a rifle butt to the face, and I heard something crack super loud. I let my rifle dangle on the sling and used my knife to finish her. Seyfert and I began to pull bodies off Danny, then Ship was suddenly there, and I let him do the heavy lifting.

I may have mentioned, Dear Reader, that my friend and bestest-buddy-pal is a big dude. He simply grabbed the center of a dead thing's shirt, effortlessly lifted it up, and tossed it over the side of the escalator until we were able to pull Danny to his feet. He brushed himself off, looked himself over and gave us a thumbs up. I don't know why, but we all burst out laughing. Great big guffaws, which as I write this sounds ridiculous as we should have been trying to enforce noise discipline. It was that moment that cemented trust between our two groups, and I knew that my life was worth something to these people. Strange that means so much nowadays.

There were three other shops and a couple of cafés on this level, and we cleared them all. Simple raps on the glass doors of the shops yielded nothing. The raps couldn't be heard by the hordes of infected outside because the crowd was fucking *loud*.

Seyfert sat in a café chair and stretched out, placing his rifle on a table. He tried his radio but couldn't get a signal. We all tried and suffered from the same problem.

"Must be some interference from the structure," Kev surmised.

Seyfert let loose with a heavy sigh. "I am very open to ideas at this juncture.

"We're in a giant fucking building," I told him. He looked at me like he didn't understand. "Place seems empty. Let's look around. If we can secure this place, imagine what an FOB it would be. And," I added, "it might look down on the bad guy's hideout. I mean, we think it's that warehouse thingy across the street, right? The one with the clock tower?"

"Yeah," he answered, "that's what intel tells us, but we're not a hundred percent on that one."

"So then let's get up a couple floors, take a peek through a sniper scope, then start shooting pricks in a barrel."

Ship signed to me, and I nodded. I was getting better at the sign language, in fact I was pretty good, but there was still one word I didn't get just then.

"Ship wants to know if the submarine has any... I don't know that word buddy."

He wrote something quickly and passed me his book.

Tomahawk was the only thing printed, and I said it aloud like I was asking a question.

Literally everyone smiled, and I felt left out. I *hate* being the stupid one. Until I met Ship and Remo, I was always one of the smartest guys in the room. Now I'm always one of the dumbest. That shit isn't fair.

"It's a missile," Remo told us. He had said it to everyone, but I think it was meant for me.

I shrugged. "So nuke 'em then."

"It isn't a nuke," Kev told me. "It's—"

I interrupted him, "I *know* it isn't a nuke. *Nuke* was a figure of speech." I rolled my eyes in impatience, "Big boom, makes the bad guys dead? Nuke?"

"So, we clear the upper floors," Danny proposed, "get a vantage, call it in, and watch the fireworks?"

"I like it," Seyfert said. "The radios should work once we access a higher elevation."

Anna squinted in thought. "But what if we open a door in here and there's a thousand infected on the other side?"

"I don't want that door," I told her. "You can have it,"

The SEAL harrumphed, "We'll be careful."

In three minutes, our group of eight was standing in front of a big, green, granite desk in the elevator lobby. We had come in on the higher side of the street level, and now stood on the lobby level kind of half a floor up. The building we were in was called Four Embarcadero Center. What a stupid fucking name. They could have just as easily called it Joe's Building, or the Vagina Center, or something cool, but no. Forty-five floors of offices and convention areas; this building was big. Like huge and stuff. A bunch of shops, a bank, a post office, and a movie theater sat on the lower three levels, the top being the Promenade level. I looked up and to the right. Those same glass-walled walkways spanned the empty air above us between shops, escalators, and stairs. A couple dozen businesses including two restaurants were on the floors above us. Yay.

We could hear the dead outside, but we couldn't hear them in the clothing store we had come through anymore. The best news is that we didn't hear them *inside*.

We followed Seyfert to one of the doors at the end of the elevator lobby. A little brass placard adorned the wall next to the door. STAIRS TO FLOORS 1-45. We took up a pyramid firing stance as the SEAL put his hand on the door handle. It was a fire door with the little lever for your thumb. He held up three fingers, and we all aimed our rifles at the still-closed entrance. He counted down with his fingers and yanked the door open when his fingers were a fist.

Nothing came out of the darkness except for the stink of the dead. It wasn't overpowering, but it sure as shit wasn't the smell of cotton candy. That growling hiss that the dead make came to us as well, but it wasn't loud, and it didn't sound like there was a football-stadium sized crowd in there. All our tactical lights were shining into the stairwell, and in a moment a dead woman tumbled down the stairs to the bottom landing. She stood, one foot missing and limped toward us. She got out the door before Danny stabbed her in the back of the head.

We listened intently but heard nothing else in the stairwell. Seyfert pointed at Remo and the two of them moved into the staircase, flanking left and right. Remo whistled and tapped the end of his rifle on the steel handrail, the sound echoing up into the darkness. Nothing came at us or made any noise.

Seyfert glanced up. "If they're in here, they're quiet."

We all moved quickly into the stairwell. The first thing I looked at was this side of the door. It was a push-bar type that could easily be opened from this side. The next thing I did was shine my light up into the stairwell. It seemed to go on forever.

As did we. When we reached the sixth floor, we found dead-lady's foot. It was still inside her filthy sneaker and it could stay there forever as far as I was concerned. I was tired as hell and my legs were aching by the time we reached the twentieth. Seyfert called it on the thirtieth floor because every other door on the way up here had been locked and there was a desiccated dead man propping the door open with his body on the floor above. It was mostly a skeleton, with a hole in its forehead. There was dried goo spatter on the stairwell wall behind us as we approached the steel door.

The SEAL held his fist up and we stopped. He took a quick peek past the door and pulled it open. We moved inside the thirty-first floor as a unit with our rifles at the ready, left hand on the person in front of us. We stopped when Alvarez, the last in the line, entered. He pulled the body out of the doorframe and let the portal close.

We were on an office floor. A Little greeting desk stood opposite the stainless elevator doors just to our left. The letters VEP adorned a plexiglass plaque in gold letters with a circular emblem on the front of the mahogany desk. It was pretty. It also looked brand-new. The only thing out of place was the single .45 caliber brass on the gray carpeted floor.

Seyfert tapped his left palm with his right index and middle fingers. We grouped into two firing lines side-by-side and moved further into the floor. The elevator area opened into a large cube farm with neck high cubicle walls made of a madras-gray colored fabric that reminded me of technicolor puke. Offices dotted the exterior walls giving the higher-paid workers windows to look down on the city from. I glanced out one window and all I could see was fog. It must have rolled in while we were in the lobby. Seyfert used his left hand to indicate my line should go left. Remo, Anna, Danny, and I went straight down the cubes, while Seyfert, Ship, Kev, and Alvarez went right.

We cleared offices, closing frosted glass doors as we did so. The cubes were a bit more daunting as they were too high to look over and we had to pass by the open ends of them in order to look in. We saw nothing indicating a plague of the living dead had swept through here forever ago. Other than a small bit of dust, everything looked like we were invading an office on a Saturday when everybody had the weekend off.

Remo was on point and when he threw up a fist, we all stopped panning our weapons around. On the ground in front of us, sticking out from behind a corner cubicle wall, was an arm, palm up, fingers relaxed. The arm was moving, but it didn't look as if it were in control, almost as if someone were shaking the body the arm was attached to.

Ragged breathing and a fevered, wet, ripping sound emanated from around that corner as well and I'm sure you can see where this is going.

Remo nodded at me, and I nodded back. I drew my SOG Seal Pup, (the best blade on earth) hoping to make this quiet. We both stepped quickly around the cube-corner, our suppressed weapons ready should I not be able to use the knife. We were immediately plunged back into a nightmare. Blood covered the exterior cube wall, the floor, and the opposite office door. There was some arterial spray on the ceiling that I had failed to notice previously.

A dead man lay on his back on the ground, his glazed eyes looking directly at me. Perched atop him, with its back to us and its hands rummaging around in the poor, eviscerated bastard's thoracic cavity was a younger woman, maybe twenty-five by the look of her. She was turned away from us, but she looked young from the back.

I don't know what revealed us. Neither of us gasped or moved in any way. Maybe it was a change in the air currents, or a smell, or some inherent sixth sense these things have, but the infected horror tearing into this guy turned her head quickly and looked directly into my eyes. I was correct; she had been in her mid-twenties. Now the evil in her was ancient.

Blonde and surely pretty at one time, her lower face and the front of her sweatpants and t-shirt were dripping with gore. She had a string of something the color of rotten eggplant in her hand that ended inside of the guy on the carpet. Her mouth was full, but she didn't continue chewing as she made to leap at me, claws at the ready. Remo fired, her cranium snapping back as the suppressed round took her just below the right eye. The shot would ultimately be fatal, but she wasn't done yet and scuttled up on all fours, not really giving a rat's ass about the new hole in her face. We both shot her, this time one of us getting her in the dome. The thing crumpled immediately, her head coming to rest in a blood puddle which had come from her victim.

The dead guy's hand latched onto Remo's pant-leg and he cursed. It began to roll over, but before it could, I stabbed down with my knife into the thing's eye, re-killing it.

"Report!" came through our radios in a hushed yell. It was Seyfert, who must have heard the suppressed shot.

I spoke into my shoulder mic, "One Runner, one pus-bag down." I looked the dead guy over. The fact that he had been being eaten gave us a ton of information. "Both were fresh," I added. "I think we'll have uninfected in here someplace, so stay frosty."

"We found a dead one that had been put down recently," he shot back, *"it's still gooey, and it has fresh blood on its face. You stay frosty too."*

There were no other surprises, and we met up with the others in five minutes. We had cleared all the offices, the considerable cubicle area, the bathrooms, two meeting rooms, and the breakroom. A small duffel of food was found abandoned in the breakroom, but other than that the place was clean.

We gathered in the larger of the meeting rooms, Danny and Alvarez absent as they were on watch by the stairwell doors.

"So, we're in a building with forty-five floors and we've cleared the lobby, which is totally unsafe with the glass windows, and one other floor?" Anna asked.

"Yeah," Kev answered, "yeah, that's right. Oh, plus the stairwell."

Everybody looked to Seyfert. Before we got to San Francisco, everyone in my group always looked to me. You should know, Dear Reader, that I never know what the fuck I'm doing, so the team silently asking Seyfert what to do was a huge relief.

"We clear a few more floors above and use this as our forward base. The hostile breathers either haven't been in here, thought it was too dangerous, or they were here long enough ago that they think the place is cleared." He put his feet up on a beautiful mahogany table and leaned back in a wheeled office chair. He rubbed his calf and made a face. "But first we rest for twenty. After that we get comms up with the Rock, then we check out the assholes below us. The swarm down there, plus the fact that they are missing a team now, will have them on alert."

A half hour after we had made contact with Alcatraz, the fog burned off enough that we were peering through binoculars and scopes at the Ferry Building Marketplace about six hundred feet to the east of us. A big, red plaza sat between our building and theirs, and it teemed with the dead, as did the streets around it and a big area with some kind of art structure to the north.

The SEAL harrumphed, and Ship pointed at the same time. "Huh. Smart," Seyfert blurted.

Remo passed the binoculars he was holding and told me to look at the clock tower. Four guys moved around these column-like structures at the very top of the tower. They also had binoculars and sniper rifles, but their attention was on the massive swarm of undead shuffling around outside of their huge enclave. Our shenanigans of a couple of hours ago must have drawn the crowd below, and they didn't want to stumble off without a snack. Danny had one eye focused on one of the assholes through his sniper scope, no doubt the crosshairs on the douche's noggin.

"It'd be sooo easy..." he whispered.

Seyfert shook his head no. "And then they would know we're around." He grabbed his radio. "Rock, this is Sabre. Enemy stronghold currently under surveillance." The SEAL read off some grid coordinates.

"Rock copies, Sabre. What is your distance from target?"

"Less than three hundred meters."

"Recommend you exfil ASAP. Confirm when Sabre reaches minimum safe distance of five hundred meters."

"Sabre copies all." Seyfert clicked his mic off. "We need recon on the other three sides of the building."

"I gotcha, buddy," I told him. "Ship, if you don't have anything pressing, wanna come with?"

The two of us moved into three different offices to check the street below. North and south were a definite no, as those directions were wall-to-wall infected. West had significantly less undead, but they were still streaming by the dozens to the east.

"Looks like ex-fil is going to have to wait a bit," I said aloud.

Ship touched his head then pointed at me. Sign language for "think same". He agreed with me.

We reported to Seyfert, and he let Alcatraz know. We would have to sit tight.

"Anybody got a deck of cards?" I asked.

ENCOUNTERS
ALCATRAZ

"Ya think?" Kyle asked as he stared into the dark maw of an abandoned tunnel under the power building.

Chloe shrugged, "Yeah, why not?"

"Have you ever *seen* a horror movie?" the tall boy demanded.

Richy answered for her, "Our parents weren't too keen on those, why do you ask?"

Kyle looked at the three of them like they were all nuts. "Cuz the only thing worse than heading into a dark tunnel is splitting up." He pointed at the tunnel. "That's exactly what we shouldn't be doing."

"Which is why we're gonna do it," Vanessa said, producing a flashlight. "I don't like the zombies, but I'm gonna die if I don't do something fun." She flashed the light into the tunnel, the beam slicing the darkness and illuminating abandoned detritus on the dirty brick floor. "Or at least something scary."

The other three clicked their lights on, the shafts of light moving at odd angles and crossing each other. Richy took a tentative step forward, but both girls pushed past and started down the bricks. The quartet almost collectively shit themselves when they heard a small voice behind them.

"Can I come too?"

They spun quickly, the flashlights focusing on the person behind them. A young blonde girl stood in the light cast from an ancient broken window in the power house. Her forearm blocked the light from the flashlights and the other four quickly lowered them. A multicolored cat sat next to the girl licking one of its paws.

Chloe strode to the kid. "Of course you can come. You're Sam, right?"

"Yeah, and this is Pickles." The cat continued to lick itself, finding something particularly interesting on its right paw. It chewed the paw for a moment then went back to licking.

The kids, who had only met Sam briefly prior to now, introduced themselves. Sam was about eleven, so she would be the youngest of the group.

Chloe took her hand. "Come on, Sam, let's break the rules." Sam smiled a huge smile and the five of them started down the incline.

It grew dark quickly and in moments it was pitch black. They came to a bend in the tunnel with a door blocking the way in a minute or two. The door was thick iron and had a semicircle window with vertical bars three-quarters of the way up its rusty surface.

"Well, this was fun," Kyle said quickly. "Let's go back to where we won't get eaten by zombies in the dark."

Richy shined his light through the bars then tried the door and was able to pull it open with some effort. The rusty hinges squealed loudly, and Chloe helped him push the heavy iron open enough to allow access.

"Relax," Chloe said to the group. "This door hasn't been opened in forever."

Pickles weaved through the legs of the kids and darted through the partially open door. The kids followed, the darkness getting to them as they began to move down the slight incline. The beams from the flashlights sliced the darkness, the white of the brick turning to red as they progressed.

"Look at this!" Kyle said and stooped to pick up an object. He showed them what he had via his flashlight.

"Wow, that's pretty cool!" Richy told him. They were all looking at a rusty revolver as Kyle turned it over in his hand. He tried to cock the hammer with his thumb, but the rust wouldn't allow it.

Kyle beamed, "I bet this thing is a hundred years old!"

"I bet this is too," Chloe challenged. She was holding an equally crusted cutlass, the elaborate handguard covering her small hand. Vanessa and Richy immediately panned their lights across the floor, searching for valuable booty.

The five of them jumped when one of the lights came across a human skeleton dressed in some type of uniform. The bones had been in this tunnel for fifty years at least. One of the eyes held a spider web, and Sam said, "Ick."

"He can't hurt us, Richy told her."

"I know, but... ick."

Kyle gave a nudge to the thing's boot. The kids had another fright when the jaw fell away with a clatter on the bricks. Kyle laughed nervously, the rest of them following suit. Vanessa made to pick up the jawbone, but Sam put a hand lightly on her arm. "Don't. Let him rest in peace." Vanessa nodded.

Richy smiled, "More like in pieces."

Other items littered the floor; an old frying pan, an empty wooden barrel, mostly rotted away, odd pieces of unidentifiable metal, and the bones of several small mammals.

"Rats," Richy said and smiled again.

Vanessa and Sam looked scared, but Chloe punched her brother in the arm. "Yeah, *dead* rats. Probably been dead since the dinosaurs. Quit trying to scare us."

"We're in a pitch-black tunnel during the zombie apocalypse," Kyle demanded, "and rats are supposed to scare us?"

They moved further down the tunnel, Kyle and Chloe holding their prizes close. The tunnel opened into a larger room, the far end under water. The floor sloped into the inky liquid, disappearing five yards from where they stood.

"Anybody for a swim?" Richy asked.

The other four looked at him as if he were crazy. He smiled, shaking his head. "I was just kidding." Chloe punched him in the arm again, the boy rubbing the impact spot. He pointed at her, "That shit stops now!" They began to playfully argue, and Sam asked for a flashlight. Vanessa handed hers over. Sam swept the beam around until she saw her cat sitting on an old cast-iron stove. The animal was staring intently at the water, his tail curled around his feet. He stood slowly and took a step back from the water. He arched his back and hissed, but the kids were talking amongst themselves and didn't hear him.

Sam saw the action though and flashed her light on the black water. Soon enough, eddies in the water began to form.

"Look!" Sam whispered loudly and pointed. The other four kids turned to stare at the water too, all four flashlights now focused on the water.

Pickles gave a low growl, jumped down from the stove, and bolted back up the tunnel. A head broke the surface of the water, followed by another, then two more. The kids stood transfixed until one of the figures opened its mouth to growl and seawater poured out.

"I fucking knew it," Kyle whispered, and the kids chased after the cat.

Bobby and Hal stood on the ferry dock overlooking the bay. They were on patrol and were happy to pitch in. Both had been members of the Alcatraz family for almost a year now. A crazy guy named Billy had saved them from a group of infected, gotten them to a boat, and told them to tell the folks on The Rock that he said hi.

The guys were milling about on the wooden planks, talking about Billy when Hal noticed someone crawling up the rocks to the south. He pointed at the man crawling.

"Wassat?"

"That, Hal old buddy, is a dead fella." He looked cockeyed at his friend, "It's why we're on this here patrol thingy. To spot dead fellas."

Hal returned Bobby's gaze but remained silent. He unclipped his radio from his belt and made a quick call. "Command, this is Patrol Three. We have one down here. It's outside the fence, but on the rocks. We're moving to engage now."

"Copy, one. What's your exact position?"

"At the ferry dock moving south."

"Sending assistance now, stay in contact."

Bobby cast a sideways glance at Hal who shook his head. "Nah, I think we can handle it," Bobby told the radio. "There's just one."

"Negative. Only engage if you're threatened. A team is on the way. Keep the hostile in sight."

"Gotcha. We'll wait."

Hal pointed again. A dozen or so heads broke the water each with hands gripping the cut stone embankment. "Oh shit…" The entire length of the breakwater crawled with the dead. They scrabbled up the stone and onto the flat area immediately in front of the black chain link fence that encircled most of the island.

"Call it in!" Hal screamed. "Call it in now!"

"Command, we have hundreds of infected scaling the southern embankment! We need firepower down here now!"

Bobby didn't wait for an answer. He raised his rifle to his shoulder and fired off a round. His bullet struck a dead woman in the shoulder and he bolted another round into his hunting rifle. Hal fired slowly, picking targets with his scoped AR15. He dropped three before Hal could get a second shot off.

The front ranks of the dead reached the top of the rocks and were stymied by the four-foot chain-link fence. Several fell backward into the growing crowd, but most pushed and pulled as their brethren flowed out of the water behind them. The fence buckled in one area, then it came down in a fifteen-foot section. The dead poured onto Alcatraz.

"What do you mean stuck?" Kyle demanded in a panicked voice.

Richy and Chloe continued to frantically push on the ancient iron door. "Stuck, as in it won't open!" Richy shot back sarcastically. "Do you need a friggin' dictionary? Help us push!"

Pickles sat with his tail wrapped around his legs. He looked back and forth nervously from kid to kid.

"We just came through here!" Chloe said, looking over her shoulder. "How can it be closed?"

A chill ran down Sam's spine when a familiar voice chimed in, "You just never can tell when one of these old doors will stick." It took all of Sam's willpower to keep from peeing herself.

The five kids looked through the bars of the door to see Mr. Martingale's face peering back at them smugly.

"Maybe a few hours in there will make you appreciate—"

Kyle screamed at him, "There's dead in here with us! Open the door!"

Martingale raised his eyebrows in disbelief. "Sure there are. Not only are you degenerates, you're lying degenerates.

Vanessa shined her flashlight behind them, searching for the dead, but there was nothing back there.

"Listen," Richy began, "I'm sorry I put you in the wrist lock, I am. There really are a bunch of dead down here, and we need to let the soldiers know. If you don't open the door, they're going to tear us to pieces!"

The adult rolled his eyes. "You're a liar. The whole island was searched more than a year ago. There are no dead."

The cat started to meow and pawed at the door. He began looking in several directions.

Sam began to cry.

The rasping sounds of infected began to echo softly up the tunnel. Martingale glanced over the top of the kids heads as the hacking noises grew louder. Vanessa kept her light shining down the tunnel as the kids pleaded with the man to open the door.

The flashlight threw eerie shadows on the walls of the underground passage as its beam was blocked by the rusty objects scattered throughout. Vanessa gasped as the first dead man shuffled into view not forty feet away.

"Do you believe us now?" Richy screamed past the bars and into his face.

Martingale's eyes grew wide as he saw the dead rounding the bend in the tunnel. He began to breathe fast, then turned and ran, bumping his leg on something big and metal in his haste. The kids screamed after him, but he limped quickly away.

"What do we do?" cried Kyle.

Richy drew his combat dagger and moved past the other kids. "Get the door open. Throw your weight against it, all of you."

Rather than push on the door, the four children began to propel themselves against it, the impacts of their shoulders raining dust from the bricks above.

Richy moved a bit down the dark corridor, his light trained on a particularly nasty specimen of dead. This thing was missing its left arm and a gaping hole existed where the abdominal and chest cavities used to be. Strings of discolored flesh hung from the top of the rotting hole.

Kyle, Vanessa, and Chloe kept throwing their shoulders against the heavy iron door and Sam moved toward Richy. The boy looked to the side when he heard her coming. "Stay back, Sam, I got this." The kid advanced toward the nasty dead man with no belly. He did a quick count, noting fourteen infected slogging up the tunnel. He sighed. On his best day he could probably get three before they swarmed him. He glanced back at his sister. He would keep her alive until they brought him down.

NEWBIES
JOURNAL ENTRY 3

"Go fish," I told Anna. She drew from the pile. I glanced at Seyfert, who shuffled his cards in his hand. "So, when does the Florida rain death down on the douches?"

"Once we're clear." It was his turn. "Got any threes?" I handed him two cards and grumbled about it.

I pressed him a bit, "But isn't that building kind of nice? I mean it's keeping the dead out right now, isn't it?"

"Yeah, so?"

"So, what if we could take it? It's right on the water, there's a ton of boats if we need a quick out, and we would have a foothold in the city."

He shrugged. "We're here to figure out where their base is. We figured it out. I don't think the captain would want an armed incursion into an enemy stronghold..."

There was a big thump on the ceiling directly above us. Everybody looked up.

Seyfert was still looking at the ceiling when he said, "But he does want us to clear this building if we think we can do it." He stood, tossing his cards on the conference room table, "Shall we?"

We all stood, and the SEAL radioed to Remo and Kev, who had been keeping an eye on the bad guys, to tell them we were heading upstairs. We met up in the cubicle area.

"Six of us will go up, two stay and keep this floor secure. There's definitely something on the floor above us."

"Sounds like people moving around," I added. When I noticed everyone looking at me, I continued, "Well, I would imagine it takes a considerable impact for us to hear it a floor below in a building like this, right?"

"That's true," Anna said, nodding.

We were standing in front of the door to the stairs in just a minute. Kev and Danny would stay behind to keep the thirtieth floor secure.

Seyfert pressed his ear up against the door and listened for a full twenty seconds. He shrugged when he looked back at us and pushed the door open. He and Remo moved into the stairwell quickly; he peered down the stairs, and Remo moved up so fast it was amazing.

"Clear," they both said into their mics at the same time.

I was the last one into the stairwell after Anna. "Good luck," Danny said and clapped me on the shoulder as he shut the door quietly.

My nuts clenched when that door closed with a *snick*. Everybody was already moving up, and I was to cover our rear, so I moved slowly, panning my light back and forth down the steps behind us. It was fairly dark in the stairwell, and the only sound was our careful footfalls, but to me every step sounded like cannon fire.

I followed the group, trying to be as quiet as possible. There was nothing lumbering up the steps behind us, or worse, sprinting. The door to the thirty-first floor was, of course, locked. It didn't matter though, because it opened just as we surrounded it.

A woman's face peeked through the crack in the door. She screamed and tried to pull the door closed, but Alvarez stuck his boot in the way. Ship put his considerable hand on the door and pulled. The poor woman lost her grip and went on her ass, but let's face it, if there were a contingent of people pulling on the other side of the door, Ship could pull it open without breaking a sweat.

We stared into the desperate faces of about eight skinny people all armed with makeshift weapons ranging from a paper cutter blade to a sharpened curtain rod. One guy had a pencil in his fist. No shit, a pencil. We moved into the room as a unit, filling the door briefly then I closed it behind us. The office building people backed up as we spread out. Remo checked behind a big front desk. "Clear," he told us.

"You better leave!" the guy with the pencil yelled at us. "Or there's going to be trouble!" He swallowed so hard it must have hurt.

Seyfert aimed his rifle at the group. "How about you drop your weapons, or we kill all of you? If we wanted you dead, trust me, you'd be full of holes already."

The guy with the paper cutter blade, a tall, very thin man with glasses and male pattern baldness, began to raise his weapon a bit higher. Danny aimed his rifle right at the guy's face, "Don't."

This guy swallowed hard too.

"Drop 'em," a short-haired woman told her crew. Every one of them put their weapons on the carpeted floor immediately. Clearly this woman got it. She could see the hardware that the other morons either failed to see or didn't comprehend.

"On your knees, now," Seyfert demanded. I wrote *demanded* there but really, he asked nicely. "Lace your fingers on top of your heads and cross your ankles."

37

Each of the folks did as instructed except the guy who had threatened us with the pencil. "I've got a bad knee," he told us.

Seyfert nodded. "It's ok. You can stand, but just you. Anna, Alvarez check 'em." Anna and Alvarez slung their rifles and stepped forward. As they were frisking each of the office people, the woman in charge piped up.

"Are you here to help us?"

"Depends," Seyfert answered. "Are you with those assholes in the marketplace building below us?"

She shook her head. "No. They tried to get in here a few months ago, but the dead chased them off. We've seen them come and go out of their building, but we didn't really like what we saw, so we never tried to signal them."

"Why are you in this building?" Remo asked.

The woman shrugged. "We've been here since the start of all this. A bunch of our coworkers tried to leave, but none made it that we know of. We've lost a dozen more trying to forage." She looked down. "We've been out of food for days."

I pushed on the door with my palm to ensure it was secure. It was a fire door and it wasn't opening unless somebody used the push bar from this side. I shouldered past Remo and Anna to stand at the front of our group. "Door is secure," I informed Seyfert. I took off my pack and offered energy bars to each of the office people.

They accepted quickly, the tall, bald dude tearing into one of the peanut butter bars greedily. "Thank you," he told me while he chewed. His friends also muttered thanks, each of them obviously starving.

"They're clean of weapons," Alvarez told us as they chewed.

"All are malnourished, but there are no bites or scratches that I can see. I should do a more thorough exam on each of them one at a time, though."

Seyfert nodded. "Agreed. Let's clear this office and set up a triage station. Let me know who's the worst off and we'll treat them first."

"Two of our group just went on a food run," the short-haired woman told us. "They were only supposed to go down one floor because we weren't able to get in there before. Have you seen them?"

Seyfert and Remo glanced at each other briefly before the SEAL answered. "There was a fast one tearing into a recently killed guy on the level below us. They left a bag behind." He looked to Ship, who was carrying the heavy, red bag with handles on it. He passed the bag to Seyfert, who passed it to the woman.

She sighed and turned to her group. "Sara and Allen didn't make it." Several of them began to sob and the tall guy shouted, "Fuck!" and ran his palms across the sides of his head.

"Sorry," Seyfert told her.

Twenty minutes later saw most of us sitting in a huge meeting room at a beautiful mahogany table. Even after a very long while, the table had a freshly polished surface. I thought that was weird, but who knows what people will do to occupy themselves when they're trapped in an office building. I was standing because there weren't enough seats. Ship also stood.

We had cleared the floor in five minutes. No bad guys or infected hiding anywhere. We found several makeshift sleeping areas, but the place was pretty tight on personal space. Anna was examining each of the office dwellers near the front desk, one at a time, while Alvarez and Ship watched over her.

Seyfert radioed Kev and Danny to sight tight while we talked to these folks.

The short-haired lady was named Joan, and we began to question her.

"So, you've been in here since the beginning?" I asked Joan.

"Yes. We only recently ran out of food because there was a huge amount of non-perishables in the storage room for the restaurant on thirty-six. We were able to get a bunch of the food back into this office on multiple runs, but we suffered losses."

"Infected or assholes with guns?"

She looked down. "The dead."

"What about the other floors?" asked Seyfert. He rubbed his calf and made a face. I would have to ask him about that later.

The tall guy, Brad, piped up, "Other than the thirtieth, the eighteenth, and the forty-first , we've been able to get into all of the floors from sixteen all the way to forty four. We haven't been able to access the roof because we keep getting chased out by the dead. They hold all the floors below the sixteenth we think. They also hold most of the floors above us, and occasionally some will stumble into the stairwell."

Remo nodded; "And you've managed to stay alive for this long with just the supplies that were in the building?"

Brad glanced down for the briefest of moments before he said, "Yeah. It hasn't been easy, and we're out of food now."

"But you can take us out of here, right?" asked one of the office workers. Her name was Jill.

Seyfert was about to launch into a tirade about how we had a mission and that these folks would have to wait, but I cut him off.

"Yup," I answered, "we sure are. We've got guns, people, and food on Alcatraz, and after a quick quarantine, you folks will be members of that community."

Another woman was holding the hand of the guy sitting next to her. They were both looking a bit nervous with all the hardware surrounding them, and I felt it would be nice to look less like we were going to kill them all. I shifted my rifle around to my back on its sling. "What are your names?" I asked them and the other two people.

"I'm Lynda and this is Steve," the woman said, and they both stood, sticking their paws out for a shake. It was funny because Seyfert, Alvarez, and Remo all tensed when they stood.

"I'm Jon."

"I'm Bob."

"I'm Kayla"

The other three said at the same time. It was fuk'n funny that they all spoke together and we all smiled.

The last one of them, a lanky, younger man, didn't speak at all. He just sat and listened.

"That's Gary," Joan told us. "He hasn't said a word since more-or-less the start of all this."

Guy didn't look nuts. He looked like everybody else, he just didn't want to talk. I could live with that.

We all shook mitts, then Seyfert indicated Remo and I should follow him while conversation ensued. Alvarez and Anna would keep watch on the newbies.

We moved back down the hall to the elevator lobby and Seyfert spoke to me. "What if we can't get them out?"

I shrugged, "We have to. Can't leave 'em here, right? Besides, if we can't get them out it's because we're dead. I don't wanna die today."

He smiled and pulled his radio. "Rock, this is Sabre."

"Saber, Rock, we read you."

"We found nine breathers, they seem to be friendlies. Request additional orders."

"Copy, Sabre. Rock Actual is on station."

A different voice came over the radio, it was McInerney and there was surprise in his voice. *"Hell of a discovery, sailor. Nine survivors?"*

"Roger that, sir. Skinny, but uninfected. Also, not associated with the hostiles, at least as far as we can tell."

We didn't hear it, but I just knew the captain sighed before he said, "*Copy that. Bring them home, Ensign. Abort code is three-alpha-mike-foxtrot.*"

Seyfert knew the code, but he opened a little envelope he had removed from his Velcroed breast pocket. He read it out loud, then spoke into the radio. "Three-alpha-mike-foxtrot confirmed. See you tonight, sir."

"*Copy that, Saber.*"

Smiling, and already knowing the answer, I asked, "What just happened?"

"Change in mission," shrugged the SEAL. "Elimination to evacuation. We're going to get these folks to Alcatraz. The captain has the coordinates on the bad guys anyway if he wants to engage."

I immediately felt a million times better. As I had said before, I had never hunted the living. I had killed many asshole breathers since the onset of this little apocalypse thingy, but only ever in self-defense, or to preserve the lives of my family. I didn't want to kill the douches in the other building, but douches they were. Murderers and rapists. Preying on the weak. That pisses me off which is why I signed up for this mission.

But to be honest, I would much rather help people than kill them, so what we were about to do was better.

Our group had increased two-fold in size. Eight folks with battle rifles and tactical gear, and eight people with sharpened sticks. We would now escort these people back to Alcatraz. Should be fun.

After Anna had checked everybody out one at a time and given them clean bills of health, we told them what was up.

"Leave?" asked Bob. He was the one who had threatened us with the pencil, and he had a bad knee if you remember. "You want us to go out there?" He pointed to the window.

"Not going to make you," Remo told him. "You don't want to come, stay here."

They all decided to join us, even Bob. The office dwellers gathered some of their shit, and we gathered them at the fire door near the stairwell and the elevators, so the newbies could listen to Seyfert.

He told them to keep quiet unless not doing so would endanger us. He told them not to run unless all of us were dead. The not running and the noise discipline were the only directives. The eight of them would stay between two groups of four of us. They had no questions and in under two minutes, Seyfert had his inspection mirror poked out the door.

"Clear," he said, and I felt like shitting myself. You'd think, Dear Reader, that by now I would be all calm and shit when it came to leaving a safe place to face the dead. Nope. I was scared shitless every time.

We started down the stairs, trying to make as little noise as possible, but fourteen people just can't move silently. Seyfert gave a double squelch when we were outside the door to the thirtieth floor, and suddenly Kev's face was staring at us. He and Danny joined Seyfert and Alvarez in the front. Ship, Anna, Remo, and I held the rear.

We made it three floors before the caterwauling shriek of a Runner echoed through the stairwell below us. Three of the office folks turned around to run back up the stairs, but Ship was between them and the way up. Short of a battering ram, or maybe a freight train, nothing was getting past Ship when he planted his feet. Bob and Jon tried, but it wasn't happening. Bob drew a big breath like he was going to shout, but Ship clamped his hand around the little guy's face.

Picture, if you will, grabbing a tennis ball in your palm. That is about the dimensions of Ship's hand on Bob's face. Ship leaned way down and looked into the guy's eyes. He let go of his face and then put a finger to his lips. Loosely translated: *Shhhh.*

Bob nodded, and he and Jon turned back around. We started moving downward again, slowly. Seyfert's group passed the door to the eighteenth floor, and I realized my legs were tired. I was in the best shape of my life, but these stairs were kicking my ass. As I write this now, I remember thinking then that I should write *the stairs were kicking my ass* when I was able to sit down with a pen. I remember that because I associate it with the exact time the door to eighteen pushed open and the stairwell flooded with infected.

BATTLE
DANK AND DINGY TUNNEL BENEATH ALCATRAZ.

"How's the door?" Richy asked calmly over his shoulder.

"It's moving," Kyle almost screamed, "but not enough!"

When the large infected with no abdominal cavity got within fifteen feet, Richy ran up to it and stabbed it in the eye as it lunged. It collapsed immediately, the boy extricating the weapon as the creature tumbled. Something long and skinny slithered from its belly, moving back down the bricks behind the infected. One of them stooped and reached for it, but it slipped away.

A former woman, short, perhaps five feet, reached for him and he put his hand on her slimy throat. He stabbed the dagger down on the crown of her head and she dropped as well.

Two of the others lunged and the kid backstepped quickly. This wasn't going to work. There were too many. Richy sprinted the twenty feet back to the door and threw his weight against it with the others. It scraped open enough that they could fit through, but only one at a time. "Go, Sam!" Chloe screamed as the cat shot through the opening.

The little girl slipped through, followed by Vanessa. Kyle noticed Richy turn around, and he picked up an ancient piece of pipe from the brick floor. The dead were ten feet away when he brought the pipe over his head with both hands and threw it at them. The piece of lead glanced off the shoulder of the dead young man and struck a thing with long hair in the face so hard it took a step back.

"Come on!" Vanessa screamed at the boys.

"Go!" Richy said, and Kyle squeezed his tall but skinny frame through the space in the door. Richy followed as best he could, but the dead had reached him. He thrust his weapon into the opening mouth of the nearest creature, the thing clamping down on the blade with its teeth. Slimy, mottled hands grabbed the boy as he tried to slip through the gap. Two of the things had his T-shirt and they were reaching in with their mouths. Kyle and Chloe pulled him through the door, the poor kid leaving a bit of skin on the brick next to the door frame. The dead still had hold of his shirt though, which resulted in a brief but victorious tug of war for the kids.

The dead thumped against the rusty iron, fingers and a hand reaching through the bars. One of them attempted to squeeze through the space the kids just had, the soggy skin on the side of its face sloughing off on the bricks. Chloe thrust her knife into the creature's skull, and it hung head-down in the opening.

"We're good," sighed Kyle as he pushed against this side of the door with the girls. "They can't get us."

Richy sighed, "Maybe not that good." He had been holding his right hand over his left bicep. He lifted it off and it came away bloody. Two small furrows had been dug into his arm. They looked like they had come from fingernails.

Chloe swallowed, "Rich, no…"

"We'll deal with it later. Right now, we need to seal this door and then tell somebody that there are dead down here and that they can get in."

This side of the door had a large piece of rusted iron placed against it. The kids could see the drag marks where Martingale had pulled the piece across the floor.

"They can't reach us," Kyle repeated, "and they aren't strong enough to push the door with us pushing back. We can hold them here until help comes."

"Vanessa, you and I will go get help," Chloe said aloud. "You guys got this, right?"

Richy, Kyle, and Sam leaned on the door with both hands. The heavy iron didn't move either way.

Richy looked through the four iron bars into the crimson orbs of a dead man six inches away, "Yeah, we're good. If the door starts to move, we'll make a run for it."

Chloe nodded in the gloom, and she and Vanessa ran up the slight incline toward the island proper.

"You scared, Sam?" Richy asked her.

"A little, but like Kyle said, they can't get us."

Kyle stared into the same dead eyes Richy did. "I sure hope not."

There are dead on the island! Martingale thought as he sprinted toward the end of the tunnel. Those brats would definitely die, but it wasn't his fault. They shouldn't be down there in the first place. They'd been told. They'd been told not to wander into unknown areas. If he had opened that door, he might not have made it out of the tunnel alive.

Initially he thought that the rest of the Alcatraz community would understand his actions, but the more he mulled it over, he realized they would blame him. They would blame him for the deaths of those ungrateful little monsters instead of thanking him for preventing the real monsters from using that tunnel to access the island.

No, he wouldn't be able to tell anyone. He would just say he heard something in the tunnel and requested backup to check it out. With the kids dead, nobody would be the wiser. Really, he had done the island *two* favors.

He put his hand against the cool bricks of the tunnel and nodded while he took a quick breath. Martingale had never believed in exercise as a means of staying in shape. He just thought that if he ate right he would be fine. He looked down at his belly and smiled. He had lost twenty pounds since his escape to the island. Nobody would give him the extra food portions he asked for, and maybe that had been a good thing. *I look good*, he thought, but he knew he still couldn't run for extended periods of time.

He withdrew his palm from the bricks and continued up the tunnel. The sunlight at the end was a welcome beacon for him, and he strode forward, triumphant. His smile vanished when he saw that horrid cat sitting in the sun looking at him. He sneered at the animal. "If I could just catch it…" he said aloud.

When he got within ten feet of the feline, it spun its head to the left, then bolted away to the right.

Martingale huffed as he navigated from the tunnel through the basement of the power building. He really wanted a pizza. Hadn't had one in ages. Pineapple and pepperoni. He salivated, and could almost taste the…

Were those gunshots? He listened harder if that were possible. Four more shots sounded outside the building, then the firing became sustained. It sounded like there was a war going on out there.

He reached the south door, cracked it open and peeked out. A frightened man was limping up the brick walkway toward him, waving his arms. One of those arms was bloody.

"Martingale!" the man, Hal if he could remember correctly, yelled to him. They're right behind me!"

The walkway behind Hal flooded with dead. They gave a slow but steady chase after the flesh in front of them. Martingale took a final look at Hal then slammed the door. He shot the upper and lower bolts home to give him as much safety as possible.

Hal reached the door and began pounding his fists on it. "Let me in! What the hell are you doing?" He pleaded for another fifteen seconds or so before he began to scream.

Martingale took a few steps back as he listened to the man outside the door be consumed by the infected. When the hammering on the door switched from two fists to two dozen, he turned and fled back into the power building, searching for another way out.

Five men stood speaking to each other in the command center. They were awaiting confirmation of the initial reports from the southern dock. Meara, Pitt, McInerney, Dallas, and Rick Barnes. "Where the hell is Martingale?" asked Rick, his eyes darting to all corners of the room.

Dallas harrumphed, "Lil sumbitch is supposed to be here, ain't he? To… was' the word, liaise?"

The radio came to life as McInerney searched the room as well.

"Command, Detachment Alpha. We're going to need backup on this one. The count looks to be in the hundreds, over."

"Bravo concurs," McInerney heard through the radio. *"Request permission to engage?"*

The captain leaned down to speak into the microphone. He depressed the send button, "Granted. All teams, light 'em up. He turned to speak to his XO. "Mr. Pitt, send two more squads, then begin evacuating civvies to the boat. I want all the kids inside before any adult steps foot on the gangway."

"Aye, sir," Commander Pitt replied as gunfire erupted from the southern end of Alcatraz. Pitt began to scramble his attendants, barking orders and pointing.

McInerney glanced at his radio man. "Jennings, get the Reaper up. I want constant surveillance."

"Aye, sir." Jennings spoke into a different microphone and got to work.

"Captain Meara," McInerney began, "would you please help facilitate the evacuation? The civilian population looks to you."

Meara nodded, grabbing Rick as he hurried from the room. Dallas followed.

"C'mon, shitheads, we ain't gettinn' paid by the hour!" yelled ensign Strohl. The three others in his fire team, Li, Brown, and Devine looked nervous. Two were civilians, which Strohl was not in favor of. The sailors from the Florida had been training the civvies for quite a while on tactics and the use of weapons, but they still lacked discipline. Li was the only other sailor, and Li was the only man Strohl trusted. Strohl's detachment consisted of eight men divided into two fire teams. The squad had split up when they noticed infected travelling in two directions. Nothing had been heard from the two men on watch since they first called in the trouble.

An infected stumbled from the right side of the concrete path. It looked directly at the group of four men and growled. Strohl sighted and fired his rifle. The creature dropped, but dozens more rounded the southern bend, trampling the pretty flowers and shuffling up the walkway. "Brown, cover our backs. Make sure nothing is coming from behind us. Li, Devine, fire at will!"

The three men selected targets as they had been trained and began to fire into the small horde of infected. The creatures dropped to the ground, their brethren tripping over them in their slow plod toward food. At twenty feet, Strohl called a retreat, and the men withdrew further back up the walkway. When Strohl deemed they had enough range on the dead, he spun and resumed firing, as did Li and Devine.

Strohl heard Brown yelling something, but the sustained fire from he and the other two men had his ears ringing. He dropped his expended magazine, slamming a new one home and Brown grabbed his shoulder and screamed in his face. Strohl glanced at Brown who was pointing behind them. A smaller contingent of infected were shuffling in from the rear. There were only fifteen or so, but Strohl decided that they needed to bug out.

"Switch targets and press to the rear!"

The men did as they were told and fired into the horde behind as they walked toward them. More infected streamed down the trail from the northeast.

"Shit!" Strohl bellowed as he realized there were too many. They would be out of ammo before they made a dent. *There must be hundreds of them*, hhe thought. "This way!"

The living men made a break to the east, the dead ones closing in. One managed to grab hold of Li's T-shirt but the material ripped and the infected was denied its meal. At the base of the old guard tower, Strohl stopped and turned around. The dead were twenty feet behind and he sighted on them selectively firing and destroying targets. Not needing to be instructed, his fire team clanged up the iron spiral stairs toward the top of the tower. When the three of his men made the first bend, he followed. They reached the third bend as the first dead woman put her foot on the bottom step.

A steep set of iron stairs met the men at the top of the spiral staircase. Li climbed the steps and shouted "Clear!" when he poked his head through the open trapdoor. When Strohl climbed through the aperture, Li and Devine dropped the heavy trapdoor down and shot the iron bolt home.

The four men looked out at their home from the guard tower. The dock area and picnic areas teemed with the dead. Infected milled about on the Agave Trail until the walkway bent out of sight to the west. Li watched as a contingent of rotten former humans smashed their way into the bookstore and giftshop. Dead streamed both north and south on the trails and walkways.

"There's got to be a thousand of them," Brown breathed.

"Command, Spartan Platoon Detachment Bravo. Four-man fire team is cut off and in the guard tower. From here we can see Limas all over the eastern edge of the island. Can't see any on the parade ground yet, but they're on the way. I can see as far as the power house and there are Limas up there as well. Running low on ammo. Request evac or orders, over?"

"Bravo, command. Sit tight and continue with intel. Take out any tangos you can. Reinforcements are inbound. Command out."

"They're leaving us here?" demanded Devine.

Li rounded on him. "What the fuck do you want them to do?"

Strohl put his hand on Li's shoulder. "Easy, buddy." Li nodded. Strohl looked to the command center by Eagle Plaza and the lighthouse. "If they aren't sending anybody right now, that means they have problems of their own."

A thump on the bottom of the trapdoor gave each of the men a jump scare.

Strohl ejected the magazine from his rifle and checked the load. "Alright, Bravo, here's the plan: We take out as many as we can. I would suggest we each save one round."

"But how are we gonna get down from here if we're using up all our ammo on the ones on the ground?"

Strohl sighted on an infected in a Golden State Warriors basketball tank top. "Where are we going to go? If we thin the herd, maybe help can get here. Otherwise... well, like I said, save a bullet."

"We're five short," Juanita told Pitt as she double checked her clipboard.

His brow furrowed. "Where are they?"

"I don't know. The twins, the tall kid Kyle, Vanessa and…" she looked at Rick, "Sam."

Rick nodded to Dallas and Pitt, "Come with me." The three of them moved into the group of civilians until Rick saw a ten-year-old boy. "Quincy," he said, putting his hand on the kid's shoulder. "Do you know where Sam is?"

"Uh-uh."

"How about the twins, or Kyle and Vanessa?" asked Pitt.

The boy looked nervous. He clearly didn't want to tell the adults where the kids had gone. He swallowed hard, his eyes wide and scared.

"It's ok, Quincy. You're not in any trouble and neither are they. Not for this. They could be in real danger though." Rick got down on his haunches, his patience holding. "We need to know where they are, so we can go get them and bring them to the sub."

The boy nodded. "They went to go check the tunnel under the power building." He looked down. "I told them I wouldn't say nothin'."

Rick thanked the kid. He stood and nodded to Pitt, who nodded back. Pitt checked his sidearm and spoke to Meara as he watched Rick and Dallas make for the door.

"You've got six sailors to help you get everybody on board the Florida. I'm going to help your friends. He started after Rick, then stopped, pointing a finger at Meara, "Do not let these civilians make a mess of my boat!"

Vanessa and Chloe burst from the tunnel running for the command center. The girls almost collided with a small contingent of undead as they milled about near the tunnel entrance. A decaying hand made a swipe for them but was woefully short. Chloe screeched as she juked the hand and the girls darted away. Six of the things began to plod after the girls, but two stopped and stared briefly into the tunnel before shuffling into the entrance.

Chloe cupped her hands together and screamed toward the tunnel, "Rich! There's more out here! You got two coming into the tunnel!" Both she and Vanessa grasped their blades firmly in their fists. Chloe banged her knife on the iron railing, egging the creatures toward her.

"Come on you dead A-holes, this way!"

One of the infected who had entered the tunnel stumbled back out and began its chase.

"Behind!" hissed Vanessa.

Two more of the things were coming from the opposite direction, pinning the girls between them and the larger group. Chloe continued banging her blade. "When they come for me, you run around them! I'll be right behind you!"

The infected did indeed head for the banging sounds and Vanessa was able to duck off to the right of them. "Come on!" she screamed.

Chloe abandoned her railing and sprinted to the outside of the reaching hands. This time one of the things was able to latch on to her shirt, and before she could pull away, it had her. She grappled with it for a moment before she twisted her arm up and over its elbow and broke it. She tried to turn away, but her foot got tangled in the thing's legs, and they both went down in a heap. She struggled to keep the creature's mouth from her but noticed the other one fall to its knees next to her in an attempt to feed.

She thrust her blade at the head of the creature atop her but missed and stabbed it in the neck. The other one had grabbed her arm and was pulling it to its mouth when a streak hit it from the side. The growling that came from the combatants was not that of the undead, but from a ninety-five-pound bloodhound that was shaking the infected to pieces.

Chloe saw an arm fly past her and heard the dog barking furiously. The canine let loose with a loud bay, and suddenly the thing atop her was dragged off. A two-foot long length of rebar crashed down on the infected cranium, driving it to the ground where it remained motionless.

"Get up, kid!" shouted a man in a southern drawl. The man thundered forward and smacked the now armless creature the hound had dragged off. The big man hit it twice in the head before it stopped moving.

"Dallas, back on the line!" a man shouted. It had been Commander Pitt, and Rick was with him.

Chloe smiled as she looked up into her friend's face. Dallas helped her stand and the two of them sprinted from the oncoming horde, dog in tow. Rick and Pitt fired into the crowd dropping infected with headshots. Dallas joined in and fired with his shotgun until there were none left.

Dallas got down on one knee next to Clyde, the bloodhound. "Good boy!" he said when the gunfire ceased.

Rick was about to ask Chloe and Vanessa where his daughter was when Vanessa pointed, telling the grown-ups there were kids in the tunnel with the dead.

Rick and Pitt ran for the tunnel, Pitt calling back over his shoulder, "Dallas, get the kids to the boat!"

The dog started to move toward the tunnel, but Dallas called to him, "Clyde, you stay with me, now." The pooch about-faced and trotted back to the Texan, padding toward the USS Florida with the girls.

"Why do they call submarines boats?" Dallas asked the kids. "I mean, they go *under* the water, right?"

"It scratched you?" Kyle asked over the din of the infected.

Both boys pushed against the rusty iron door, and it seemed the dead would not be able to open it from their side. Only two of them could push on it at once, and the bottom of the ancient metal was stuck on the bricks.

"Yeah, but we can't worry about that now." Richy glanced at Sam and smiled. "You ok?"

"Fine," she said in a small voice. "You sure they can't get through?"

"We did, so, no." He looked at the heavy piece of metal that Martingale had used to block the door. That was helping, but if the kids left, the dead would be able to push open the door and gain entry to the island.

Hands reached through the opening between the side of the door and the bricks, but they couldn't reach the warm flesh.

"What was that?" Sam asked when she heard gunfire echo down the tunnel.

Kyle crinkled his face up. "Sounds like somebody shooting." His eyes went wide. "But that means…"

"We don't know what it means," interrupted Richy. "We do know that the girls went to get help. They'll be back soon with some soldiers and a bunch of guns."

The children spent the next few minutes in silence, the wet, rasping hacks of the dead just on the other side of the door the only sounds in the tunnel. Shouting bounced around the tunnel walls briefly, then the bob of flashlights appeared and suddenly Commander Pitt and Sam's dad were standing staring at the kids.

"Sam!" Rick yelled and ran to her. "Are you ok?"

She nodded and threw her arms around her father.

"What the hell is this?" Pitt demanded in a stern voice.

"This is us stopping them from getting on the island!" Richy retorted.

"How did they get in there?" Rick asked as he scooped up Sam.

"There's a bunch of water at the end of the tunnel!" Kyle almost shouted. "They just walked in!"

"Good work, you three," Pitt congratulated as he put his hands against the door. "You're also in a world of trouble. Rick, get 'em out."

"What about you?"

"I'm right behind you. Kids!" he added quickly, "There's a body in the tunnel back there. One was coming up behind you and we took it out."

Rick put Sam back down but held her hand as he trod up the tunnel. Richy and Kyle were immediately behind. When they were out of sight, Pitt took his hands off the door and hurried to follow them. The heavy iron door began to scrape across the brick behind him.

When he made the first bend in the passageway, he flashed his light back the way he had come. Three of the dead were already through the gap and more were squeezing past. The door slid further open and infected spilled onto the bricks.

Pitt harrumphed. "Eat this, assholes," he said under his breath. He removed an object from his tactical vest, pulled the pin and threw it underhand down the corridor, the metal making pinging sounds as it bounced across the bricks. Immediately, the sailor sprinted toward the entrance of the tunnel. "Fire in the hole!"

He could see Rick and the kids running into the sunlight when the explosion behind him almost knocked him over. Dust rained down and several bricks fell from the ceiling. Pitt dove out of the dank tube followed by a dust and particulate cloud that sprayed out of the maw behind him.

Ears screaming, he wafted his hand in front of his face to push the dust away. He stood, Rick aiming his rifle at him. Rick screamed something, but the confined blast had replaced Pitt's hearing with a painfully loud ringing noise.

The sailor felt a hand latch onto his shoulder but only briefly. He spun to see a dead woman collapse behind him, but Rick hadn't fired. Three other dead people materialized out of the dust and Pitt could see other shapes moving toward him. He ran back to Rick and the kids, Rick covering with his rifle. Now Rick was popping off rounds. Pitt could hear the gunfire, but it sounded like he was hearing the rounds while he was under water.

Several dead moved through the settling dust cloud with malicious intent. Rick took them one at a time, but several became dozens which turned into a hundred or more.

Rick tapped Pitt on the shoulder. He was speaking to Pitt, but the sailor couldn't hear him. Rick got what was happening and pointed behind them. The five Alcatraz survivors raced back up the walkway toward the anchored sub. Rick noticed a pile of fresh bloody rags in front of the door to the power building and he knew there were going to be casualties today.

EIGHTEENTH FLOOR: COSMETICS, LINGERIE, AND SHITLOADS OF ZOMBIES
JOURNAL ENTRY 4

Jill was in front of the door to eighteen when it exploded outward. The force of the door knocked her into the railing, the infected took her over it. She fell screaming onto the stairs a landing down with one of the things latched onto her, her shrieks ceased with a crunch. Jon went down almost immediately, his neck now displaying a ragged, spurting hole in the right side. He fought briefly, but there were too many. Joan took a bite on the arm but was able to fight the things off until we were able to assist.

We hadn't thought it through. We had considered what could happen if infected came from above or below, and even thought about a couple from an open door. We hadn't thought about an attack en-masse from the side. My team below brought their rifles up, and so did we, but we couldn't fire. The dead were between us, and the rounds would cut down the living as well as the dead if we fired into them.

Ship took one step down and decapitated two infected with one swing. Remo thrust his blade into the side of the head of one of the things and it collapsed, then he did draw his sidearm and fire into the open doorway. Seyfert and Alvarez were also stabbing and slashing with their knives. Danny was grappling with one of the things that had grabbed Brad, the two of them playing tug-of-war for Brad's life.

Lynda and Steve pulled their weight by destroying two infected with their bare hands. Well, hands and feet. Steve smashed the noggin of one of the things into the railing, and Lynda stomped on the face of one that had fallen.

We destroyed eleven infected in twenty seconds. Remo's gunfire had our ears ringing, but not badly enough that we couldn't hear what was coming up the stairs below. The scream of a Runner preceded it as it sprinted up the stairs two at a time. It rounded the corner, saw us, and tried to climb over the railing instead of continue up the steps. Danny shot it and it fell backward, clutching its chest.

"Up!" shouted Seyfert. "Back up!"

"Can't!" I countered. "They're above us in the stairwell too!"

Ship started tossing dead bodies like rag dolls over the railing. Remo started helping him, then I finally got the idea: We were going to enter the door the dead had come from.

It only took a few moments to clear the door enough to get through. Ship and Remo moved into the doorway first, with Anna and I behind in cover formation.

"Clear!" Remo shouted.

It wasn't long before the fourteen of us were standing in another elevator lobby. Anna was tending to Joan, the rest of us with firearms pointing them all into the office. It smelled awful. Terrible. Like, BAD in there. There were blood smears and drag marks all over the place. A lady's shoe, some tattered remains, bones, and some of the shit the dead leave behind when they shuffle about were strewn in the lobby.

The pretty of the green granite lobby was overpowered by the stench of what had been in here. A dead thing stumbled from the cubicle area of the office. Remo shot it quickly, then tapped his suppressor on the granite desk. Nothing else came.

Seyfert had the back of his wrist covering his nose. "We can't stay here."

Bob, one of the office workers, grabbed Remo and yelled in his face. "You idiots should have left us where we were! We were fine!"

Remo didn't say a word. He looked at Bob's hands on him, then shifted his gaze to Bob's eyes. The office guy let go immediately and I understood why. I had been on the other side of Remo's *don't fuck with me* face, and it was unnerving as hell. I'm sure he could have used his glare as a weapon to melt this guy had he wanted to.

Joan was getting a bandage on her bicep from Anna when she piped up. "We would have been eating each other in a few days."

"But Jon and Jill!" Bob nearly shrieked. "They would be alive right now if—"

Joan cut him off, "It doesn't matter. We all would have been dead if…"

Thumps sounded from the door we had just come through. The dead had reached our floor.

"Remo, Ship, Alvarez," spoke Seyfert, "we need to properly clear this floor." He pointed at me. "You, Danny, and Kev watch them. Don't let them wander off. If anybody moves toward the door, shoot them. Anna, check everybody for scratches, you can check us when we get back."

The four of them slunk off, weapons at the ready. I rounded on the office folks, "We're gonna get out of here. It's what we do."

"Tell that to my friends who just died," Bob almost sobbed.

"I feel bad about that, but if they died so that you could live, then honor their sacrifice by living."

Lynda and Steve were holding each other tightly.

"You guys ok?" I asked.

"Yes, thank you," Steve told me.

"Can they get in here?" Brad asked staring at the door. There was considerable thumping going on, and we could hear the other sounds of the dead.

"It's a steel fire door and it opens out," Kev told him. "And you guys were in an office just like this for a long time; did they get in there?"

"No, but they never pounded on it like they are now."

Kev shrugged. "Life's a bitch."

"So's death," I said aloud.

Joan smiled, showing us her bandaged arm. "Guess I'll find out soon."

We heard a suppressed shot, then four men said *Clear* into the radio.

The boys showed back up, Ship in the rear.

"So, what's the plan, Navy?"

Seyfert looked tired. "We clear the stairwell and exfil the civvies back to the Rock." He peeked at the door being thumped on by the shitheads, then pulled his radio. "Rock this is Sabre One, how copy?"

This was the first time in my short stretch in San Francisco that Alcatraz hadn't responded immediately to a radio call. Apparently Seyfert was a bit put off too, because he made a face.

"Rock, Sabre One. Come in." Seyfert glanced up at us. Something was amiss.

I was about to ask what was up when the radio answered "Sabre, this is Shark. Switch to the alternate frequency now."

"Who's Shark?" I asked, confused.

Seyfert didn't even look at me. He fumbled with his radio for a moment, then nodded at Danny, "With me," was all he said. The two of them moved off into the bloody cubicles while the rest of us stared at their backs.

The office building people began to fire questions at us, but Remo held up a hand and they fell silent. "We know as much as you do," he told them.

Seyfert and Danny returned in less than a minute.

"Alcatraz is under attack," the SEAL told us.

I moved toward the door. My hand reached for the lever-style handle before Ship's massive mitt came down on my shoulder.

"We gotta go, buddy. Our family is on that island."

He nodded that he understood but kept his hand on me. Had anybody other than my loved-ones put their hand on me like that, they would have drawn back a stump, but this was Ship. Firstly, he was family. Secondly, I had neither a chainsaw nor Excalibur on me, and that's what I would need to cut this guy's hand off.

I looked way up at him. He pulled his hand off me to sign some stuff. He told me that we would have to think this through, and that we would most likely die if I opened that door.

I couldn't help my family if I was chewed chunks of meat.

I moved to Seyfert. Remo and Ship stood with me. "What's the plan?"

"Kill everything and exfil."

I thumbed at Seyfert while looking behind me at Ship and Remo, "I love this guy."

Seyfert shrugged out of his pack and placed it on the granite elevator lobby desk. This was a pretty green granite with gold veins. I liked it. He fished around in his pack for just a second until he came out with a length of black rope. He pointed at Danny who did the same, then the SEAL spun to regard the stainless-steel elevator doors.

He rounded on the office folk. "Any idea what floor the elevator stopped on before you lost power?"

"No," replied three of them at once.

"So then if I pry those doors open, there could be an elevator full of infected right on the other side?"

Joan shrugged, Steve asked *why*, and Brad said *yeah*.

I could see where this was going, and I didn't like it, but what choice did I have? We either opened the door and fought infected in a six-foot wide stairwell eighteen floors down to the lobby, used the elevator shaft to climb down, or jumped out the fucking window. I glanced at the tactical rope and could see that both men had twenty-five-foot lengths.

"I've seen this movie," I said. "In fact, I was the fucking star in it. In my movie there was a ladder in the elevator shaft."

"Nope," Brad said, "no ladders. I checked months ago."

I sighed, "Buzz-kill."

I smelled something burning so I glanced at everybody's favorite bigfoot. He was staring intently at the silver of the stainless elevator doors. He shifted his glance to the granite desk, then whipped his head around to look at the cube farm. The wheels were turning in his giant dome, I could see it. He snapped his fingers, and everyone looked at him expectantly. He pointed at Remo and made a writing motion in the air.

Now, as I've stated countless times in my other journals, Ship is Mute. He is not deaf, and he is the polar-opposite of dumb, he just can't speak. So, when he looked like he was demanding a pen from Remo, when I absolutely knew he had at least two on his enormous frame, I was confused.

Remo instantly produced the same black Sharpie he had used on a million occasions and passed it to Ship, who took one stride and was hastily drawing on the elevator door.

That pissed me off. I could speak mostly-fluent sign language and had known both Ship and Remo much longer than they had known each other, but every time one of them wanted or needed to convey information, the other knew *instantly* what the first one was saying. This is a superhero power. I am not even fucking kidding.

My superhero power is remembering porn star names. That shit just isn't fair. What's worse is that these two guys, smart and empathic as they are, still look to me to make decisions. What the fuck are they thinking?

I knew what Ship was thinking. We all did. He drew the shit out of it in black marker on the silver door. It was artwork. A damn Rembrandt. No, more than that, a fucking Da Vinci. After he finished wrecking the stainless steel, he gave the marker back to Remo and began writing in his notebook. When he finished, he passed the book to me.

I read it aloud for all to hear: *It is extremely unlikely that the elevator car stopped on this floor at the onset of the plague, but we should prepare for that eventuality before we open the doors. If we utilize the granite desk and some of the cubicle walls, we could create obstacles to force the dead to the elevator. If the car is not too close below us, the press of the infected to obtain food (us) will force the vanguard into the obstacles, where they will ultimately be funneled into the shaft. Even if the dead are not destroyed by the fall, they will be rendered incapable of attacking us at the bottom of an elevator shaft... unless the door at the bottom is open. Any who get close to crawling past our barriers, or any stragglers left behind, can be picked off with the rifles.*

Ship didn't wait for approval or infighting. He ran back to the cubicles and began looking at the floor near them.

"Where did you *get* this guy?" Seyfert asked me.

"Internet."

As I rushed off to help Ship, I heard Seyfert talk to Danny, "Stand by the door to the stairwell. Anybody goes near it, shoot them. The rest of you come with me."

Joan and Anna stayed behind, but everybody else did as ordered and we were soon dismantling cubicles with several multi-tools. When we had twelve five-foot cube walls, we stacked them by the lobby. Four of us stood behind the granite desk with Seyfert and Kev in front of the stainless elevator doors.

"Good?" asked Seyfert. I have no idea how he wasn't shitting himself. He and Kev had volunteered to open the doors. We would blast anything that came out, but those two were most definitely in harm's way.

"We're good," I answered speaking for everybody. I was trying to be tough.

"What about us?" demanded Brad.

Remo did not take his eyes off the door when he replied, "If they get past us, kill as many as you can before they eat you."

Seyfert did not wait for the civvies to cry before he and Kev pried the doors open.

We looked in on an empty elevator shaft. Seyfert stuck his head into the shaft and cautiously peered up and down. He used the magwell button on his rifle to activate the tactical light which he shined in both directions.

He shook his head. "I can't see the elevator either up or down."

In a half hour, Ship had devised a tiny labyrinth from the stairwell door to the open elevator shaft. There were four of the formerly white cubicle walls at an angle from the stairwell to a long fall. They were braced in the back by two others placed vertically and attached by the cubicle hardware.

Four feet from that wall was another double set of cube walls set all the way across the lobby. It was fourteen feet in total, and we made a bit of a sliding door with one of the walls. The heavy granite desk, which took six of us to move was braced behind the sliding partition, and three more vertical walls would prevent the dead from pushing the barrier back at us.

We hoped.

There had been two flag poles standing and one lying next to the desk. Remo picked up the American flag, he and Seyfert folding it into a triangle, which they placed with reverence on a chair on this side of the barricade. Even with the country in shambles, this flag still symbolized everything these guys valued. I felt a bit of guilt that I had spent the last few years prior to this little apocalypse thingy as a criminal instead of in the military. I really think I would have fit in with that lifestyle, and for the briefest of moments shame pushed its way past the guilt.

Then Ship snapped one of the poles in half and handed it to me. It had a nice pointy end, perfect for skewering the rotten noggins of a bunch of festering dead cannibals. I asked him why he didn't break the other two and he told me we could use them as prods to assist the things into the elevator shaft. He had both signed and showed me what he meant, and I got it immediately.

"When I open the door," Seyfert began, "they should flood this little area." He looked at me. "Make damn sure I'm back through our gate here before you shut it."

"Gotcha," I nodded. I was the guy who was going to slide the gate home.

The SEAL continued, "When I'm through, we do everything we can to get them into the shaft. The difficult ones will get shot or stabbed. You guys good?" He raised his eyebrows while he looked at the civvies.

"What can I do to help?" asked Steve. I could see he was shitting himself, and my respect for him shot skyward.

I reiterated Remo's statement from before: "Kill any that get past us."

"But if they get past you—" Kayla began.

"Then they're done eating us and they're coming for you," I finished for her. "So fucking kill them all. Keep in mind these things have already killed pretty much everyone you know outside of this room, so be pissed and take out your anger on them."

She nodded. She really did look mad. That was good.

Seyfert moved to the door. He put his left hand on the silver handle and let out a big breath he had been holding. He turned to face his army. Thirteen of us stood ready. Well, Joan was sitting in a chair looking ill, but the rest of us stood.

"On three," the SEAL told us. He counted down, and when he got to one, he pushed the handle down and kicked the door. It moved about four inches, then slammed closed. Seyfert was already halfway back to the gate before he realized the door was not open.

"Shit."

He moved back to the door. He let out that same breath, pushed the handle down, kicked the door, and this shit was on. Bunches of fingers, hands, and arms forced their way into the crack between the door and the frame. They did not belong to nice people.

The problem was, the dead were too stupid to act as one. Some were still beating on the door and some were trying to pull it open, so they kind of stymied themselves.

Seyfert was back through the gate and I slammed it home behind the heavy granite desk in five seconds. We might have been able to order a pizza before the dead douches pulling on the steel actually won the fight and the door moved open enough for the things to spill in.

And spill in they did. They shuffled forward, slamming into our barrier with all the force they could muster. Arms reached over the cube walls, but the things couldn't get any type of purchase as the walls were five feet high. The ones in the front were crushed against the barrier as the ones in the back flooded the lobby.

Ship is a fucking genius. I've said that many times, and I'm sure I'll repeat it until the day I die. If the next few paragraphs don't cement the fact that Ship is a genius into your brain, you should go find a container of bleach and make some margaritas with it.

The tops of the cubicles had these pretty, opaque-blue glass partitions on them. I saw one of the things press its rotten face against the glass as it tried to reach over and grab me. Our eyes locked and we regarded each other as the thing slid to the right. There were two-inch-wide gaps in the glass, and when the thing reached one, its skull was briefly caught. Half the thing's face peeled off as it slid past the slit. The thing's left eye skated across the corner of the partition and let go with a wet squirt. I watched in awe as the dead in the back pushed the ones in the front and the ones in the front slipped to the right.

The angled cube walls did their job well. Half-face looked back at me with its remaining eye for another moment before it disappeared into the shaft with a few others.

I glanced at Remo, he looked at me at the same time. We both shrugged and continued to stab at the more industrious of the pus sacks who tried to climb over the walls. None of them made it.

I don't know how many of those rotten things took the plunge, but it was quite a few. All I could picture was each of them hitting the bottom of that elevator shaft with a wet splash. The floor we were on now was pretty stinky, but can you imagine the stench from that friggin hole in a month?

Ew.

It was over in twenty minutes. There were a couple of crawlers on the other side of the wall, mixed in with any of their re-killed brethren who hadn't fallen to their wet end. Ship used one of the broken flag poles to end the two legless things and we were suddenly out of zombies. We waited five minutes, not hearing anything from the stairwell. Seyfert tapped his chest, pointed to his eyes and then at the open fire door. He pointed at me and I nodded. Ship slid the makeshift door to our barricade open, Seyfert and I slipping through quietly, sidearms ready. We stepped over a baker's dozen of the stinking corpses and slunk to the wide-open fire door prepared to sprint back if need be. We hunched over, using our inspection mirrors to check outside the door. Seyfert checked the right, down the stairs, my direction was left and up. I have no idea what the SEAL saw in his mirror, but mine caught the reflection of a pair of knees. As I angled the mirror up, I could see a tall, thin man. He stood with his back pressed against the concrete wall of the stairwell, palms flat, head back. The fucker was trying to hide behind the open door. I had no idea how this guy hadn't been shredded and consumed by the sixty or so undead that had been in this concrete tube not six minutes before.

Until I angled the mirror up a bit more. The man's tank-top was covered in gore as was his beard. He had that twitchy, feverish look that only meant one thing. When he dropped his gaze and looked directly into the mirror with his red, bleeding eyes, it was confirmed. My sanity checked out for a split second, my mind simply not prepared for this.

But wait, there's more!

I gasped, and the thing shrieked, tearing around the door and leaping over the re-killed thing that had it propped open. It grabbed the door frame with both hands, its long arms propelling it into the elevator lobby. It smashed into me, knocking me off balance, then plowed into my new buddy. Seyfert's weapon clattered away, the man and the lanky infected going down in a thrashing heap. It straddled him, the two of them fighting for the SEAL's life.

"*YES!*" it screamed in a voice not remotely human, and it brought its hand up high to slash downward into Seyfert's face. Four bullets impacted the Runner simultaneously and it flew to the left, smacking its noggin on the doorframe. Seyfert scrabbled backward on his ass like a crab, but he only made two feet before he hit the wall next to the open elevator doors. Five feet to his left and he would have joined the infected at the bottom of the shaft.

The Runner put its nasty paw on the floor and began to push itself up. It only got halfway before I shot it in the back of the dome with my sidearm.

I stood, moving into the stairwell to cover Seyfert until *his* sanity returned. This was some fucked up shit right here, and it might take a minute for him to process. Nothing was coming from above or below that I could see or hear. I dragged both things out of the doorway and pulled the door closed.

"You ok?" I asked, holding a hand down to him to help him up.

Seyfert looked up at me blinking. "You... you heard..."

"Damn skippy. Fucker spoke." I waggled the fingers on my still extended hand, and he got the message. I helped him up and the two of us stared back at the group behind the safety of the cubicle walls.

I began to ask, but Remo cut me off, "I heard it too."

"Me too." said Anna.

We all did," Kev added. "What in holy fucking hell was that?"

"Dunno," I shrugged. "Maybe he was a Jeopardy winner before he was infected. Ya know, all smart 'n shit."

Conversations started between pretty much everybody. Even Ship was furiously scribbling on his pad.

"Hey," I said.

The conversations not only didn't stop, they got louder.

"Hey?" I asked a little louder.

Nothing. Dicks.

"Hey!" Everybody looked at me like *I* was being rude. Gaggle of douches. "I know talking infected are a cool new apocalyptic topic and stuff, but I have family on that island, and I'm pretty sure all of you office critters want to get the hell out of this building." Murmurs of assent and some nodding fueled my chastisement. "Let's book."

PERCHED
ALCATRAZ

How did these people live on this thing for months at a time? Chloe marveled. She looked all around but the walls just seemed to want to crush her. The quarters were tight, and everything smelled like stale air, stale people, and stale oil. The place was packed full of people, and as this was the apocalypse, there wasn't a lot of deodorant to be had. She helped Vanessa as the girl reached the bottom of the ladder.

"I want every single person who wasn't on board before the attack checked by the corpsman inside of an hour." Chloe heard from above. It was the captain's voice. "Get him any help he needs to do the inspections. Don't miss *anybody*!"

"Aye, sir!"

Chloe grabbed her new friend by the hand. "You ok?"

"Yeah, but…" Vanessa looked around as Chloe had. "This is… tight." The girl swallowed hard.

"I know, but we're safer in here than out there with all the dead."

Vanessa nodded, still surveying her surroundings.

Clyde began to bay as he was lowered into the sub on a line. He looked miserable, and Dallas grabbed him before he was able to put one of his four massive paws on the deck.

"Hush now, ya big galoot!" Normally Clyde did what most people told him, but he didn't like it inside the submarine and wanted to let everyone know.

A sailor with a clipboard stepped up to them. "Keep it moving, girls." He raised his voice to compete with Clyde's baying. He smiled, "Follow everyone else to the galley. They'll set you up for a bit in there until we figure out what's going on." He produced a stick of jerky and pointed at Clyde. "Sit." The dog not only complied but became instantly silent. The sailor passed the pooch his jerky and the bloodhound gobbled it down quickly.

"Thank you," Chloe told him, and they moved on.

"He was cute!" Vanessa whispered, looking back over her shoulder.

"He's like, *thirty!*" Chloe shot back, nose wrinkled.

The girls moved down the corridor and a set of stairs, keeping in line with the other civilians until they reached the galley. There were no seats left at the tables, so they stood with dozens of others. One of the sailors pointed to a family and said, "You're next, come on." The man wore a surgical mask over his mouth and nose and was flanked by two other sailors carrying wicked looking black guns. The family stood and followed them out.

"What's that about?" Chloe asked Vanessa.

A woman behind them answered, "They're checking everyone for bites. It would be pretty horrible to have an outbreak inside this thing."

Chloe instantly thought of her brother and his scratched arm.

Commander McInerney stood on the hull of his submarine, staring at Alcatraz through his binoculars.

"Where the hell is Pitt? Try him again."

The sailor next to McInerney adjusted the sling on his sub-machine gun and placed a radio call. There was no answer.

"Command, Spartan Platoon, Detachment Bravo. I Saw Pitt and a group of civvies run out of a tunnel near the power building. I lost them when they rounded the corner. They have a shit-ton of Limas on their six."

The sailor passed the radio to his Commander. "Copy that Spartan. What kind of enemy presence are you seeing from up there?"

"Difficult to get an accurate count, Command. I would estimate about four hundred, but they're moving all over the place. They have no focus, so the count could be off. They've stopped coming ashore though and there are only a half dozen milling about on the dock."

"Excellent intel, sailor. Sit tight, we'll get to you when we can."

"Copy that, Command. Good luck."

Pitt, Rick, the boys, and Sam rounded the bend near the Model Industries building. Dozens of infected were in front of them and Rick realized they would never make it to the inflatable boats which would carry them to the submarine. The dead in front hadn't seen them, but the ones in back were hot on their heels, maybe a hundred feet behind.

"Up the hill!" he hissed. "We get to the water tower and climb."

"Good idea." Pitt agreed, the five of them scrambling up the steep rocks. It was a difficult climb, but no one slipped even once.

Kyle glanced back down the hill when Richy helped him over the edge at the top. "Holy shit," the boy breathed. The rest of the group peered back down the steep slope. Several dozen infected were scratching their way up the hill, but they couldn't get purchase. They would get a few feet up and tumble back into the legs of their counterparts. If any of the survivors had fallen like the infected had, they wouldn't have had time to scream before they were eaten.

Pitt had seen enough. He reached for his radio, but it was missing. "Damn." He rubbed the stubble on his chin. He hadn't shaved since the day before yesterday. He *hated* stubble, but shaving equipment was hard to come by now. "Let's get to the top of the tower and do a proper recon. You kids up for another climb?"

The group of them stood beneath the massive water tower looking up. The top of the tower would be the highest point on the island, and it had a 360-degree view, but it was dangerous. The metal had been painted recently, and Chloe had told Richy that the government had spent a million dollars to restore the tower in the past few years. They had even re-lettered the graffiti scrawled on the tower by Native Americans during a time called the Occupation of Alcatraz. Rick's friend and SWAT sniper Pablo Martinez had used this very tower to scope out an attack from hostile humans a year ago. Martinez had been killed en route to Boston, and Rick felt a moment of sadness.

Pitt put his left hand on one of the rungs of the blue-painted ladder. I'll go first. Let me get a few rungs up before you start after me. Boys, you're next, then Sam. Rick, you follow at the end." Pitt glanced back toward the Model Industries and Power buildings. The dead were on the way up the steep ramp to the water tower. They would arrive in a few short minutes. The sailor began to climb, his boots making a clanging noise on the steel rungs as he ascended. A protective cage encircled the ladder all the way to the crest of the water tower.

The boys followed when Pitt was about ten feet up. Sam began her ascent with Rick immediately behind her. "You ok, honey?"

"Yeah, this is easy."

Soon Sam was extending her hand to Pitt, who assisted both her and her father onto the wire mesh walkway. Four feet of catwalk would keep them just under a hundred feet away from the gnashing teeth and tearing claws of the infected dead.

Pitt smiled, proud of the sailor who had had the idea to put caches of supplies all over the island. The Commander used his multi-tool to snip the cable ties which kept two ALICE packs, covered in plastic sheeting attached to the railings. The packs had a few day's-worth of food and water, two hundred rounds of .556 ammunition for the rifles, clips and line to keep stranded survivors from falling off the catwalks, and most importantly, two marine radios. He would need the radios not only to communicate with Command, but for the combination on the footlocker which contained an M40A5 sniper rifle and two hundred rounds of .308 ammo.

Pitt smiled again. "Now we're in business."

There were only four sets of clips and line, so Rick clipped the kids first, then tried to give the last set to Pitt. "You clip in," he told Rick. "You have a daughter up here."

The sailor switched on one of the tactical radios, tuned into the proper frequency, and depressed the send button. "Command, this is Pitt. How are we situated?"

"Pitt, Command. What is your location?"

"Staring at you through these giant binoculars from the catwalk on the water tower, sir."

Pitt watched as his captain and good friend shifted his gaze with his own set of binoculars. He noticed a visible sigh of relief leave McInerney even from a few hundred feet away.

"Glad you made it to safety. Who's up there with you? I want to check them off the list. Also, you should be able to see Spartan-Bravo in the guard tower. Coordinate with them."

"I've got Rick Barnes and his daughter Sam, one of the twins, Richy, and the tall kid, Kyle."

Pitt could see his captain confer with another sailor with a clipboard on the foredeck of the Florida. Pitt's boots clanged on the metal catwalk as he circled the steel of his tower to check the guard tower. He stared at a man aiming a rifle at him. The man used the scope to survey his Commander and lowered the rifle when his check was done.

"Got you, Commander."

"Copy, Spartan. Where's Alpha team?"

"Haven't heard from them. Bravo will keep trying."

"That leaves sixteen unaccounted for," McInerney's voice cut in, *"not including the mission fire team in the city. Dammit, where's Martingale? He's supposed to help facilitate the civilian evacuations."*

Richy and Kyle glanced at each other while Pitt continued his radio conversation. "Mr Barnes?" Kyle asked tentatively

Rick was hunkered down next to Sam and he raised his eyes up to the standing boy, staring at him expectantly.

"We were in the tunnel, all of us. Chloe and Vanessa were there too." The kid seemed hesitant, but he continued. "Mr. Martingale must have followed us into the tunnel. When we saw the dead coming out of the water at the end we ran for it, but the door was locked behind us. Mr. Martingale was on the other side. We told him there were dead in the tunnel, but he called us liars."

"It's true," Richy confirmed quickly. "You can ask Sam."

Rick didn't need to. "It's true," she told him. "He said that, then he ran when he saw those things coming behind us."

"He *ran?*" Rick asked incredulously. "What do you mean he ran?"

Richy folded his arms. "He saw the dead and took off. He left us to get eaten."

Pitt finished his radio conversation, glaring at the kids. He slipped the walkie-talkie into his pocket. "He *left* you? He *left* you there?"

All three kids nodded.

Commander Pitt shook his head in disgust. "We'll deal with that later. Right now, we have more pressing concerns." He dialed in a combination on the locker and extricated the firearm stored within. It was a greenish rifle that Richy thought didn't look overly impressive. There were two full ten-round box magazines and an ammo can in the footlocker as well.

Pitt slapped in a magazine and bolted in a round. He brought the rifle to his shoulder and took a sideways glance at Rick. He grinned a half smile. "Captain said to fire at will. Stick your fingers in your ears kids."

Dozens of the undead had made their way to the base of the water tower, but most of them would be difficult to hit from his vantage. He aimed the weapon toward the power building. A group of nasty specimens were milling about slowly on the stone walkway. The scope's crosshairs settled on the head of a burned and blackened corpse. It turned and looked directly at Pitt, the white of its teeth in stark contrast to the blackened flesh on its face. The teeth exploded when the .308 round entered just below the burned-off nose.

"Huh," Pitt thought aloud. "Little low."

He fired six more times, scoring four headshots. "This will take all damn day."

Rick aimed his rifle into the crowd and began firing. Shots from the guard tower echoed across the island as well.

OH SHIT!
JOURNAL ENTRY 5

We made the lobby of the office building without seeing another infected. It was a damn long walk, even going down instead of up. The cube critters were breathing heavy, not just from the climb down, but from the constant terror of being outside their environment. They had lived in the building, barely leaving that floor, since the start of all this shit.

We emerged from the stairwell and surveyed our surroundings. Right back where we started in this friggin' building. I glanced at the silent escalators and the equally silent infected we had taken out a few hours ago. A glance out the gigantic floor-to-ceiling windows yielded two infected milling about outside. Two was significantly less (and better) than the two thousand that had been out there earlier. It was also eerily quiet as the noise from the hordes of dead had moved on with them.

Seyfert and Remo were on point as we moved through the darkened lobby. There were tons of places to get ambushed and I didn't like being here. Shadows had lengthened as the day drew on, and the place was shrouded in gloom. The sun tried its best to penetrate those huge windows, but they must have been polarized.

Kev and I were in the middle of the pack with Danny and Anna. Ship and Alvarez closed out our little group at the rear. The surviving office folks were scattered between us.

"Not feeling great," Joan told us. She had been bitten less than a half hour ago but huffing down a million stairs had probably pumped whatever shit she was infected with throughout her small body quickly.

We were passing a support column when a dead thing snaked its arm out and latched on to Kev's collar. Six people had walked in front of us, and this thing couldn't have been bothered, but when I take a step near it, it decides to lunge. Kev gave a frightened yelp, spinning to try to see what had grabbed him, although let's face it he already knew.

I grabbed the thing that had seized Kev. The human pulled away, and when he did, the buttons on his shirt popped off, spraying everything with little round pieces of plastic like a button spewing machine gun. The rifle sling kept his shirt on him, but Kev would need a tailor if he wanted to keep that shirt.

I stabbed the thing in the side of the head, but my blade skidded off its noggin leaving a deep gash that didn't bleed. It leaned in for a bite, but between the two of us, we had slowed it down enough that Kev was able to dispatch it with his own blade.

I picked a piece of plastic out of my tactical vest and handed it to my friend. "Here."

Kev accepted the button and glanced down at his partially bare chest. He lifted the left side of his shirt up. "Don't think this is going to be salvageable."

"Pity you couldn't figure a way to weaponize those buttons," I told him. "They would have destroyed that infected." I had an epiphany and smiled a face-splitter. "I'm gonna call you Buttons from now on."

He nodded. "Me likey."

"Quit the fucking grab-assing and let's get back to the boat, yeah?" That had been Danny, and I had to wonder why he and everybody else in front of Kev and I had gotten a pass from the re-killed infected I was checking out now. It looked like any other dead thing.

We made the front doors in a few minutes. It would be dark in an hour, and the sun had already dipped down low to the bay. A dead man stood trapped in the revolving door. He pawed at us but made no noises as we moved past him. He would probably be stuck in there forever.

Joan drew her forearm across her forehead. "I… I need to sit down."

She looked horrible. Her pallor was the color of rancid cream, her eyes bloodshot. She blinked a few times and wiped her eyes. I could see she was about to take a digger, so I grabbed her arm and helped her to the floor. I could feel the heat coming off her before I had even touched her skin.

"How long?" she asked me.

I can't even fucking begin to tell you how many times I'd been asked that. A hundred at least. Everybody, even folks who didn't know me, just assumed I knew the answer to that.

And I did.

I sighed. "Anywhere from thirty seconds to about nine hours. It will get bad long before that though."

"Worse than this?"

I smiled and looked at her helplessly, nodding. "Much."

I saw her eyes glance at my sidearm and I covered it with my hand.

"We don't have shit loads of time here," Seyfert said. He wasn't trying to be a dick, but Joan was already dead. It would just take a bit for Death to cement his hold, and the rest of us were in imminent danger.

Joan started to cry. "I need you to do it," she told me.

"Do what?" I asked quickly, clenching my hand harder on the polymer grip of my Sig Sauer handgun. I had played dumb, but I knew exactly what she meant. She wanted me to kill her.

The double bitch of this was that not only was she correct in asking me to blow her brains out, but I would absolutely do it for her. I got the chills for a moment when she asked me, but that moment was brief. The brevity of my feelings is a testament to the world I live in now.

"What are you talking about?" Brad demanded in a hoarse whisper.

The group had gathered in a small circle with Joan and I in the center. I sighed again, "It's a long way and she can't make it. She's infected." Brad and Kayla took a step back, but Gary got on one knee and put his hand on her shoulder. He didn't utter a word. "She wants me to kill her," I finished.

The group looked stunned. "Kill her?" Brad demanded again. Lots of demands out of this guy. "Are you fucking insane?"

I stood and drew my Sig. "She can't come with us."

"I don't want to be one of those things!" she hissed at all of us. She clenched her fists, "Just do it!"

"You're going to shoot her? You're actually going to shoot her?"

"Yes, Brad." I pointed at the dead thing pawing at us through the curved glass of the revolving door, "Or she turns into that and tries to kill every living thing she comes across."

Everyone in the group looked at the pathetic thing trapped in that stupid round door. Its face was pressed against the pane and vile fluids ran down the glass in black rivulets. It was disgusting. Everything about it was horrible.

"Every person she bites after she becomes one of them becomes one of them," Remo said.

Joan tried to stand, and I helped her. She grabbed my wrist; the fever in her gave off heat like a furnace. "C'mon," she croaked through her tears and pulled me through the group. We moved fifty feet or so back into the lobby, out of sight behind the rounded wooden bar of a small café. She let go of my hand and surprised me when she covered me in an embrace. I hugged her back.

She let go and looked me in the eyes. One of the capillaries in her right eye let go and the white began to fill with red. "Thank you. Get the others to safety."

She turned, clasped her hands together, and looked at the ceiling. "Our Father, who art in Heaven…"

"Where is she?" Brad asked through a whisper when I came back to the group alone. He looked past me, then right at me. "This is your fault!"

"I know," I said and moved to the center of the group.

The civvies knew the drill. If they spoke, we all died. If they panicked, we died. If they fucking breathed loud, well, you get it. Seyfert did take a deep breath, let it out and pushed through the exit next to the revolving door, leading with his rifle. We filed out after him in silence, me glancing one more time at the thing scratching at us. It looked sad we were leaving.

We slunk down the tan granite walkway outside the office building single-file like a line of giant ducklings. Steve and Lynda held hands but the rest of us just held weapons.

We got to the end of the building and Seyfert peeked around the corner of a little annex of the structure. He whipped his head back quickly and used his hand to point back the way we had come, then he started running. Most of us didn't need to see what was around that corner, we just ran for it. Thankfully, the office folks figured it out quickly.

I have no idea how we hadn't heard them. I mean they're fucking *loud*, especially when there are so many. I didn't see them come around the corner as I was running the other way, but I sure as shit heard them. When I glanced back to assess how fucked we were, there were already a hundred or more behind us with substantially more rounding the corner every second.

Now they were loud. We were in California and I have little doubt this particular horde of undead could be heard in friggin' China. They got louder when they saw us too.

The cubicle critters bemoaned what they saw but kept up with us as we sprinted down the street. We were passing the undead occupied revolving door when Brad peeled off running back toward the building. The dumbass was going back to the prison he thought was safe.

I started to go after him, but Ship grabbed my shoulder. He quickly nodded no, and I had to agree. Brad was already through the door before we made the far corner of Four Embarcadero Center. Above us was a pedestrian walkway between this building and the one next to it, probably a different number Embarcadero Center. I couldn't help but think I wouldn't mind being up there right now, but then I remembered Brad, and how he was now both trapped and alone.

There were several dozen abandoned vehicles near this area, parked on the side of the road. Some had their doors open, and one blue Toyota

Camry was occupied. A hand shot out like a striking serpent and latched onto Danny's pantleg as we passed. He brought his rifle down on it and I heard the undead bones crack from ten feet away. The thing began to extricate itself from the car, but we didn't hang around to exchange phone numbers.

The street behind us was thick with the dead now; they stretched all the way across the pavement and onto both sidewalks. There were thousands. They had begun to come from our left and in front of us too, effectively giving us one direction to run.

When Seyfert was done with his corner peeking on this side he turned to assess all directions before he regarded the rest of us.

"This is going to get bloody. The best out is to the right." He snapped a folding baton out and held it with his left hand which was also on the magwell grip of his rifle. He rushed around the corner and, God help us, we all followed him.

"Oh shit…" six of us said at the same time.

"Can we make it back to Harrison?" Kayla begged.

She meant the business she had been holed up in back in the office building. Nobody bothered answering.

There were at least fifty of the things in front of us. They were already looking in our direction and let us and everything else in the vicinity know they had seen us. Those hacking rasps and hissing cackles always shrink my nuts and send shivers down my spine, but this time it was worse because of their proximity. Seyfert didn't bother holding back and began firing his rifle immediately. The noise would call every dead thing in San Francisco down on us, but honestly, surveying what was surrounding us, I thought they were already here.

We all began firing. I selectively sought out targets, wishing I had spent more time with Donna and the kids before volunteering for this stupid fucking mission. I had wanted to help the Alcatraz folks rid the area of a hostile threat. I had set out to kill people and now I was going to get eaten for it. Clearly Karma had it in for me.

I sighted on a gray woman with no arms. When she was down, I shifted my aim to a guy in a suit. Then another guy in a suit. I couldn't believe how serene I was with what was coming for us. I hadn't seen this many in a while. Seyfert was on the radio, but I couldn't hear what he was saying as I dropped a dead tattooed guy with half a beard.

Steve and Lynda were suddenly at my side. "I was deployed in ninety-six," Steve yelled, "Gimme a fuck'n gun!" He sounded like he was from Boston with that accent. He didn't wait and yanked my Sig from my hip holster. Then he did something I didn't expect; he passed the weapon to his lady, who ejected and inspected the mag, slapped it home and dropped a rotting teen with no lips.

Ship was suddenly next to me and he looked nervous. He immediately passed his M4 to Steve, who didn't eject the mag, but shouldered the weapon and fired into the diminishing crowd in front of us. Both civvies had scored headshots on their first attempt.

There were eighteen infected remaining in front of us when Seyfert yelled, "Run!" He fired once more and slung his rifle. We followed him, sprinting towards the infected. The bass boom of Ship's shotgun sounded, an infected blown off its feet.

The SEAL had two blades, and he was going HAM. Thrusting two at the same time, he took out both infected that were near him. Remo was also using his big knife which he slammed down on the dome of one of the things which had gotten too close.

Kev and Danny fired once more each and pulled their blades.

I glanced behind and almost had a full code brown in my skivvies. The horde from the side and the one from behind were mixing together like they were being poured through a giant funnel. There were thousands of them.

We dodged the ones in the front and sprinted up the street. When we were a few hundred feet from the horde behind us, Seyfert yelled for us to drop to the ground and cover our ears.

I had no idea what the hell he was talking about, and I think I should say for posterity that I thought he was fucking nuts for wanting us to *stop* running but I instantly dropped on my belly and put my hands to my ears.

Good thing too, because two contrails appeared in the sky above us and in two seconds corpses were tossed in the air from the resulting explosions of the missiles fired into the crowd. Glass from the buildings around us exploded, but it was all pushed inward so none of us were injured. I saw the Reaper bank left and it moved out of sight behind the building we had just left.

Seyfert was on his feet quickly helping up Gary, who had been blown off his feet when he hadn't hit the ground fast enough. Gary, Kayla, and Bob were standing dazed and Bob was bleeding from his right ear.

"Come on!" the SEAL shouted, and we pulled the civvies with us.

Ship was moving his jaw around and I knew that the overpressure from the explosions between the buildings had messed up his equilibrium. The dust was beginning to settle behind us, and between the small fires we could see the dead stirring. They were on the way.

We continued running and soon were entering a huge, overgrown park. There were infected here too, but they were spaced out pretty well. Several of them were stuck inside the five-foot metal fence that encircled a kid's playground. They would probably be ensnared for a long time.

A lone infected sitting on one of the park benches stared at his trapped comrades. Seyfert was about to shoot it when it turned to regard us.

"Is that you guys blowing up the city?" it asked. The man tilted a Pepsi to his face, then wiped his mouth with his forearm. "It would be super cool if you would like, stop blowing up the city."

I smiled. "Hey, Billy."

FLORIDA
ALCATRAZ

Richy smiled and looked sideways at Kyle. "This thing is *sick*!"

The boy put his eye back to the rifle scope and settled the crosshairs on the head of an undead.

Pitt checked that the boy had the rifle butt pulled tight to his shoulder. "Looks good," he said. "Pull the trigger."

Click.

"Now bolt in another round."

Richy used the bolt action of the rifle to simulate bringing up another bullet into the receiver. He kept his eyes on the prize and the thing with the crosshairs on its head turned around. It was gaunt and white, the sunken eyes not focusing on anything as it shuffled around. It suddenly directed its gaze toward the boy and the upper lip curled into a sneer. Richy smiled and clicked the trigger again.

"Splat," he said under his breath.

"He's ready," Pitt told Rick. He took the rifle from the boy, slapped in a magazine, and passed it back. Richy accepted it with a gigantic smile.

"Keep it to your shoulder or you'll hurt yourself," Rick re-iterated. "And don't put your eye right up to the scope or the recoil will smack you in the face."

"Got it," Richy said and wrapped the sling around his forearm. He found the same undead that he had exchanged glances with and put the crosshairs on its face. It was moving, so he adjusted and tracked it.

"Fire at will," Pitt told him.

Even after all the shots he had witnessed, after all the pistol and rifle fire he had dished out himself, and the training he had received by Remo, Alvarez, Ship, and Javi back at the Double Hoof Ranch, when Richy pulled the trigger, the buck of the rifle was unexpected. He had been firing M4s or MP5s up to now, and this was his first .308 rifle.

He had hit himself in the damn eye with the scope. He pulled the little green ear plug out of his right ear to hear what his teachers had to say.

He rubbed his eye with his thumb while Pitt and Rick chuckled. "Happens to everybody the first time," Rick chortled. "Look." Rick pointed at the spot that Richy had fired the rifle.

On the ground was the lanky undead the boy had sighted on. Pitt was impressed. "Bullseye. Hold it tighter, but not too tight, and keep your eye a half inch off the scope."

Richy replaced the ear plug and bolted in another round. He sighted on a dead woman with broken rib bones sticking out of her side. The rifle shot was loud, and the infected dropped like a rock. The boy took eight more shots, dropping six more infected before he passed the rifle to Pitt. Pitt slapped in a fresh magazine.

"Not bad, son." The commander smiled. "Your turn, Melman."

Richy and Kyle both smiled. The kids had taken to calling Kyle *Melman* after the giraffe in a popular kids' movie that had played when there was a world. Kyle was already six foot five and he was only sixteen. He also weighed 135 lbs soaking wet, so he was skinny.

Didn't matter because he scored five kills. *These kids are naturals*, Pitt thought.

"Think you can hit the ones over by the guard tower?" the kid asked Pitt.

Pitt shifted his gaze to the guard tower. He couldn't see the base of it, but a baker's dozen of the infected milled about on the stairs leading up to the trap door. A few were scratching at the door. He sighted on a few of them, then passed the rifle to Rick.

"Bravo, this is Pitt. You'll have incoming fire in a moment. We're going to thin the herd on your stairs."

"Copy, Commander. Good luck."

"You mind? Rick asked. Pitt waved him on, and Rick brought the rifle to his shoulder.

Ensign Clarey shifted on his bunk. The tightness in his chest was becoming irksome and he moved his shoulders to try to relieve it. He had been working a lot on the sub since the plague started, and rest was a difficult thing to come by when he was forced to hot-rack with several other sailors. He had been forced to sleep in the torpedo room with nine other sailors when he had finished checking behind an instrument panel earlier this morning. His sixteen-hour shift had been over for three hours, and he was back on in another five. He needed some rack time. With all the civvies pouring into the sub, he was glad to be as far from them as possible. There would be a bit of quiet in the torpedo room.

Normally it would be all hands on deck for such an event, but he and the other nine guys had been stretched thin recently as there were issues in the machine shop.

He shifted again, thinking he would need to see the doc soon. Chest pains were nothing to mess around with, and he had been having them sporadically for a few months now.

Millavich, one of the machinists, began to snore in the hammock above him. Clarey smiled as the snore was better than the noise the throngs of civvies were making in other sections of the boat. He drifted off thinking about how the Skipper and Gilligan used to sleep just like this in their hut fifty years ago.

Clarey suffered a segment elevation myocardial infarction sixteen minutes after he fell asleep. The infarction led to cardiac arrest eight minutes later. He made a slight noise during the event, but the nine other guys didn't hear it as they were all asleep as well. His life force left him shortly after the heart attack and something else invaded his body. His eyes opened exactly thirty minutes to the second after he had fallen asleep.

He would be the only one who died peacefully in the torpedo room.

The thing that had been Clarey got out of its bunk and surveyed the area using the soft, overhead lights to see. It focused on the noise in the room that didn't belong; a snore. Millavich's hammock was at chest height to the undead and the creature that had been one of his friends a mere half hour previous, leaned in and bit him on the Adam's apple. Millavich's struggles weren't silent and two other crew members, Mabius and Kaplan, grunted grievances at the noise.

Kaplan switched positions in his hammock to see what the commotion was and stared into the dripping face of the undead Clarey. As the Clarey thing ripped his throat out, Kaplan noticed Millavich sitting up.

"Where the hell is Clarey?" demanded Chief Petty Officer Ricks, looking at his watch. "He should have been here half an hour ago. Marshall, go get Clarey, he's asleep in the torpedo room with the rest of the A-gangers."

"Aye, sir," machinist mate Marshall told his superior and friend. Marshall began to make his way from the machinist bay to the torpedo room. He took his time, knowing that Clarey probably needed the rest. They had all been stretched thin, but they did need Clarey to mill those last eight suppressors for the handguns and to fabricate the rungs for the exterior ladder they were going to install up to the solar array on the roof of the cellhouse building. No small task and they only had three days to do it or the commander would shit a brick.

With the undead attack currently happening on the island, Marshall was damn happy he was on the sub. There was no way the things could gain entry from the island. All they had to do was pull the gangways and those dead fucks would just scratch at the steel if they didn't sink to the bottom of the bay.

Marshall fought the crowd of civvies as he moved down the tight corridor to the torpedo room. He didn't mind the civvies, some of them were nice to talk to, but when he was tasked to do something, he couldn't hang around, he needed to work. He stepped over a knee-knocker and pulled the hatch closed behind him. This resulted in a bit more quiet. The damn civilians were loud on his boat. He didn't throw the handles on the hatch because why would he?

He reached the hatch to the torpedo room and heard movement on the other side. At least somebody was awake. Only one hatch handle was in place, so he pulled it out of the locked position and the hatch flew into him, hitting him in the face. Blood spurted through his fingers when he brought his hands to his ruined nose.

The pain in his nose was forgotten when eight of his former friends and fellow sailors flooded from the torpedo room and swarmed him, biting and tearing. The things finished with him when he sat back up just a few minutes later. They shuffled off toward the muted sounds on the other side of the hatch at the far end of the corridor.

The Marshall thing attempted to stand, but there was no muscle left on its arms or left leg. It began to drag itself toward the sounds its brothers had followed.

Back in the torpedo room, exhausted machinist's mate Jon Moe shifted on his bunk. He yawned and pulled the light blanket off his head. He stared up at the dim crew lights hung from the ceiling, then spun his wrist and turned a bleary eye on his watch. Four hours until his shift started. He sighed and pulled the blanket back over his head. The green earplugs did wonders to keep out the noise of the boat, especially with all the civvies on board. He was asleep again in seconds.

This sub was AWESOME! There were so many things to see inside and all the sub-guys knew what to do all the time. They all had guns, but everybody had guns since the rottens started killing people. Eight-year old Caleb glanced at his six-year old little brother Noah. When they had

had to flee their home in the city, Noah had shutdown and clung to his mother for half a year. Nothing would get him off her leg, even trips to the bathroom. He had just come out of his shell a few months ago, but now that there were so many people in the crowded submarine, Noah was on his mom again like a tick.

Caleb rolled his eyes. Noah was just a baby. This place was *exciting.* The eight-year old moved away from his mother's side to look at the gleaming metal tables. They had metal tables! They were all attached to the floor too, and so were the stools. The boy pouted. It stunk that he had to stay in the cafeteria of the sub. It was like his old school except for the cool tables and stools.

He glanced at his mother, but she was talking to some other lady. Caleb made his escape and threaded through the legs of a dozen people to make his way to one of the sub-guys. He stared at the wicked looking black gun the guy had. It was so cool! Caleb wanted a gun too. He had gotten to shoot one of the handguns, *that* had been really cool, but the sub-guys wouldn't let him keep one for himself.

He slipped past the sub-guy and stood in front of a black door. Even the doors on the sub were cool. They started at his thigh and he had to step over the bottom bit of it to get through. Cool. This door was shut though, and it had six little handles on it but only one was closed. He heard something on the other side. Was it something even more cool? Maybe there were guns or… maybe torpedoes! He had never seen a torpedo before! What if he could touch one. He smiled. Noah would never believe he had touched a real torpedo.

He put his hand on the hatch lever and something exploded into his mind. Rule number one: Never go anywhere alone, and if you're a kid, you have to be with a grown up. It was dangerous with all the rottens stumbling around all over the place. But he was on the sub! The rottens couldn't get on the sub, everybody said.

Rules were lame anyway. He didn't have any of his toys or video games from his house. He didn't even have any Legos. The only thing he could do was play made up games with the other kids. Dave was the oldest and was kind of in charge of the other kids.

But I bet he's never touched a torpedo… Caleb thought and made his decision. He pushed up on the handle but it didn't move. Frowning, he put more effort into the push and the handle slid up. The scratching on the other side of the steel had to be seen. He had to know what a torpedo felt like. Three seconds and a quarter inch from the freedom to explore the sub, touch torpedoes, and be a legend, someone scared the pee out of him.

Seriously, a bit of pee eeked out.

"What are you up to, little fella?"

Caleb whipped his head around to see a sub-guy with his hands on his hips. The guy had a smile on his face, but Caleb knew that he had been busted. This guy stood next to the guy with the gun and they were both looking down at him.

"Nuthin'," he answered. He put his hands behind his back and looked down. If he didn't look at the guy and the guy couldn't see his hands, maybe he wouldn't realize that Caleb had been about to open the door.

The guy's smile evaporated. "Nothing huh? It's my experience that when someone says they're up to nothing, they're up to something. Where's your mom?"

Caleb swallowed, knowing that the jig was up, but also knowing he hadn't really done anything. He pointed wordlessly at his mother, still talking to the lady next to her with Noah still so close to her they looked like conjoined twins.

A thud from behind him made Caleb almost add a bit of poop to the pee he had already set free. The sub guy glanced away from Caleb and at the hatch behind him. "Get to your mother," he said, not looking away from the door. For the second time in five minutes, Caleb made his escape, but this time he ran back to mom.

Ensign Talbot shifted his MP5 on its sling and smiled. "Damn kids." He shook his head, his disdain for children evident on his scowl. Both he and CPO Ricks were watching the boy flee back to his mom. Talbot huffed and threw the hatch handle the rest of the way open.

Ricks whipped his head around as he heard the handle move. "No! Wai—"

The hatch flew back into Talbot with the weight of several infected behind it. They tumbled over the knee knocker and spilled into the galley. It didn't take long for the civilians to see what was happening, the screams of terror flooding the steel enclosure.

REUNITED
JOURNAL ENTRY 6

"Billy!" Anna yelled and Seyfert looked like he was going to dive for his foxhole.

"Hey, Anna! Hey, Danny! Hey, Gossamer! Hey…" He looked at me quizzically for a moment, "I never did get your name."

I was about to tell him when Seyfert told us we needed to move. "Now!" he admonished.

"Whoa," Billy breathed lifting an eyebrow. "Who's Captain Serious?"

"I'm not a captain, I'm…" Seyfert trailed off for a moment then jerked his head up to stare at the blond kid. "Billy?" He looked at Anna. "*The* Billy, the one you guys are always talking about?"

Billy beamed. "I'm a *the*? I have a *title*? Wait… am I famous?" He stood and gave Anna a huge hug.

"You're about to be lunch, kid," Steve told him.

"No, he won't." Anna, Danny, Alvarez, and Remo said at the same time.

Seyfert glared at all of us. "What, does everybody know this friggin' guy except me?"

"I don't know him," replied Lynda quietly.

Seyfert glanced back at the corner we had rounded a minute ago. There were still no dead yet. He pointed at Billy, "You're coming with us."

Billy sat on the bench, crossed his legs and folded his arms. "No."

Seyfert raised his rifle and pointed it at Billy. I didn't know what was going on, but the guys on both ends of Seyfert's M4 had saved my life, so I was a tad conflicted.

Anna grabbed the barrel of the weapon and shoved it to the side. "You're not shooting him. If you did, you would have to deal with half the population of Alcatraz when you got back."

"I don't want to shoot him. He's mission-optional, but I'm supposed to bring him if I find him."

"But what if he doesn't want to go?" Billy asked in earnest.

Seyfert shook his head. "That wasn't discussed."

"We don't have time for this," Remo stated, checking our six.

"He's right," I added. "Alcatraz is under attack and I want to get back and help."

Billy's brows furrowed. "Attack? Like, an undead attack?" He directed his gaze at Anna. "Where's Sam?"

"She's there, Billy, and so are a ton of heavy-hitters like these guys. SEALs and stuff."

"I don't care about aquatic mammals." He pointed at Seyfert. "I need your boat."

Seyfert's eyebrows shot skyward, "You're coming with us?"

Billy pulled the Samurai sword from the sheath on his back. "Incorrect. You're coming with me." He stood and began a confident stride toward the east.

"Billy!" Anna called to him.

"Yeah?"

"It's this way." She pointed north-west.

"Gotcha." He switched directions and proceeded to lead our group toward the boat.

Infected with smoking clothing began to round the building we had passed a few minutes ago. The horde saw us and began its arduous trek in our direction. I had to give it to them; they might be fucked up on a ton of levels, but they never quit.

We began to thread through the overgrown park, the dead trapped inside the fence reaching through the black bars toward us. The things began to come out of the woodwork, likely because of the blast from the Reaper. It was beginning to look like a Black Friday sale and we were the hot ticket item.

"Rock, this is Sabre, how copy?"

Seyfert repeated his ask into the mic, but there was no joy. He glanced at Remo, who made the same call, but there was nobody there.

"I gotta tell you," I piped up, "I don't like that."

"What are you guys waiting for?" Billy demanded. "Let's go!" He thrust his sword down into the tall grass. "Watch your ankles."

We all immediately stared at our feet. I brought my eyes up and stared at the park in front of us. Shambling forms were making their way in our direction, but they were spread out. I was more concerned with moving through the tall, brown grass and having a crawler take a chunk out of my leg. I was pretty sure I would survive it what with the whole immunity thing, but nobody else would.

"Seyfert, I'll take point with Billy."

"Negative,   I'll—"
I interrupted him, "Double negative! Trust me on this, I'm better suited
to—" Ship put his heavy paw on my shoulder. He shook his head, *No*.

I shrugged out of his grasp, a monumental task considering he could
palm a small moon. "Lay off, *Mom*. We need to get back and this is the
best way."

He hated it, I could see it, but he knew I was right.

"Do what you gotta do, Seyfert, but my kids are on Alcatraz." I caught
up with Billy and we stood about five feet apart, trudging through the
grass.

We made it about half way before it went to shit. Kayla let out a yell
as Billy was decapitating a particularly rotten specimen. We both turned
to see what was going on, and that was when something grabbed me from
below. I let out a very unmanly yip and stumbled to the ground. I heard
Kayla screaming over my own roaring ears as I fought off a dead thing
which was trying to crawl up my legs to my face. To this day I have no
clue why some of them will bite the first thing they can, and others want
to go for the good stuff.

I tried to scrabble backwards like a crab, but the thing had me. My
sidearm had taken a tumble with me, jarred from my grip when my ass
impacted the ground. I frantically reached for it with the hand not holding
the infected cannibal at bay, but realized it was out of reach. I drew my
SOG, the best knife made by man, just as Billy yanked the collar of the
dead thing. The creature, which had no face but did possess fuck-tons of
teeth, was weightless for a moment until the rotten collar of the shirt it
was wearing tore loose and it came back at me, choppers first. I slid my
SOG into its dome and the fight was over.

I could hear the dry hack of several of the things and knew we weren't
as alone in the grass as I had hoped. One of them loomed over me but
before I could do anything, Ship was there. He swung his airplane wing
sized machete and turned one infected into two, but neither would walk
again. The top of the thing's noggin flew away like a demented bird.

I expected either Ship or Billy to extend a much-wanted hand down to
help me up, but both stepped out of sight. I got to my feet and saw why.
Dozens of the things were on top of us. They couldn't have reached us
from the street so quickly and I noticed that the street infected were still
in the street, albeit significantly closer. My gargantuan intellect told me
that these things had been in the grass before we got here. Had they been
lying in wait? That would mean they were capable of setting traps and

that shit wasn't funny. More likely they had just sat down as they sometimes do.

I wasn't the only one to stand. As I surveyed our surroundings, I saw several of the dead things stand up out of the tall grass, search for a moment, then come plodding toward us. One of the things was five feet from me, so I strode to it and stabbed it in the forehead.

Remo was dragging Kayla with him; she looked injured, but I didn't have time to see how badly.

"On me!" I heard Seyfert yell, and we moved as a group to him.

"We're going to need the rifles on this one," Remo suggested.

Danny nodded quickly, and Buttons (fucking Buttons, that shit is gonna stick) agreed as well. "Yeah, our secret is out, boss."

"Firing line," Seyfert grunted. "We move northwest. For fucks sake watch your feet!"

The dead things came slowly but steadily. We began to fire, selecting targets who would get in our way as we moved toward our destination. The *pffft* of the suppressors still echoed across the park we had thought was empty. As I have mentioned on many occasions, the shots were significantly quieter than without suppressors, but definitely *not* silent.

Billy chopped downward with his sword twice, then continued forward. I noticed one of the things lying in a puddle as I moved past. It had been a little girl.

One of those yowling screams rent the air, the prelude to a Runner who burst through the grass. Nobody could do anything as it leapt atop Danny's back, slashing and biting. He threw the thing to the ground hard and gave it three shots. He put his hand to his neck and brought it back to check it out. "Fuck!" he yelled.

"Bitten?" Remo asked him.

"Scratched."

Another scream sounded, then another, two more, then another.

Anna was pointing the business end of her rifle in all forward directions. "I don't see 'em!"

"They aren't back here!" Buttons said. There was a twinge of panic in his voice. "But there's a shit-ton of the dead ones!"

I had to concur with his assessment. To steal the verbiage of a long dead biker douche, it looked like a Patriots game had just finished and the fans were all headed toward the parking lot. Forward of us wasn't looking tons better. They were really coming out in droves now.

A shadow fell over me and I glanced up at the sasquatch. He said all he could with a look: *We're in it now.*

A few months ago, I had lost a good friend of mine in this exact situation. That shit was not happening again. Fuck these dead assholes.

Seyfert had had enough, "Move!"

We moved forward tactically, rifles to our shoulders and firing where possible. The pops of rifle fire seemed to spur the dead on. More of the screams sounded, much closer this time. I whipped my rifle barrel to the left, the scope to my eye. My scope was an ACOG, with a 3.5x zoom and this little chevron on a stick on the inside to help with bullet drop compensation. The sight showed me the rustling grass fifteen feet away a half second before a Runner burst forward. The horrid thing screamed and slashed at the air as it sprinted toward Bob.

The guy stood his ground with his desk leg at the ready, but I gave the Runner two in the side before it could get to him. The thing collapsed, trying to crawl toward us but too fucked up to do so. Bob glanced at me and smiled in silent thanks. I nodded and began to search for more targets when two more of the sprinting horrors exploded from the stalks right next to us. The thing which used to be a woman leapt onto Bob, slashing and tearing. He smacked her with his desk leg, but she was already on him, so his swings were ineffective. Danny gave the thing a rifle butt to the head, but the second thing hit Bob at his midsection, and they all went down. Danny rolled away as I got to them, but Bob began to yell. I shot the tackler point blank in the head before something hit me like a freight train and I went sprawling.

I could hear Bob yelling and bullets firing over the screaming of the thing on top of me. It had been an average-sized guy, and I could see inflamed holes in its right shoulder and arm where someone had hit it with buckshot days before. I guess these things could get regular infections. That would be stored in my memory bank for later if I survived the next ten seconds.

Gripping my rifle by the buttstock and the barrel, I pushed up and hit the fucker in the chest when he tried to chew on my face. I bucked, and he flew to the side, but he still had me by the shirt and my single-point sling. Hitting him in the jaw with the butt of the M4 rewarded me with a satisfactory crack, and his grip slackened a bit. These assholes could feel pain, but I think they just give a shit a whole bunch less than an uninfected person. I hit him again and I saw his jaw dislocate. Bite somebody now, dickhead.

Another smash with the rifle and I reversed the weapon and shot the prick in the throat. It clutched at the wound and fell on its back, a gaping hole where its Adam's apple used to be. I tapped it again in the dome and it ceased moving.

Ship extended a hand down to me and I accepted it. He dragged me to my feet like you would a six-year old kid and I shot the two things on Bob. He looked at me blinking, bites and scratches all up and down the guy. He was fucked, but he stood anyway, looking himself over.

I realized we were all going to die. We would all look worse than Bob in a few minutes. There were hundreds of the things coming from all directions. Sprinters were fighting the crowds of dead to get to us, our rifles sighting on them first. I joined the fray, the round from my weapon finding its mark on a Runner's chest. I took out three more before I executed a tactical magazine switch. I had lost count of my fired rounds and needed to charge another.

As I did so, I saw Billy slashing with his sword, Seyfert firing his rifle, and Remo guarding Kayla against two dead ones who had gotten close with his sidearm. Lynda and Steve were using their guns and they were doing well. Gary and Danny battled a dead one that had grabbed Gary, and Buttons was changing magazines.

Alvarez and Anna fired their weapons as well and I watched Alvarez reach for a mag, but he had none left.

"Shoot the fast ones and follow me!" Billy yelled. He had a sawed-off shotgun in his left hand and slashed sideways with his sword. As a group, we ran after him, firing, the crowds of infected closing in where we had just been fighting. They had converged and were now one massive horde fifty feet to the rear of our position.

There were thousands and they were still coming. Where was the fucking Reaper now?

As we jogged toward a few hundred of the things, I turned to speak to Ship and Remo. "Good thing we came to San Francisco, huh?"

Remo smiled. "I was thinking the same thing."

Ship didn't say shit.

"I'm out!" Buttons yelled.

"Billy, hold up!" Seyfert yelled. "Danny, it's time! How many you got?"

"Three!" Danny let his rifle dangle, and he slid the fat shotgun around to the front. He released it from the sling and reached into one of his tactical pockets. "Two HE and one frag." Danny pulled out a big, fat, green shell with a gold tip. He cracked the weapon in half and shoved it in the back of the barrel.

Seyfert looked back and smiled. "Put an HE round right in the fucking face of that thing!" He pointed at a speedy fucker fifty yards from us, screeching and slashing through the dead crowd to get at the good stuff.

"What is that?" I asked out loud.

"That," Remo answered in a soft voice, "is an M79." I could barely hear him as my ears were still ringing from the sustained rifle fire. It was no trouble hearing his next little missive, as he was standing right next to me and he yelled it loudly, "Cover your ears!"

We all did what we were told, and Danny brought the weapon to his shoulder. I heard a *FOOMP*, saw Danny kick back a little, and was then witness to one of the coolest things I had ever seen. A tremendous KA-KRACK accompanied the dead who were thrown like ragdolls fifteen feet into the air in a circle where the round had hit. Those not tossed into the sky were blasted to the ground in a twenty-foot swath. Bits of the Runner were visible, I think, but fuck hanging around for an attempt at identification.

"Now!" Seyfert screamed and bolted right at the horde. When we were almost at the recently constructed clearing of dead folks, I heard Danny scream "Fire in the hole!" and I covered my ears again. It was a bitch to do so because we were still running. You try covering your ears while sprinting and holding a rifle. It's tricky as fuck.

Another explosion ripped through the undead ranks, and suddenly there was smoking gap we could shoot. So, picture this in your post-apocalyptic mind: There are smoldering bodies all over the ground with a forty-foot gap in between like Moses had parted the Red Sea. A group of survivors is sprinting through that gap with the bodies beginning to stir. Arms, legs, bits of intestine, a jaw bone, half a rib cage, and gallons of black, infected blood cover the path and its slippery. Several of the things are starting to get up, all of whom are very interested in the group of folks running past them. We were halfway through when the first one got to its feet, but it was behind us. The ones next to us were starting to rise though. One of them reached out a two-fingered paw and tripped Remo, who fell on his chest. I had never seen Remo fall before.

I stopped to help him up, and one of the things grabbed me. Alvarez shot it, and we were free, the hordes behind us pissed off and hungry.

It was about then that we heard gunfire in front of us. Everybody else we knew was on Alcatraz, probably fighting for their lives, so there was only one explanation: The fucking bad guys had found us.

I saw one muzzle flash from the street at the end of the park and raised my rifle to sight it. Six men with hunting rifles and two more with military rifles were firing. Remo already had his rifle up and I could see the look on his face when I glanced at him. Somebody was getting a full-metal-jacketed ventilation in short order. Remo didn't know how to miss.

Before he could fire, two Runners screamed in from his left. He spun the business end of his weapon toward the closer proximity threat, but the lead Runner took a bullet in the side and half its guts blew out the other. The second Runner stopped, looked at the first like it was its soul mate, screamed at the sky, its head jerked sideways, and it collapsed.

I spun my rifle to fire at the dickheads in front of us, but Remo told me to hold on. The dudes were wiping out infected that were getting too close. They were not shooting at us. One of them stood from his firing position and began to run to us. The others followed suit quickly, and soon our groups were running toward each other. Us away from ten thousand infected, these guys *toward* them.

What. The. Fuck.

We had outdistanced the dead by a hundred yards, and as we ran, the newbies in front of us picked off the Runners that had given chase. We got to within about thirty feet from them and they did the most curious thing. Every single one of them raised their rifles over their heads with both hands.

"Friendlies!" they all started screaming.

Billy wiped his dripping sword on the tall brown grass, stood and pointed at one of the guys. Just a kid really, early twenties and lanky.

"I know you, but the beard is new."

The guy was smiling, but still had his rifle over his head.

Anna squinted at the guy Billy had been pointing at for a sec, then her mouth went slack. She was still able to stammer out one word two times, "Chris? Chris!" She ran at the kid and threw herself at him in a colossal bear hug that would have made even Dallas blush. "We thought you were dead!"

A big biker-type guy looked at Seyfert. "Can I put my arms down now?"

Seyfert smiled and shook his head. "Lower your weapons, they're friendlies." Everybody on our side did and the new guys brought theirs down too. "You are still friendly, right?"

"HAW!" guffawed the biker. "For a Navy guy, you sure as shit can't find a boat, can you son?"

They clasped hands. "Good to see you, Teems."

"And you, but let's go someplace else and talk, ok? 'Sides, these two need a room." He chin-wagged to Anna and her friend who were embraced in a public display make-out session like a couple of fifteen-year-olds.

"Follow us," Seyfert said, and we all made towards the boat, me confused as fuck.

STEEL AND BLOOD
USS FLORIDA

As his shipmates started to eat him, Talbot's high-pitched screams reached a crescendo then abruptly ceased with a gurgle. Ricks' yells were more dignified as he fought off a red-eyed and very dead Kaplan. Ricks landed a vicious uppercut and his former friend bit off a huge chunk of his tongue, spraying Ricks with contaminated blood. A hand grabbed the living man's ankle, both he and the infected Kaplan tumbled to the deck hard. As he fought off the dead thing, he noticed his other shipmates reaching into Talbot's abdominal cavity and biting the man over and over. Clarey pulled his head away from Talbot's belly, the thing's face dripping crimson. It looked right into Ricks' eyes and began to crawl toward him.

Ricks tried to roll to his left but Kaplan had a firm grip on him and was trying to chew on his face. The Clarey-thing reached a bloody hand toward Ricks' face, but a plastic dining tray came down on its head. Once, twice, three times, and the platter broke on the fourth. The person wielding the tray abandoned the shards and drove a blade into the base of the dead shipman's skull, the creature collapsed instantly. The same person kicked the Kaplan-thing in the side of the head. For half a second the infected was stunned and Ricks pushed it off him.

The submariner gave a panicked glance at his rescuer. A teenage girl had her hand extended toward him. "Come on!" she said loudly. "Get up!" she yelled when he didn't' move immediately. He grabbed her hand and she pulled him away from the dead thing coming at them. The other six dead had decided that the living people were more appetizing than the now extremely dead Talbot and they stood, one at a time.

Chloe pulled the sailor up, she and Vanessa helping him to his feet. The three of them backed away quickly, then surveyed the two-dozen panicked people all trying to funnel through a single hatchway at once. There was no way they would all make it out before the dead reached them. Talbot's weapon was on the deck behind the advancing undead, Ricks' sidearm also out of reach.

Chloe brandished her blade in her fist, looking trapped and terrified.

"Give me that," Ricks demanded.

"As if!" she yelled at him and darted forward. She gave a snap kick to Kaplan's knee, the joint bending backwards. The dead man fell forward though, and Chloe caught it at the throat as it tried to get to her. She drove the blade into its eye, Kaplan's misery over. The momentum of the creature took it into her and they both went down, the thing partly on top of her. The other dead were going to reach her before she could extricate herself from the one atop her.

Ricks ran full bull rush into his oncoming shipmates. All he could think was if the stupid assholes that were all trying to escape just picked up something and smashed the dead down, they would have been gone in moments. The first bite came on his shoulder and he yelled. The second one tore half his ear away and he screamed. The dead had him, and they would never let go. The kid had gotten out from under the Kaplan-thing with the help of her friend.

"Go through the hatch behind them!" he screamed at the girls as he fought the dead barehanded.

Chloe grabbed Vanessa's hand and they ran past Ricks and the dead. The girls leapt over the knee-knocker. Chloe tried to go back for Ricks' sidearm, but one of the dead sailors suddenly loomed in front of her so she pulled the hatch closed.

A hand closed on Vanessa's ankle, her scream of fright short. She kicked off the hand and stabbed the crawler in the back of the neck with her knife but it wasn't done. Chloe kicked it, its head snapping back but its remaining eye keeping focus. She stabbed it in the eye as it reached a ravaged arm toward her, ceasing its struggles.

Both girls threw all the hatch handles to lock out the dead. "What do we do?" asked Vanessa in a small, quick voice.

Chloe didn't answer. She stared down the short hallway. There was blood everywhere, the bloody footprints on the deck-grate coming from the direction of that hatch.

She put a finger to her lips and Vanessa nodded. Vanessa was wearing sneakers, but Chloe only possessed a pair of boots, so her footfalls sounded like cannon fire to the girls as they padded toward the unseen through the hatch. Both jumped when a thud sounded on the steel behind them. Several others followed and soon there was a steady thumping. Whatever had transpired in the room behind them was over and the dead wanted in.

"Don't touch anything," Chloe whispered. Both girls brandished their blades as they decided what to do. Staring briefly back at the steel being pounded on, Chloe nodded in the negative. "Can't go back that way." She chin-wagged toward the open hatch at the end of the corridor. They moved forward toward the lighted maw, fear creeping even further into their minds.

In just a moment the girls stood apprehensively in front of the torpedo room hatch, the light throwing odd shadows into the darker corridor. This hatch was different than the oval hatches behind her. It was smaller and circular. Applying some of the hand signals she had learned from Remo, Chloe told Vanessa to stay behind her and the girl nodded in understanding. Chloe moved her head extremely slowly until she could peek into the room with one eye.

She had thought the corridor was bloody. This place looked like someone had taken buckets of the stuff and had liberally chucked the gore everywhere. What she didn't see were any infected. Blue bunks, covered in blood, were strapped to massive blue and black cylinders on one side of the skinny room, while twisted hammocks hung from the other. There was a lump on one of the bunks up forward, but it didn't seem to be moving. She moved her head so she could look closer at the room. Vanessa also poked her head around the edge of the circle for an assessment.

An alarm began to sound and the lump on the end of the makeshift bunks sat up. It was a shirtless man, who did not appear to be infected. He stared around for a moment, confused, then focused on the girls. "You're not supposed to be down here."

"Are you friggin' kidding me!" Chloe shouted. "Look around!"

He pulled the plugs from his ears and scrunched his face up. "What?"

"Look!" both girls shouted, pointing at the blood dripping from pretty much everything.

He did. This time he did not fail to notice the gore. He also heard the thumps coming from the closed hatch twenty feet away. He shot to his feet, bumping his head on what looked like an upside-down valve handle which came from the ceiling.

"Ow! What's going on?"

The girls stepped inside the room, carefully avoiding as much of the contaminated blood as they could. It was impossible not to step on some of it, but a lot had dripped through the grate in the floor.

"A bunch of dead just came from in here and attacked us in the room back there!" Vanessa pointed back the way they had come.

"And you slept through it!" Chloe added.

Seaman Moe rubbed his head as he moved toward the girls. Both became wary and raised their blades slightly. The sailor continued to stare amazedly at the dripping and pooled blood as he reached the girls. They looked frightened, which frightened him.

He held up his hands in supplication, then pointed to a wired receiver on the wall. He reached over, picked it up, and spoke into it. "Conn, torpedo room. I've got two kids and a shit load of blood down here."

A reply came back instantly, *"Torpedo room, Conn. There are hostiles near your position. Seal the hatch and sit tight. Perform a weapons check, we may need intel."*

"Torpedo room copies all. How many hostiles?"

"Unknown. Unknown amount of crew members and civilians have been infected." There was a slight pause, *"Watch your ass."*

Moe hung up the receiver and shifted his gaze to the kids. "I just told the conn there were civilians in the torpedo room and they didn't even blink..."

"Maybe they're more worried about that," Chloe told him as she pointed to the thumping on the steel behind them.

Vanessa, after a quick survey of their surroundings, raised her hand. "I have to pee."

Moe sighed. *Terrific.*

"They hold everything forward of the galley except the officer's mess and some of the berthing areas." Kimball told McInerney as the corpsman bandaged his forearm. "A few civves were able to get into the O-mess and seal the door."

"How many civilians were down there?" asked the captain.

"I don't know, sir, maybe thirty stretched out over the galley and the corridors?"

"Twenty-eight, Captain," Harris, another sailor holding a clipboard told him.

"And how many got out?"

"Eleven. They all jammed the forward hatch trying to get out and the dead ripped into the ones in the back."

The captain glanced around the room at the people there, leaning against the bulkheads or sitting on the deck. He ran his palm across the stubble on his head. He would need a haircut soon.

"And they came from someplace forward?"

"Aye, sir. Probably the torpedo room. We had ten men in there using the deck, hammocks, and the fish as bunks. We had another six in the galley area."

The captain sighed. "Right. We're secure up top?"

"Aye, sir. The Conn is secure and there's no gangway to the island. The dead are being pushed into the water reaching for us. They just sink and have no way on board."

"Then let's get these damn dead off my boat."

The sailor with the freshly bandaged arm stood. "I should help, sir." He held his arm up, the bandage plain for all to see. "I'm dead already," he harrumphed. "Doesn't even hurt."

The phone on the wall near them blinked green and a sailor picked it up. "Sir!" He handed the corded receiver to his captain.

After a quick conversation, McInerney passed the receiver back to the sailor who had handed it to him. "We've got at least three alive in the torpedo room. Two civvies and Moe."

All the sailors smiled.

The sailor with the freshly bandaged arm looked up. "Sir?"

The captain raised his eyebrows.

"Let's get them."

"The torpedo room?" asked Harris. "But isn't that where the attack came from?"

Fifteen minutes later eight heavily armed sailors took positions outside the hatch to the galley. Blood dripped down the white steel of the knee knocker and red streaks of it were on the deck and the bulkheads. The sailors could hear the dead moving around on the other side of the hatch. There were muffled thumps as the creatures pounded to be free of their metal prison.

Shotgun and MP5 barrels were aimed at the sounds.

"I'll open the hatch," volunteered Kimball. "No matter what, we have to hold them here. If they get past us, we'll lose the boat. Firing positions."

"Jesus fuck," one of the men breathed when Kimball gripped the twist handle.

He looked each man in the eye as they hugged both sides of the short corridor. "Shottys will get them down so shoot 'em anywhere," Kimball told them, "but SMGs to the dome only, got it? Let them plug the hatch and fall over the knee knocker to slow them down. For fucks sake don't shoot me when I run back to you. Fall back when you reload and the next guy steps up."

His men nodded and he shifted his gaze to the open hatch fifteen feet behind them. His eyes locked with Harris', who stood well back with his sidearm drawn ready to slam the hatch closed if things got out of hand. Kimball nodded to him and Harris spoke into his radio, "Permission to engage, sir?"

"Light 'em up," echoed the captain's disembodied voice.

Kimball threw the handle up and pulled the hatch door wide.

KEEP IT GOING
JOURNAL ENTRY 7

A lone undead crawled out from under an abandoned UPS truck. It made that horrible noise that they make as it reached for us when we jogged past it. Oh, if you didn't know, the Embarcadero is just a road. It's two three-lane streets separated by a curbed median strip with some palm trees and street lights here and there. It's pretty.

It seemed everything was called Embarcadero around here though.

We juked the undead thing and took a brief rest near an overgrown hedge across from the water.

"Where's the rest of your gang?" Seyfert asked Teems.

"The rest of the Steadys are across the Golden Gate at a Marine Mammal shelter or something," the biker told us as we jogged. "They're waitin' on me to give them a heads up. I didn't want a hundred and fifty bikes tear-assing down the streets of the city and making too much noise." The new guy looked at Seyfert with concern as we moved quickly across the Embarcadero. "Where's Dallas?"

Seyfert huffed, "He's on Alcatraz. We just got a call from them though. The island is under attack by the dead. We were on the way home when we ran into you."

"We'll help," the big biker said.

I liked him immediately.

Ship snapped his fingers and we all looked at him. He pointed back behind us. The dead were streaming out of the park and across the street. Thousands of them. That pretty curb with the pretty trees was about to have about ten thousand ugly feet stepping on it.

"What's that?" asked Lynda, pointing forward.

I squinted down the Embarcadero... you know what? Fuck it, I'm just calling it *the street* from now on. If you haven't caught on by now, that's on you. I squinted at what she was pointing at, then peered through my little binoculars.

"Fuck."

I passed the binocs to Remo.

He sighed, "I concur with that assessment."

Seyfert, Danny, Anna, Steve, and the new kid Chris, all echoed my *Fuck* at the same time.

A horde of infected, equally as large as the five thousand or so that were behind us, was coming down the street in front. We had dead to the front, dead to the back, dead to the left, and water to the right.

So, of course it had to get worse.

Bullets began to whizz past us, and we could see dickheads up in one of the buildings laughing and shooting down at us through a broken window. They had royally fucked up though.

Every one of us holding a firearm returned fire, and the floor to ceiling windows near the shooters exploded. One of them fell through the new opening about six floors to the street below.

Infected would be eating human pizza over there.

No more bullets came at us, but a couple of Runners did. We dropped them and Ship whistled loudly. He got us all to gape at him, and he silently pointed toward a ferry boat moored at the pier a bit down the street.

It was going to be close but we would have to run for it right now.

"Come on!" Billy shouted and we sprinted for the dock.

Seyfert and Remo took point with Buttons, Ship, and yours truly at the rear. Bob was with us as well. He clutched his table leg with one hand as we ran. He was slowing significantly before we had made it halfway. I grabbed his arm to pull him, but he howled, dropped his weapon, and covered the spot I had touched with his hand. My hand had come away sticky with his blood.

He was bitten, and it wasn't just one of those little tooth-mark jobbies. A hunk of his triceps was missing.

"I can't run anymore," he said and slowed. Ship scooped him up like a two-year old and threw him into a fireman's carry.

"Ow! Damn it that hurts!" he groused.

I pointed at the crowd in front of us and shouted at him. "Better than being eaten!"

Our group now numbered more than a few. It was iffy that we were all going to make the dock. The dead were very close now in front of us. The group with the guns made it to the entrance and through the open chain link door under a pretty arch. This barrier looked like it had been hastily erected probably during the onset of the plague, but it had held. Remo, Alvarez, and Seyfert began firing into the crowd, selectively eliminating the closest targets.

They didn't get them all. One of the things grabbed Kayla as she limped through the tall chain-link gate. Danny brought his machete down across the thing's wrists and she was free, but we weren't going to make it. We knew it, our friends knew it, and the dead knew it. Remo pulled the gate shut when we were thirty feet away. They all kept firing to give us a better chance. Billy tried to make it back to the gate, but Buttons and Seyfert held him fast. The kid was wiry and looked like an octopus when they held him but hold him they did.

Bob was not a huge guy. I would call him average. I'm a bit above average in the weight capacity, but I'm tall. I weigh maybe 220 right now. Bob was a bit smaller than me and maybe weighed 180lbs. Ship is the barbarian in every movie or video game you ever played with wizards and thieves and knights and shit. Ship literally threw Bob over an eight-foot chain-link fence.

Fortunately for us, he and I were able to climb up the galvanized links and other shit that had been piled there as an obstacle to the dead. The whole shebang groaned and protested under Ship's bulk (let's face it, I was an afterthought with this guy next to me) but we made it. I did feel a few of those rotten fingers brush my boot as I scurried over the top.

Unfortunately for Bob, he hadn't the foggiest what had been about to happen to him, so he hit the ground damn hard on his chest. He was able to get his palms down to absorb a bit of the impact, but he absolutely did not stick the landing.

The dead were starting to pile up on the fence and they were already about five deep. The horde that was behind us was going to hit the links in less than thirty seconds, and when that happened this fence was coming down.

Bob was not moving when we got to him, Remo, Steve, and Lynda getting to him at about the same time.

"Ow," he breathed from the ground.

Remo and Steve made to pick him up, but Ship, astonishingly fast for a guy who could beat a Yeti at arm wrestling, picked him up by his arm pits and began to throw him into another fireman's carry.

"No!" Bob shouted. "Fuck that, I can run." He wiped blood from his scraped chin.

Ship nodded and we all sprinted to catch up with the others.

We moved forward toward a glass-front restaurant with the name Hard Water in orange on the glass. Seyfert called to us and we skirted right. A small, paved catwalk, maybe fifteen feet wide sat between the side of the building and the water. We chose that and ran out onto the dock proper.

I keep calling the thing I was now standing on a dock, but really it was a pier. Maybe 120 feet wide by 600 feet long, it was basically a huge parking lot that stuck out into the bay. Several open structures, like car ports, dumpsters, and an abandoned FEMA tent also adorned the cemented ground. There were cars haphazardly strewn about like a gigantic kid had left his massive Matchbox and Hot Wheels toys on the rug. A few undead, maybe twelve, wove their way in between the vehicles.

We had a choice of four boats at our disposal. There were five, but the one closest to us was half sunk. Two huge ferries sat on the left side of the dock, The sunken thing, and a smaller ferry sat on the right, and at the end was a smaller ferry-type boat. Billy, Buttons, and Danny took care of the things coming from our forward. When we were halfway down the pier, we heard the things behind us. They were using the same walkway we had. I guess the barrier had let go. They also were built up against the giant back windows of the restaurant we had avoided, and the glass gave way after only a few seconds, spilling the things onto a pretty sun deck with overturned umbrellas.

Why hadn't anybody used any of these vessels to escape the city? I mean three of the boats here were huge. One of them had to be 300 feet long. As we passed the one on the right, I answered my own question; the boat was jam-packed with undead. I could see them scratching at the tinted glass on the starboard side of the boat not fifty feet away.

I spun my head to look at the huge ship on our left. San Francisco Belle looked back at me in tall gold letters. It was a fucking massive riverboat complete with a huge paddle wheel.

It didn't seem to creep with the dead, but I was pretty sure I was going to be the captain of whatever boat we purloined to escape the clutches of the infected behind us, and I would have no idea how to pilot that big bitch.

We made it to the end of the pier, and we had maybe five minutes before the dead would be on us. I glanced back at them and could see individual faces in the crowd.

As luck would have it, the boat we chose had Alcatraz Cruises on the bow. It was still a big boat, eighty feet probably, but our choices were limited.

Seyfert and Billy were doing what they could to open the locked gangway but were coming up a bit short. Ship looked back at the swarm and shook his head. I followed his glance. "We're swimming in three minutes," I shouted back over my shoulder. "We're dead in four."

Seyfert didn't even turn around when he yelled back, "Working on it!"

"Come on, Come on…" I heard Steve say under his breath.

Teems echoed the sentiment, "Anytime, Navy."

"Hundred meters out," Remo said quietly. A scream from inside the crowd lanced through the mid-morning air. It was echoed by two more, and no human had made those calls. Remo eyeballed the crowd through the ballistic scope on his enhanced battle rifle, "Two I can see fighting the crowd, but I heard three calls"

I glanced at Bob, he didn't look great. "We all heard three, buddy/"

One of the speedy infected had fought its way to the vanguard of the dead and began its tireless sprint toward us.

"Firing," Remo said casually, and his rifle kicked out death at eighty meters. The Runner dropped where it was, the dead behind it stepping or tripping over it in short order.

"Fuck! I can't get this stupid lock!" Seyfert bellowed.

Billy looked at him sideways. "While I don't appreciate the profanity, I can't either."

"Danny, blow it open with your shotgun."

Danny moved forward to follow Seyfert's command, but I stopped him.

"Hang on, boys. Ship can pick any lock. Ship, old buddy? Can you save our lives please?

Ship strode (really, he only took two steps) to the door and gave it a once over. He nodded, took a step back and lashed out with his meaty foot. The steel locking mechanism on the wood and metal door bent under the force of his kick and the door almost broke free of its hinges.

Fucking barbarian. Told you.

"Secure that door as best as you can," Seyfert told us. "The rest of us will clear the boat."

"Ship and I will cover," Remo told him.

They raced up the long gangway to the boat and went into tactical positions as they boarded it, then moved out of sight.

I looked up at Ship. "Fucking ape. You broke the shit out of this door." I shook my head in disgust and gave Remo a sideways glance. He was smiling too. I searched the ground and there was fuck-all to secure the door with. I grabbed a length of paracord out of my pack and began looping it through the aluminum door and its frame. Ship slung his rifle and removed his bracelet. He unraveled the paracord and began to tie the other side of the door as well. By the time Remo had sniped the other two Runners, we had made about fifteen loops each on the door. Ship bent down to do the bottom of his side, and I did the same. The dead were a hundred feet away and loud as fuck by the time we had made four locks on the door. It wouldn't stop them, but it would definitely slow them down. At least I hoped so.

I spoke into my radio, "Seyfert, the door is as secure as it's gonna get."

"Copy. Boat is almost secure. You guys head forward and check the top deck. Stay frosty."

Ship, Remo, Bob, and I moved up the gangway and took a right. The boat was big, but not big enough for an infected to hide where we were. We had the place scanned and secure in less than a minute.

"Clear," we all said simultaneously, and Bob smiled.

"That was cool."

Half the group showed up in a moment or two and they were asking for me.

Buttons threw me chin wag, "Can you fly this thing? Alvarez said you could."

"Dunno. Let me at the controls and we'll see." I followed him up a steel stairwell toward the wheelhouse. "Plus, the diesel is two years old by now, and that might be a showstopper."

From the wheelhouse I could see the dead had reached the gate and were clawing at it. They had fanned out along the length of the boat, but the gunwale was too high for them to climb over. They reached their filthy hands through the over-sized scuppers, but that was about all the purchase they were getting. I could hear a Runner screaming, but I wasn't sure if it would be able to climb up the side of the steel.

There was already a small group of people waiting for me.

"Where'd you get them fancy radios?" I heard Teems ask Seyfert as I moved in front of the controls.

"They recharge on board the Sub," he answered. "We have a few dozen."

"Yeah, so this is doable if the fuel is good," I told no one in particular.

One of the bikers raised an eyebrow. "And what if it ain't?"

"Then I hope you can swim." I flipped the switch to start the blower, and it came on immediately.

"It didn't start," Seyfert alerted me. He pointed at the controls to make sure I saw that the craft had remained off.

"Yeah, that's the blower. It needs to run for about five minutes before I try to start the engine."

"We don't have five minutes!"

"If I try to start the motor and there's two years of fuel fumes in the compartment... well you do the math."

"Alvarez, Buttons, Danny, with me. We're going to cover the gangway with Ship and Remo until he gets this thing started." They moved off to do just that.

The start switch had a locked cover on it, but it couldn't withstand the butt of my M4. In three minutes, I hovered my finger over the green button for a moment. "Here goes nothing..."

Nothing was exactly what we got when I pressed that green piece of plastic.

"Well, shit."

"Can you fix it?" demanded the same biker."

"Absolutely, if I knew what was wrong. I need to get to the engine room."

"You guys stay here. If anything bad happens... Well, fuck, I don't know. Try not to die."

The civvies stared at me helplessly as I ran out of the wheelhouse and down a set of stairs in the back. I made my way as low as I could until I saw two doors on either side of the companionway marked Authorized Personnel Only. They were both locked, but I was able to persuade the one on the port side with my boot. The smell hit me immediately. Not the horrid stench of the dead, the reek of oil, fuel, and machinery.

God, I love that smell...

I allowed myself a deep breath of heaven before switching on the tac light on my rifle. I panned it around with my finger on the trigger. I had standard rounds in my weapon, so I really didn't want to throw lead around in here as I was in a steel room. Ricochets are a thing. Really.

As I moved into the engine room it got tight, so I let my rifle dangle and went to my sidearm. The Sig also had a tactical light and I used that to find what I was looking for. I found it quickly. Back by the beautiful Red QSK95 Cummins diesel engines, (there were two!) a red handle jutted out from a pipe that T'd off into both engines. This was the fuel shutoff switch and it had been put in the off position for safety. This was common practice on larger boats and the only reason I knew about it was because I had worked as an underwater welder for a few years in the northeast before the planet tanked. That was the good news.

The bad news was that the prick who had closed off the valve had been a stickler for safety and had used lock-out tag-out techniques. That means the douche put a fucking padlock through the shutoff valve.

F him, because the most important thing the apocalypse has taught me (other than there's always a zombie in the bathroom) is that I should be prepared. I pulled the neon green-handled bolt cutters out of my pack and soon the lock was in three pieces. I threw the lever up and spun to get out of the engine room.

I looked directly into the red eyes of a dead man standing behind me.

You know, I'm a pretty good judge of character. Before this little undead issue took Earth by surprise, I prided myself in being able to immediately assess a human being upon seeing them for the first time. I wasn't always correct, and in retrospect, a one hundred percent correctness on this would have kept me out of prison, but I was damn good at it.

Seems this particular trait worked on the undead as well. I had a jump scare, because if you turn around and don't expect someone to be standing behind you but there they are, you fucking jump a little. I don't give a shit if you're Iron Man, you jump.

So, I jumped.

But that was it. I know it's going to sound weird, but I knew immediately this thing meant me no harm. I could see it on his face and in his eyes. Before you get all high and mighty on me and think: *His eyes? Are you fucking certifiable? How many other people have been eaten because they didn't feel one of these things was dangerous?* you should understand a few things.

1.   Your thought is not wrong. I'm guessing thousands, hundreds of thousands of people died because of that same very trusting manner.

2.   This thing didn't lunge or growl or do any of the things that an infected would do when in close proximity to fresh meat.

3.   As much as I hated the people who took me away to experiment on me, I instantly knew I had to preserve and protect this thing. I had to do to him what those anus-breath douche-canoes had done to me.

It stood there for a second, looking at me from three feet away with my bolt cutters threateningly raised, then it did something I completely didn't expect: *It turned the hell around and made for the door.*

What in the actual fuck was going on? I had to blink a couple of times to make sure it was real. An old psych professor of mine told me to count my fingers if I was ever stuck in a dream and that would instantly wake me. I had never tried that before and I sure as shit wasn't about to total my digits now, but come on, this had to be a dream, right? I had seen at least three people who could walk through throngs of undead with impunity. Billy, the guy above decks who needed a check up from the neck up, could do this. *He* was undead immune.

But I wasn't. As evidenced by the multiple bite wounds on my person, I can tell you with extreme certainty that the undead do, in fact, wish to dine upon me.

So, I repeat my question to you, Dear Reader: What the fuck?

The fuck would have to wait. I had shit to do.

"Hey," I said. I truly didn't know if what had just happened had happened, so I put it to the test.

The thing turned, looked at me, then turned back and took two steps toward the door. Apparently, he had better things to do than speak with the likes of me and wished to go do them.

I put my hand on his shoulder and gently pushed him to the side as I cautiously moved past him. He didn't fight me at all and allowed me to move him out of the way. I quickly made it to the door and shut it behind me, trapping him.

I heard him thump into the wooden door and half expected him to either use the door handle or start banging on it like they do.

He did neither, so I called into my radio. "We have a pus-bag in the engine room," I said as I clanged up the stairs. "Nobody goes in there and nobody destroys it."

"Wait, what?" Alvarez' voice came over the coms. "You mean you found one and you didn't kill it?"

"That's a solid fucking copy. We can talk about it later. Repeat, stay out of the engine room. Nobody goes in there but me."

I ended that last sentence as I thundered into the wheelhouse. Remo and his gang of miscreants were firing into the crowd of dead that had assembled in front of the gangway. In actuality, the things were spread out the breadth of the pier with some splashing into the inky water as the crowd pushed them over the short rail. The luckier ones were pulling or pushing on the chain link of the gangway door, but that didn't last. The pressure from the swarm pushed the front runners against the door, their rotting flesh diced into cubes as it pushed through the galvanized links. The door held for another five or six seconds, then it came down with a crash. The paracord held, the door frame didn't. The dead in the back stepped over or on their brothers to get to us, the ones on the ground crushed to pulp.

I depressed the green button again and a light came on underneath it this time. I flipped the switch for the generator and the overhead lights flickered and came on. That was nice as one would usually have to go find and play with the generator in order for it to work.

Another touch of the green button and the engine fought to catch. A long while's worth of shit might be in the motor or the lines, so this thing starting would be a miracle anyway, although I left that little tidbit out when we first got on the boat.

The thing didn't' start, and I gave a nervous laugh. The entire group sans the fighters who were firing into the crowd now coming up the gangway looked to me to get this thing started.

That was totally unfair.

I jammed my finger down again and held it while the engine sputtered and bucked. It wanted to start, I could hear it.

I heard Danny yell, "Grenade!" and had to wonder where he got all those awesome toys.

Ship would tell me later that Danny chucked his 'nade over the heads of the infected on the gangway, our warriors dove for cover, then the grenade blew. I felt the boat shift to the left from the blast, felt and heard the gangway hit the side of the boat and splash into the water, and felt the engine catch all at more-or -less the same time. I couldn't see it, but I knew big black plumes of diesel belched out of the exhaust pipes to the rear of the ship.

I moved the transmission into gear and pushed the accelerator handle forward slowly. Until then, we had had about twelve feet of distance between the gunwales of the boat and the dock, but the moment I pushed the accelerator, the bow of the boat pushed right, and we slammed into the dock. Hard.

I was incredulous. Nobody had thought to untie us from the fucking dock.

"Seyfert!" I yelled into the radio. Ok, it was more of a scream, "For fucks sake untie us!"

He looked from the gunwale to the wheelhouse, then frantically searched for the lines until he and Ship found them. Seyfert tried to untie his, but Ship just used his machete to sever the line on his side. It was a hefty line, so it took a few whacks and some sawing.

I saw the SEAL reach *Fuck it* and he abandoned his untying operation and opted to saw with his knife as well.

Up by the bow of the boat on the edge of the pier, an ancient aluminum shed, clearly constructed during the Pleistocene Era, had also reached *Fuck it*, no doubt because of me smashing into the dock, and the thing straight up died. It collapsed toward my new ride with a metallic clang as it hit the steel of the boat. It was maybe thirty feet from Seyfert's position, and he whipped his head up to see what the hubbub was. Danny and Buttons were there by that time trying to assist with freeing us from the dock.

The friggin' shed that had fallen over had decided to bridge the gap between the dock and our boat. I don't think a better makeshift gangway could have been constructed in so short a time. The dead wasted none of *their* time, and flooded from the pier to our boat, stumbling and falling on the bow as they did so.

Fuckity fuck-sickles.

I was about to scream into the radio again, but Remo and Ship started firing into the growing crowd of stowaways before some of them could even stand. Buttons and Danny joined them, and in three seconds, Seyfert stood, screamed "Punch it!" into his radio, and joined the firing line.

In the half a minute it took for the SEAL to hack through the bow line, eighty or so dead had decided on a San Francisco Harbor cruise. They all were trying to stand, so I did, indeed punch it.

I threw the throttle as far forward as that little silver handle would go. The boat leapt toward open water and any dead thing that was standing took a tumble back to the deck. Unfortunately, my buddies were on the deck, and all of them except Ship and Remo hit the deck too. Short of an eight-pointer on the Richter scale, Ship was not toppling over, and Remo probably didn't know how to.

I saw Ship reach down with one hand and literally pick Buttons up by the back of his tactical webbing.

I spun the wheel to the left and pulled back on the throttle a little as the gunshots echoed across the bay. There were a bunch of dead down already, but so many more were still un-alive and ready for a late lunch.

Anna ran out of the wheelhouse and began firing from the top of the narrow metal stairway. I surveyed my company. Lynda, Steve, Gary, and Kayla stood looking scared. We'd lost Bob someplace, and I hoped he was OK. I unslung my M4 and passed it by the ACOG to Gary.

He looked at it, then looked back to me. "Do you want me to give this to somebody?"

"No!" I yelled and pointed. "Shoot 'em!"

Steve grabbed the rifle. "Gimme that!" He inspected the load and passed Gary his pistol. Steve bolted to the other door, threw it open, and chucked lead at the dead. He fired single shot instead of full auto, which meant he actually hit his targets. Yeah, this Steve guy was going to be a keeper.

"Magazine!" Anna yelled. Ship had my Molle pack, but I had two mags on me. "Somebody give her one of the mags on my hip!"

Kayla, as scratched up and probably doomed as she was, fiddled with my ammo pouch until she had both magazines. She ran to Anna, then ran to Steve.

I could see through the front windows that my guys were backing up as they fired. "I'm out!" Anna shouted.

My M4 stopped barking as well. "Me too!" Steve bellowed.

"Fall back!" I could hear Seyfert yelling. The dead were on full court press now and flooded toward the living. Up forward there had been room to maneuver, but the rotten things had driven my team down the sides of the vessel where it was more cramped. Only one or two of them could fire into the horde at once. In addition, there was an entire other side of the boat that the dead wasted no time in exploring.

"Get in and shut the doors!" I screamed at Anna and Steve. They did as they were told and none too soon. The dead had found the stairs and were banging on the door windows in no time.

This was the third time I had been on a ship crawling with infected and I've got to tell you, it still sucked.

"What do we do?" Kayla asked in a small, terrified voice. I steered the bow toward Alcatraz.

I stared into the dead faces of the things smacking on the starboard hatch, "How much ammo do we have?"

Gary had passed Steve's gun to Lynda. She opened the revolver and sighed. "Five bullets."

"Great," I said, noting that there were six of us.

DAMN THE TORPEDOES
USS FLORIDA

"What's that?" demanded Vanessa in a frightened voice.

"Gunfire," both Chloe and Moe said in unison.

Moe put his hand on the hatch. "Means they're coming to get us." *A quarter inch away are my dead friends. They want to eat me,* he thought. He thumbed his sidearm. He had eight rounds in his magazine and one extra mag.

"How many of them were out there?" he asked the girls.

Vanessa shrugged, then pointed at a small sign attached to the frontmost torpedo. "What's that mean?" The sign read WARNING WARSHOT LOADED.

"It means don't touch *anything.*"

Chloe glanced at Moe's weapon, wondering if she could get it from him if he decided to abandon them. "I don't know. They came from in here and started killing the people in the room down the hall with all the seats and tables. There have to be at least twenty by now."

She had an idea and silently made her way to the make-shift bunks. Moe was still standing with his hand against the steel when she began carefully moving blood-soaked sheets and clothing away from the bunks. She noticed a belt wrapped around a pair of boots and smiled. It was a gun belt.

"More ammo here," she said quietly. She found one of those guns where the bullets went inside a detachable thing. She knew it was a magazine, but she thought that word was dumb. She ejected the magazine, checked the load, and reinserted the mag quickly.

Moe stared at her for a moment before asking, "Why don't you give that to me." He stuck his hand out.

She nodded. "No thank you. Besides, two guns are better than one." She smiled.

He was not smiling. "That's dangerous. Please hand it over." He took two steps toward her. She pulled back the slide and a .45 ACP round flew from the ejector. She deftly caught it with her left hand. She ejected the mag, loaded the round, and slammed the mag back into the sidearm.

She lifted an eyebrow. "How many of them have you killed?"

"Huh?"

His hand was still extended toward her. She rolled her eyes. "Zombies. Infected. How many of them have you killed?"

He lowered his extended hand slightly. "Uhh… none. Haven't had to. I've been on board since the start of the plague. The only place I've been is to Alcatraz."

"I've killed sixty-one. Sixty-one of them. Sixty-one. I've used a knife four times, all the rest have been with a gun. You still want to take it from me, Mr. No Kills?"

He blinked. "You see that?" he pointed toward one of the torpedoes. "If you fire that gun and it sets off the fish, you don't just kill us. You kill everyone on board."

She looked at the torpedo. "I didn't know that." She took a step toward the green weapon. It dripped with blood. "Better not shoot it then, huh?" She held up a full .45 magazine. "You want?" She tossed it to him before he could answer.

"I still have to pee," interjected Vanessa.

Chloe didn't think this sailor would try to take the gun by force, but she wanted to change the subject anyway. "How do we get out of here?"

Moe glanced back at the hatch. "We wait for the fire teams to get to us. We can't open that hatch without shooting, and I really don't want to shoot near the fish."

Vanessa looked nervous. "But—"

"I know," the sailor interrupted, "you have to pee. There's a bucket over there." He pointed past the torpedoes.

Sometime later, Moe glanced at his watch. He hadn't been able to reach anyone on the phone in a while. The pounding had ceased on their hatch more than an hour ago as had the gunfire, but nobody had come to get them. He tried the phone one more time to no avail, and sighed.

"We have to open this hatch."

"Yeah, no. No, we don't."

"We need to see what's going on." He moved to the hatch.

"Far be it for me to interrupt your crazy time," Chloe said, "but what happens if you open that door and twenty of those things pour through it? You already said we can't shoot in here."

"Well, that would be unfortunate, but how long do you think we can hold out down here with no food or water?" He looked at Vanessa, "And no bathroom."

"More than two hours, that's for sure!"

"I can hold it," Vanessa told him, thinking of the bucket in the corner. It had not been empty. *Boys*, she thought.

110

"Alright," Moe acquiesced, "I won't open it." He furrowed his brow. "How much ammo did you say was down there?" He pointed at Chloe's feet, where the weapons had been found.

She glanced down. "Another maga—" As soon as she had glanced to the bloody deck, Moe threw the handles on the hatch and pushed it wide enough to peek through the opening.

Satisfied and smug, he turned to push his smugness on the kids. "See? Told y..." He stared down the barrel of Chloe's newly appropriated handgun. His smile evaporated.

"If you ever plan to take our lives into your hands again, *don't*." He nodded, and she stuck her left hand out. She made a casual *move to your left* motion with her palm. He sidestepped and she fired the sidearm once. Moe threw his hands up in a futile defensive move, and the two girls immediately covered their ears as the weapon had not been suppressed.

Moe felt rather than heard a body slump to the ground. He spun quickly and noticed one of his ravaged shipmates in a heap over the knee knocker.

"Next time I'm just gonna watch," Chloe told him through ringing ears.

"Fall back!" Kimball screamed. He was sweating and a bit nauseated, but he was able to plug one of the dead civilians that stepped over its re-killed brethren. There hadn't been much left of the thing's face or throat, the exposed trachea draped in shreds of dripping flesh. That sent a wave of nausea through his already queasy stomach.

He fired his shotgun and the left arm of the creature fell to the floor. Pellets peppered its bared skull and hit the creatures behind it, and it stumbled a little, but it didn't collapse. Kimball was having trouble focusing.

He was suddenly angry. Everything was gone. Everything. He would never see another movie in his favorite movie theater back home. His mom and dad were undoubtedly dead back in Des Moines. He would never see his dog, Bently, or the pretty girl who worked at the drug store again. The dead had taken it all, and now they wanted his boat.

"Well, you can't fucking have it!" he screamed.

He jacked another shell into the chamber and fired. The skull of the lead creature sprayed backward in a shower of fluids and bone fragments. Kimball fired until his weapon was empty, then he began to reload. He was shaking, he was so mad. It was difficult for him to get the shells into the weapon as his right hand kept flexing of its own accord. Not only did the bite on his arm not even hurt, he felt great. Fantastic. He absentmindedly wiped sweat out of his eyes while thinking he couldn't possibly be infected if he felt this good. He was heaving, and he hunched over, out of breath.

Kimball smiled one last time and the shotgun clattered to the deck. His eyelids fluttered in rapid succession and he looked at his hands. They were both flexed into claws. The essence of this plague flooded his mind and body. Any thoughts other than violence and the hunt left him. He needed to rend and kill. The necessity to taste flesh and watch the life leave from something, anything, became primal.

He whipped his head around to glare at the things coming from his left. They were already dead. Useless.

ET-Nav Nichols was dumbfounded that his friend would drop his weapon. "What the hell is he doing?" he asked himself and the others in his fire team. "Kimball! What the fuck is going on? They're coming!" He pointed the barrel of his MP5 at one of the incoming infected and gave it a round to the face. He had fallen back fifteen feet at Kimball's command, but clearly there was something wrong. "Cover! I'm going to get him!"

He felt a hand on his shoulder. "Wait…"

He shrugged out of the hand and took a step toward the friend he had shared his home with for the past three years.

Kimball stood with his face toward the infected. When he heard the sound of something he might be able to kill, he spun to face it. His thoughts were no longer human thoughts, but they did bear a resemblance. This new creature would kill the things in front of it without mercy or compassion. He would use his hands and teeth to tear and bite and beat them until they were bloody husks of what they once had been. He screamed that at them, told them he hated them, and he would kill them. Kill them. KILL THEM!

Nichols' bladder let go when the thing that had been Kimball let loose with its inhuman scream. No man could make that sound. Nichols stood transfixed as the thing sprinted at him, its dead cousins just behind it. He heard a noise and the Kimball-thing jerked twice, then fell. It looked up at him with bleeding eyes, reaching over the knee-knocker ten feet away. There were more noises behind him, then he felt himself being dragged backwards, his weapon and thoughts forgotten.

Nichols' shipmates pulled him away from the oncoming horde. One of them threw the navigation technician back into the rest of the fire team. "He's checked out! Get him out of here!" The man fired three more times at the things stepping past a mortally wounded Kimball, then slammed the hatch between them closed. It was mere moments before the thumps of dead fists rang on the steel of the hatch.

***

"That one," Rick said and pointed. "The one in the red shirt."

"Dude," Richy answered looking sideways. "They all have red shirts, it's blood."

Lt. Commander Pitt stepped up behind the boy and gave him a friendly cuff to the back of the head. "We don't *Dude* people in the Navy, son. Show the man some respect."

"Sorry, sir," apologized the kid then he directed his gaze to Rick. "Sorry, Mr. Barnes."

"Don't sweat it. I meant the skinny thing, the one in front of the gate post. There." Rick pointed again. Before he could finish pointing, the top of the skull of the dead thing flew off."

Pitt lowered his binoculars. "Damn fine shot, son."

Richy nodded and passed the rifle to Kyle. "Thank you, sir."

Kyle popped off a round and another thing dropped. The tall boy rubbed his shoulder. "Does it ever not hurt?"

Pitt shook his head. "It's always going to hurt a bit with these rifles. They're high-powered and not supposed to be fired over-and-over again like this."

Rick looked at his watch. "We've got several hours of light left. He peeked over the railing on the water tower, then at Detachment Bravo in the guard tower. "There are three on the catwalks under your men and maybe twenty milling around the dock. Another ten or so moving toward the structures. I can't see where the rest of them went, but that doesn't give me a warm and cuddly feeling. We can't hit the three on the catwalks from here."

"What are you suggesting?" Pitt demanded, the binoculars affixed to his face.

"You and I make it over to the guard tower, kill the infected there, get your guys down, and start making sweeps."

Pitt nodded, "I like it. If we could clear most of the island before nightfall, we could get a ton more fighters to help run sweeps in the morning."

"What about us?" Kyle asked.

"You three will stay up here and shoot anything that comes near us," Rick told him. "Make sure you know they're infected before you fire. I don't want you shooting anybody living." He held up his radio. "Can you use one of these?"

"Yeah." He glanced at Pitt. "I mean yes, sir."

Pitt called to Spartan platoon and told them the plan.

"Sir, you're going to be covered by a sixteen-year-old kid?"

"A sixteen-year-old kid who hasn't missed a head shot all day? Affirmative. Christ's sake, he's two years younger than some of the kids who went through BUD/S."

"Copy that, sir."

"Daddy…"

Rick shifted his eyes to his little girl.

"Be careful."

Rick hugged her and he and Pitt climbed down the ladder and were soon on the ground. Many bodies littered the area, but nothing moved. Detachment Bravo had done as a good a job clearing the water tower as Rick's group had of destroying infected underneath the guard tower.

"Don't get too close," Rick told Pitt. "I've seen them look dead but grab at the nearest passerby."

"Copy that."

They moved through the pile of bodies slowly, checking as best they could to ensure each had a hole in its cranium.

Rick noticed a contingent of infected about twenty yards in front of them. The dead were between them and the guard tower. "Commander."

"I see them."

Both men moved forward as quietly as possible. The dead were milling about and didn't take notice of the living. Rick and Pitt skirted an elevated walkway and heard something above them, but they couldn't see it from their vantage.

"Two above you, they don't see you," Richy's voice whispered through the radio.

Pitt glanced back at the water tower and gave a thumb's up. "I like those kids."

Rick smiled. The kids had gone off and done something they shouldn't have when they had explored the tunnel. They would answer for that. But they had also saved Sam's life at their own personal expense. He smiled again. He didn't know how, but he would personally reward them for that too. His smile evaporated as a single thought penetrated his mind: *Martingale.*

A woman's scream sounded from their right and both men spun to regard the sound. It was in one of the buildings a bit higher up the island than where they were. Unfortunately, the dead in the area had heard the cry too, all of them turning to stare right at the two men.

Donna leaned with her shoulder against the rickety door. Thumps and pushing came from the other side, as did the moans and cries of the dead. She had been at a yoga class in the former farming building with some of the other ladies from the island. "Yoga" actually meant "women's discussion about life on the island with a little stretching." All the women loved to talk to each other once every few days with no men around.

"Juanita! Can you get that desk over here?" Juanita and one of the newer women began pushing the ancient, rusty, heavy metal desk toward the door. It screeched across the concrete floor, seeming to fuel the horrid sounds of the horde outside.

Abbey and Ali had four hands on the door as well. The top hinge had barely been attached to the frame and just last week Abbey had said they needed to fix a bunch of the doors in the buildings on Alcatraz. The hinge gave way just as the desk was pushed up to the backs of the ladies' legs.

"We can't push it anymore!"

Donna grunted out a reply as she continued to push, "If we let it go to move, the damn door will come down!"

An arm came through the gap in the door, followed by a second, and then two more. Donna did a weapons count in her head, but she also knew that she had the only firearm in the group. Ali had a compound bow, but it was twenty feet away on an ancient wooden table. The rest of the women all had bladed or blunt instruments. She looked at the dead thing on the floor. It had been the precursor to the horde outside, and the only reason they had been able to get the door closed before the larger group had arrived. It had wandered in through the opening and Donna had shot it, alerting the rest of the horde to their location.

This one was fresh, all bloody and torn. She didn't recognize who it was, but the clothing wasn't the dingy gray that all the dead seemed to wear. This poor man had definitely been an Alcatraz resident. Fear gripped her as she thought of the kids.

One of the dead hands that was poking through the failing door latched onto Abbey's wrist. She pulled away, and the door opened enough for one of the things to get the top portion of its torso into the opening. The door would never close again. It started inching into the room and Donna realized that attempting to hold it shut was an exercise in futility.

"It's giving way!" she shouted, and it did. The rickety thing broke free from its top hinge and the defenders backed into the large room except Donna who pushed for all she was worth.

Abbey brought her knife around into the side of her attacker's head, but the blade skidded off. She continued to wrestle with it as the other dead poured through the now open portal. She tried to push her attacker away, but her hand went into its chest cavity and the disgusting thing leaned forward and bit her above her elbow. She screamed in pain and terror, Donna's gunshot suddenly freeing her.

She fired three more times before the other women surged forward, their weapons cleaving the air and not a few skulls. An arrow suddenly blossomed in one of the things that was reaching for a wounded Abbey, the *twang* of Ali's bow coming soon afterward.

Donna slapped her only reserve magazine into her weapon, taking aim and firing into the crowd.

UGLY
JOURNAL ENTRY 8

At one time, he had been a good looking kid. Maybe fifteen or sixteen, Asian, tall, and fit. I wouldn't call him a muscle-head, but he had distinct tone to his arms and shoulders. Certainly would have been a lady-killer.

He must have died recently as well, as he wasn't as discolored as the other rotten things around him. He had a bit of blood on the front collar of his Star Wars T-shirt, but other than that, and the fact that his eyes were blood red, he looked pretty good for a dead kid. I couldn't tell how he died, either. In fact, I wasn't entirely sure if he was a pus bag or a Runner. I guess if he were a Runner, he would be going nuts and screaming, though.

The two-dozen other pus bags that stood banging on the plexiglass windows of the ferry growled and drooled. There was a landing outside the door, with stairs leading both up and down, so only a few of them could pound on the door at once. Several hands smacked the left and right-side windows, but the creatures the hands belonged to were lower or higher than my field of vision. The ones not directly in front of the door had to reach up or down. They frantically scratched or slapped at the thin plastic barrier between us. They wanted food, and they wanted it most Ricky-tick. All had horrible wounds, most having been savaged by claws and teeth. Except this kid. He just stood there, arms at his sides, staring at me with his head cocked slightly. He would occasionally look at one of the others trapped in the wheelhouse with me, but his eyes would snap back to me in short order. He reminded me a little of the thing I had locked in the engine room.

The fact that dead people were trying to eat us was not the most fucked-up portion of today. WTF was happening? Talking Runners and dead infected who didn't try to eat me? I know I'm immune to this little plague, but I can't stand in a crowd of the dead ones without being chewed like Billy can.

The boat was aimed at Alcatraz, and we had about a half hour before we would get to the dock. I left the controls and cautiously moved near the window to get a better look at the kid. He wasn't going apeshit like the other infected.

Yup, a fucked-up day for sure.

I heard gunfire from somewhere behind our position on the ferry. I'd give the guys a few minutes to get situated before I called Remo on the radio. I wouldn't call Ship because, well, he's fucking mute.

Kayla stared at the dead, then at the scratches on her arms. She sighed and looked at me, "What do we do?"

"Still don't have the best answer for that. Gary, take the wheel." I pointed at the ship's steering device.

"I don't..."

"For fuck's sake kid, just hold the friggin' wheel. I'll be within ten feet of you if the shit hits the fan." I stared outside into the dead kid's face again, noting the fifty or so things out there with him. "I mean more than it already has..."

Anna's radio came to life. *"Anna, SITREP?"* It was Seyfert.

"Yeah, John, I can do that too," she admonished. "FUBAR. We're trapped in the... the place with the steering wheel. Is Chris OK?"

"Cute. Yeah, we're all good. From your relaxed tone, it sounds like you're safe. We got pushed to the stern but were able to make it up to the second level storage area. There's a gate the things can't figure out. Are you in danger?"

I put my hand on Anna's shoulder and she jumped half a mile. "Anna, Kayla needs a medic." Seyfert must have heard that because he asked if she had been bitten. "No, but she's got some pretty deep scratches. Also, we lost Bob, do you have him?"

"Negative. There are fourteen of us here including me and the new guys."

"We've got six. We've also got an utter fuckton of cannibalistic undead an inch away through plexiglass and steel. I don't want to speak for everybody, but I sure as hell would like it if you put some holes in them."

"Can't see 'em. There's an overhang."

"Pissa. We're also out of ammo. When you deliver our pizzas, could you also bring me a MOLLE of 5.56 for my rifle?"

"Remo and Danny are peeking over the overhang now. Looks like the things still haven't busted through the locked gate but they're trying like hell. The port side gate is wide open. They must have stopped to snack on you guys and haven't figured out there's a back door. Alvarez and Kev are going to slip down and shut the port gate. Sit tight. Hey! Hey, what the hell are you doi..."

Anna was finishing up the bandages on Kayla's right arm when I began opening all the cabinets to search for weapons. Steve and Lynda also began to look. We came up with some paper towels, a flare gun with six flares, an unopened bottle of Captain Morgan, and some charts.

"Pissa," I said again. I shifted my gaze to check out the undead kid, but he was gone.

Gunfire became sustained from our guys on the stern. The red eyes of a bunch of the dead that were glaring at me moved left and they began to meander down the stairs. They were pretty packed in, but I saw one take a step down, heard the bass boom of a shotgun at the same time its head popped. There was a commotion out there... well, I mean in addition to the dead things slapping on the window and growling. It royally pissed me off because I couldn't see what was going on. It was below my field of vision.

"Hi-YAH! Eleven-oh-eight! YA! Nine! Ten!"

"Coming up to the wheelhouse on the port side."

I smiled, knowing who was coming.

"Copy, Seyfert. You've already thinned out our herd some on this side. Be advised there are still a shit ton of—"

I was cut off by someone screaming for Alvarez to look out. All kinds of gunfire sounded at the same time, and I heard some brief screaming.

"Oh shit!" I heard Gary yell. I spun to face whatever new threat this was and saw the dead kid with his palms on the front windows. He had climbed up on the little protrusion in front of the wheelhouse and was peering in at us. Still not going nuts like infected do when they see fresh meat though. He was just looking at us. The fact that he had been able to climb up there freaked me out a little too.

Several of the dead had stayed with us and they continued to smack the port side plexiglass. Others shoved past them to get at the vittles near the stern. I saw Billy's sword poke through the throat of a dead woman in what was left of her skimpy dress. Or maybe it was only skimpy because half of it had been eaten away. The sword drew back and was immediately thrust through the face of the dead girl. Billy climbed up a few steps smiled and waved to us, then smoked another infected.

There were maybe fifteen more of the things remaining near the port side door when the window to the right of it pushed in. It dangled briefly before it fell to the deck with a clatter. The big hole in the side of the wheelhouse was at about chest height, which slowed the things from gaining entry, but there was a stairwell which ascended past it, and it was the infected on those stairs that got their upper torsos over the barrier. One of them gained entry to our little sanctuary quickly and stood, briefly sizing us up before making its move.

It opened its stinking maw wide to do that hissing growl thing that they do, and the single coolest thing I had witnessed during this entire little plague-apocalypse thingie occurred. I heard a loud *POP,* a brief but ridiculously loud whistle, and suddenly the infected dude turned into a fire-breathing dragon.

Fire exploded from its mouth as it staggered back into the now open window, the things behind it grabbing it as if it were fresh meat. They let go almost immediately, realizing the thing with the flaming face was one of their own. The flamer's face melted off in dripping gobs of fire and bright light shot from its mouth and eyes as it collapsed.

I could see Billy literally jumping up and down with glee for a quick second before returning to his swordplay. Gunfire erupted from behind him and several of the things dropped.

I turned to survey the other folks who were in as imminent danger as I was, and I saw Lynda reloading the flare pistol. Light dawned on the stupid guy (me) and I rushed to grab the window that had fallen into the wheelhouse.

"Steve! Help!"

The two of us picked up the window; it was heavier than I thought it would have been and it had been molded to fit the window frame. There was a bend and a slight bulge to it. We slammed it into the faces of the two things that were trying to climb through the hole, and I saw a tooth fly as black shit smeared all over the other side of the plexiglass. Anna yelled and rushed at us with both hands outstretched. For a moment I thought she had somehow speed-turned into a Runner and I tried doing mental calculations on how to deal with her when her palms landed on the plexiglass and she helped us push. The things on the other side reached their arms over or to the side of our barrier, but none could reach us. I glanced at Anna and thought that if she had turned, all my ideas on how to save everyone from her wouldn't have meant shit as they had been about a year too slow.

I heard a bunch of call-outs between gunshots as I pushed that window into the faces of the dead people.

"Left side!"

"Two more on the stairs!"

"Eleven fourteen!"

"Danny, cover the rear!"

Billy hacked and stabbed his way forward, shouting something in what sounded like Japanese. An arm fell to the deck, then he thrust into the chest of a thing wearing what was left of a tuxedo. Billy withdrew his weapon and brought it in a wicked sideways arc that took off the top of Tuxedo's head. The guy and the fireteam behind him wasted no time in dispatching the remaining dead, and in less than two minutes, Steve, Anna, and I let the heavy plexiglass drop to the deck.

"Took you long enough," I said through a smile to Billy when he opened the door.

"Did you SEE that? Did you see?" He stared at the thing with the melted face. It was still smoking, the flare having just died out.

He pointed at the flare gun in Lynda's hand and honestly, I didn't know what to make of this guy. "I have GOT to get me one of those! You... melted him!" He took two strides toward her, and I thought for sure we were going to have another flaming face when he held his palm up.

"High five!"

She complied.

Remo entered the wheelhouse, followed by Seyfert and the rest of the gang. It was a big wheelhouse, but it crowded quickly, especially when Ship ducked his head and stepped in helping Alvarez.

Alvarez was cradling his right hand in his left. Blood was pouring down his bare forearm from under his tactical glove in crimson rivulets.

I blinked. "No," I said to no one under my breath.

Anna caught what I had said and rushed to my buddy. I followed.

"Let me see it," she demanded. She pulled out a pair of scissors and Seyfert stepped in my way when I tried to move past the ten thousand other people who had suddenly gotten in my way.

Ship, towering over everyone, found my eyes as Seyfert began talking to me. The sasquatch nodded no.

What did that mean? Alvarez was bitten? He was fine? He didn't fucking like spinach? What?

"SITREP!" Seyfert yelled in my face, and everybody looked. He put his hand on my shoulder and shook me for a moment. I snapped my eyes to his and I wanted to rip his face off.

I yelled into his face, "Gary is driving the boat! We've got everybody except... except..." For the life of me, I couldn't remember the guy who had been fucked up by the infected.

"Bob," Lynda added.

"Bob!" I yelled, "Now fucking move!"

Seyfert focused his glare. "This boat is not secure. I need you to take the wheel and fly this thing while we do a sweep. You get me, soldier?"

"I'm not a fucking s—"

"You are today. Alvarez will be fine. Do your job." With that he spun and began speaking to Kev and Danny. He was right, and that pissed me off.

"Seyfert!"

He glared at me.

"Don't forget about the one in the engine room. Try not to kill it, it was weird. There was also a weird infected kid up here." I glanced at the forward windows. I knew he would be gone, and he was.

"Weird how?"

"Difficult to explain. It was just… different. Didn't attack and go nuts like the others do."

He shrugged. "I get it, but what are we supposed to do with it?"

"I dunno, I'm not a scientist."

Alvarez yelled in pain and I was about to juke past this Navy SEAL when Remo did what he does second best and just appeared like a friggin' ghost. "He's fine. One of them came up from the rear and got close. They went down and Alvarez got a shard of glass through his palm.

Why couldn't that Navy douche have just fucking said that? All my fears and trepidations would have melted away. Dick.

"Thanks," I said, glaring at the back of Seyfert's buzz cut. "How're we doing?"

Remo's eyebrows shot up. "Billy's pretty handy. Rotters don't seem to want to eat him, and he uses that to his advantage. Took out twenty of them by himself."

"Twenty-three!" Billy corrected. "Not my best day, but it's up there. Is there a spare flare gun up here anywhere? I need one." He scrunched up his face in thought. "Also, how did you get it to open up? Its mouth I mean. Did you do anything or was it just hungry?'

Guy was dead serious.

"Ask Lynda," I told him and moved with Remo to the ship's wheel. "I got it, kid." Gary stepped off, looking relieved. "Good job," I added, and he nodded.

Remo glanced over his shoulder. "Really handy. Like, *take with us* handy when we move on."

"What? Move on?"

"Yes. Like everywhere else, this place isn't what I expected."

He meant Alcatraz, and I had to agree. These folks were badass, that was for sure, but they wanted Billy. What were they going to do with him? The kid straight up told me he used to be a serial killer, but I don't know what that means. He was clearly a bit off, but I didn't get *murderer* coming off him. If anything, he'd saved my ass twice.

If they wanted Billy, how long until they wanted me? I had survived a bite, then stupidly had told them about it. This Seyfert guy and his crew were good folks, but what would he do if that sub captain Mac-something decided I was his new mission?

Fuck.

Alcatraz was getting larger in the front windows when Ship was suddenly standing next to me. He passed me his notebook and I started to read it aloud for Remo. Ship put his hand on the page, shook his head almost imperceptibly and looked at the group behind us. He didn't want me to read his message so others could hear. I showed it to Remo and we read it together.

You two should keep your voices down when discussing things like that. When we get back, we should talk about what happens next.

Remo tore the page out of the book and crumpled it up. "You're right, Ship."

A dead one slapped its nasty paw against the starboard side window and made us all jump.

"Alright, we're good here," Seyfert told us looking at the dead thing. "We need to sweep the whole boat to make sure there are no surprises. Two teams of four," he glanced at the big biker, "if you're up for it."

Teems nodded. "We got this." He held up his radio. "Channel four." Teems took all five of his guys with him. Seyfert took Danny, Buttons, and Remo. Alvarez piped up like he wanted to go, but I stared him down.

"Kat," was all I said, and I could see the fear in his eyes. Kat and Alvarez are boyfriend and girlfriend. In the apocalypse, that means she wears the penis. Now that I think about it, I'm having a hard time thinking Kat wouldn't have ruled the roost before the apocalypse, too. Her poor boyfriends…

I hoped she was ok. I started to think of the rest of my family on Alcatraz with all those dead things and I nudged the throttle on the boat up a bit.

"I'm coming too!" Billy announced. He held up his newly appropriated flare pistol. He had sheathed his sword and his off hand held a fist full of flares.

He made for the door, and I stopped him. "Billy, you can't fire that thing on the boat."

He frowned and I thought he was going to burst into tears. "But she did!" He pointed at Lynda.

I shook my head. "Yeah, but if you fire a flare gun where there's something flammable…" I let that hang. His raised eyebrows and expectant expression told me he had no idea what I was getting at.

"Flare gun equals boom."

"Oh! Yeah! Right! I won't shoot it until I get off the boat then."

"Good man." He started to move away, but I held him fast. He looked at my hand then at me. "And if you could keep an eye on my friend?" I chin-wagged at Remo's back."

"No problem!" he cheerily agreed.

I was trying to maneuver the bow toward the southern dock of Alcatraz when the heavy-hitters returned to the wheel house. Teems and his crew sat on the bow, taking in the mist. The sun was hiding behind some clouds and it looked like there was going to be fog tonight.

"Vessel is clear," the SEAL told us. He stared directly at me, "Except the engine room. We didn't breach the engine room."

I glanced past him, staring at our destination. My eyes grew wide and Seyfert took notice, spinning to face the island.

A shit load of unmoving corpses were splayed out in various places on the concrete. I could see several of them making their way down some of the paths toward us. There had been a firefight here, but the defenders must have retreated. Or I was staring at them.

Seyfert's radio exploded, *"To the vessel pulling up to the dock at Alcatraz; identify yourself or you'll be fired upon. You have thirty seconds to respond."*

Seyfert grabbed his radio. "Rock, this is Sabre. Sabre is on board the vessel with several civilians. Code is Zulu Alpha Niner Niner.

"Copy that, Sabre. How are you situated for ammo? You're going to need it."

"Ammo is light, can we get a SITREP?"

"Limas control all the pathways but haven't entered into the livable buildings yet that we know of. We've been picking them off as we can, but we need a strong ground force. The Florida also has Limas aboard."

That really seemed to bother the SEAL. "Fuck…"

"There's 5.56, 12 gauge, .308, and 9mm pistol rounds in a locker under the bench on the west side of the dock." There was a slight pause. *"You're going to have to hurry."*

I whipped the wheel around hard to try to dock this big bitch, but I'm me and had no illusions about my piloting abilities. "Remo, Ship, grab some of the bikers and get lines on the dock. Pull us in with the lines, but watch your ass, we've got dead inbound." Seyfert was still talking into his radio, but I interrupted him. "Seyfert! We need cover on the dock so we can tie up."

"Copy," he said to me and took off blabbing into his radio. He called out to Danny and Kev, both of whom began to follow him.

"Seyfert, wait!"

He glanced back at me questioningly.

"We're totally out of ammo here. Can you spare a mag for an M4 just to give us peace of mind while you're fucking around on the dock?"

He smiled and I knew we were cool. He nodded, and Kev threw a magazine pack with two full mags to Steve, who currently held my M4. Without missing a beat, Steve ejected the empty mag, slapped a full one home, and charged a round. He passed a magazine to Anna, who copied him.

I was really starting to enjoy this guy's company.

Ship and three of the bikers had lowered one of the aluminum gangways and were now pulling on lines they had wrapped around cleats. I gave a thumbs up to the guy with the bowline and threw the big bitch into reverse. The line pulled and soon we had a bow and stern line securing us to the dock. We also had six infected coming down the dock with shitloads of their buddies in tow. I filed it into memory that the gunwales were too high for the guys to get back on the boat without the gangway.

"Fire at will," came Seyfert's tinny voice through the comms and the gunfire began. I left the boat running, me moving as fast as possible in a run to the door. I pointed to my rifle in Steve's firm grasp and thought for sure he was going to burst into tears. He acquiesced, passed me the weapon, and I checked the chamber for a round.

"Anna, can you cover the wheelhouse?"

She nodded. In less than a minute, I was placing the chevrons in my 4X optics on the forehead of a dead thing in rags.

I saw Danny and one of the bikers make a run for the bench with the ammo box. There was a small copse of tall bushes next to the railing behind the bench. From their vantage, the guys couldn't see the contingent of dead that was less than twenty feet from them. Danny was already on one knee, pulling the footlocker from under the bench.

I started yelling and then remembered that while I had a radio, I was lacking in brainpower. "Danny! You've got a bunch right around the corner!"

Everybody seemed to hear me except Danny. The guy with him didn't have a radio, so he was also blissfully ignorant to what was about to happen. Remo shifted his aim, firing several rounds past Danny.

The remaining dead rounded the corner and were on my new friend instantly. Both he and the biker scrambled, but it was too late. Several of the things had the biker, but he fought like a badass. Danny rolled and fired his rifle. He got one of them before he was overrun. Teems and Remo got there quickly and dispatched the dead, but more were coming. Both Danny and the biker moved quickly back to the group with Teems. Both were bleeding and limping and the biker had lost his lever action rifle. Remo grabbed the silver handle on one end of the footlocker attempting to drag it and the ammo inside it to a usable position. He ducked the swiping hand of a dead monstrosity, but the one next to it grabbed him and leaned in. The thing's noggin jerked right and it collapsed, almost taking my buddy with it. Remo rolled right, barely under the reaching claws of the first thing, and the MARSOC guy scrambled away. He had to discard the ammo, or he would have gotten very dead.

"I skipped yoga to save your sorry ass, Marine!" exploded Kat's voice through the radio. "You'd better move that ass or it's gonna get bitten off!

I raised my eyes to look for her, saw what was coming down the hill, and realized that whatever was in that footlocker wasn't going to be enough. Hundreds of the things traipsed lazily down the pathways toward us. Some of the pus bags sporadically dropped, and I could see a few guys in a guard tower firing at them. I peered through my binoculars to find out that Kat wasn't with them.

She bellowed at us again, "I'm on the roof! Get back on the fucking boat!"

I wasn't in command. I was, like, ninth in command. Basically, everybody with a gun had to die for me to start issuing orders, but I could sure as shit suggest.

"Seyfert," I screamed into the radio, "we need to fall back!"

Remo and Ship, two of the toughest men on earth and afraid of nothing, both sprinted to the gangway, helping Danny and the wounded biker. Ship thundered up the aluminum behind the two injured men, and Remo covered the dock end. He began firing into the crowd, selecting the closest targets.

Seyfert had decided that my suggestions were ok in this situation. "Dammit!" the SEAL yelled. "Fall back!"

The dock crew performed a tactical withdrawal. Basically, they ran like hell. Remo covered and like everything Remo, he was the last up the gangway.

Or so we thought.

Billy suddenly appeared from nowhere, brandishing his sword. Does one brandish a sword? I dunno, but he swung and jabbed that thing like a pro and in moments was dragging the big box of ammo toward the boat, the scraping noises seeming to fuel the undead nearest him. He made it all the way to the side of the boat before he dropped his pretty weapon on the dock and tried to pick up the ammo.

"It's too heavy," he told us with a shrug.

Ship bounded back down the gangplank right into the clutches of a dead woman. She didn't clutch long because Billy took her face off with three feet of folded steel. Ship effortlessly picked up the heavy box and thundered back up the aluminum and onto the boat.

The Yeti spun, searching for Billy, but the kid had disappeared into the crowd of dead.

The fellas yanked the gangway from the dock quickly, the dead not close enough to gain access. They had used a collapsed shed as a gangway to board us like pirates last time, but this time they could fuck right off. They couldn't get up over the gunwales by themselves, but they could pile up and use each other as a ramp.

"We need to pull away," I told them, "Pull the lines or cut them."

The lines were soon removed, and I backed us off the dock about a hundred feet. The stupid asses either walked off the edge of the concrete or stopped at the edge briefly and were pushed by the shitheads behind them.

I used the binoculars to scan the rooftops to see where Kat was. Alvarez was next to me in an instant. "Do you see her? What do you see?"

"I see a scoped rifle pointing at me from the roof. I hope you haven't pissed her off lately, because you know she ain't gonna miss."

He smiled and I passed him the glasses. He smiled again and waved in a moment. "She's good. Safe up there." He dropped the front end of the binoculars to scan the horde on the dock. They were still coming down the pathways.

He pulled the glasses from his eyes, blinked in rapid succession, and peered through them again. "Holy shit…"

"What?"

He handed the binoculars to me and pointed.

On one of the stone benches, surrounded by the dead with his feet stuck out in front of him and crossed at the ankles, sat Billy, drinking a Pepsi.

"Where does he get all those damn sodas?" I asked no one.

THIRTY FEET UNDER
USS FLORIDA

He was frightened. There was one time during his childhood when he had been this terrified. During extremely cold winters, the small inlet at the marina near where he lived in Maine would freeze over and he would venture out on the ice with his buddies. He and his two friends had been iceberg hopping during one of those freezing cold events. He hopped onto one of the flat icebergs and glared back at his friends who had been too scared to follow him. He put his hands on his hips, his friends accepting the dare.

He spun around and hopped again, then again. His friend Zack made a jump, then Anthoney, but when Anthoney landed, the edge of the ice broke, and the boy went into the freezing water.

Moe threw himself at his friend, grabbing his hands in a desperate attempt to get him back on the ice. Anthoney grabbed back and as Moe pulled his friend onto the ice, he himself plunged headfirst into the water. A million needles pierced his skin at the same time. Everything, from the tips of his fingers, to his crushed-closed eyes, screamed in pain and terror at the shock to his system. He opened his eyes and they hurt worse if possible, but he was able to see. The current had taken him under the ice, his fists pounding and scratching so hard a fingernail tore off.

He was going to die. He was going to die, and his dad had forbidden him to *hop the floes*. It wasn't long before he had to take a breath. Frigid sea water filled his lungs, but he remained conscious as he tried to cough but couldn't. The water wouldn't expel from him, and he knew he was dead.

Then he did cough. He was on his back on the ice, water spewing from him like a geyser. His friends were next to him on all fours, a huge man with an equally huge beard slapping him on the back.

"Get it out, son," the man said. Moe recognized him as a local lobsterman that sometimes worked with his dad.

Moe sat up, in too much agony to cry. Besides, he was twelve and damn sure not going to cry in front of his friends. His hands wouldn't work right, and he shook so hard he bit his tongue, but he was alive.

"You're in some pretty shit now, kid," the bearded guy said and pointed. Moe's dad stood with his hands on his hips on the jetty as some of the other lobstermen fed a line out to the boys.

Death by ice cube was not as terrifying as this. There hadn't been two creatures lying in wait to tear him apart and eat him while he kicked and screamed back then.

Moe glanced back at the girls, swallowing hard. He nodded and they followed suit. The torpedo room hatch was twenty feet behind them down the corridor. The knee knocker in front of him was dripping with blood. He glanced around; *everything* was covered or puddled in gore. The hatch to a small storage room was open, as was the hatch across from it. He took a deep breath, ready to check the port side hatch when he heard a small noise behind him. The girl with the blonde braid was nodding no. She pointed to him and then to the port side hatch, then to her and the starboard side. She wanted to check both doors at the same time.

Smart kid. He nodded and they both peeked at the same time. He had almost shit himself, but the tiny room was empty. Not being grabbed from behind meant that the girl's room was devoid of *them* as well. Shapes moved in front, though, and the sound they made was unmistakable.

The plan was simple: move as far forward as they could, closing hatches along the way. Meet up with the rest of the crew in the forward area by the Conn. If they encountered hostiles, kill them. If there were too many to safely dispatch, then they would retreat to the torpedo room.

Moe knew that his shipmates, both alive and dead, were searching for him. He couldn't wait to see someone, anyone with a shotgun.

A metal stairwell to his right climbed to the next level of the sub. Further aft would lead to The Big Red Machine (a huge diesel generator) and eventually to the reactor compartment. He didn't have clearance for the reactor compartment, but he could get to the access corridor which ran the length of the sub from the reactor bulkhead to the main engines. Food, supplies, and several fully kitted MP5s had been placed in the corridor in case of an outbreak on the sub.

Moe signaled to the girls that they would bypass the stairwell and move aft. The bloody handrail told him that the infected had moved up the steps, but the red stains on the grated deck aft of the stairs told a different story.

Growling and shadows moving above preceded the arrival of two infected. The things just appeared at the top of the stairs before the survivors could move or hide. One of them glanced down and its lip curled back in a snarl when it saw the girls. Moe grabbed the smaller of the two and bolted aft as the stupid thing above them took an elongated step into space and tumbled down the ladder. Its brother was able to negotiate two steps before it too pitched down the steel. Both the things stood, cutting off Chloe from Vanessa and Moe.

The creatures started after the duo, but Chloe grabbed one by its filthy shirt and drove her knife into the back of its skull. It dropped to the deck, its sister oblivious. The dead woman made terrifying sounds as it shuffled down the grates, its focus on Vanessa and Moe. Chloe stepped past the one she had destroyed and noticed Moe raise his sidearm.

"*No!*" she pleaded, waving one hand with her pistol and the other with her knife. She ducked, and Moe fired. The dead woman's head snapped back, two ricochets echoing through the corridor before the round buried itself someplace.

She stood from her crouch, pulling her hands and weapons from her head. She spread her hands as if to ask, "*Are you kidding me?*" but Moe just shrugged. That was when the thing she had destroyed grabbed her ankle and she shrieked in surprise. The grab was weak, and she was able to pull away easily, but the damage was done. Hissing, growling, and the stumbling of many infected came from above in search of both who had fired a gun and who had screamed.

Moe turned to move aft and stared into the bleeding eyes of one of his shipmates. The thing lunged, grabbing him by the greasy T-shirt and they both went down. Having but one arm, the dead man, (probably Talbot, but Moe was unsure,) couldn't maneuver in to bite at the living man's face. With its middle missing, the weight of the creature was significantly less than its height would indicate. Moe could easily keep it at bay, but for how long? The thing snapped and slapped at him, knocking his weapon aside. Vile fluids dripped from the thing's open abdominal cavity onto Moe's midsection.

He held its throat as the girls scrambled to him.

Chloe stopped Vanessa and folded her arms. "I told you I was just going to watch," she said, glancing back to the stairs.

Vanessa was shocked, "*Chloe!*"

Chloe strode forward and slid her blade into the struggling thing's temple, the thing becoming slack. Moe pitched it to the side.

"Don't shoot in here again or you'll kill us!" the blonde girl whisper-yelled at the gore- covered sailor. "And get that shirt off, it's nasty." She held a hand down to him, helping him up. The three of them moved further aft.

Moe began to peel his blood-soaked shirt off, but Vanessa stopped him with a whisper, "Don't!"

He looked down at himself. "But it's covered in this stuff!"

"So, you're going to pull it across your face?" The young girl pulled her spring-assisted folding knife and snapped it open. "Here."

The scream of a Runner echoed across the steel. It had come from above them.

"We need to hurry," Chloe told them as she stared at the deck above.

Moe used Vanessa's knife to cut his shirt off, but his chest was still smeared with the fluids of a dead man. He used the destroyed shirt to wipe away what he could.

A dead thing exited a hatch to their left, tripping on the knee-knocker and impacting the grate with its chest. It began to push itself up, but Moe stabbed it through the back of the skull before it could rise.

The Runner's shriek flooded their ears again, the three of them casting terrified glances back the way they had come. The monster was now on their deck and hunting. They heard the slapping of shoes on the grate, but it was moving away.

Moe put a finger to his lips, the knife still in his fist, and the girls nodded. He chin-wagged that they should continue down the corridor.

Two more hatches, one on the port side and one starboard, needed to be cleared before they could reach the access corridor.

The rasps and hacks of the things that had been alerted by Chloe's shriek flooded the metal tube. Chloe spun back around to view what was behind them. The overhead lights flickered for a moment, and she squinted into the flickers. Half a dozen of the dead ones were shuffling down the corridor toward them. The dead saw the living, the moans and needful cries growing in intensity.

Two of the things stepped out from the portside compartment in front of them. They were fresh and dripping. They also moved toward Moe and the girls.

Vanessa swallowed hard. "I want my knife back."

INTRODUCTIONS

Half a dozen infected littered the ground near the door. The women had destroyed most of those that had attempted entry, but there were too many. The sea of dead faces appearing endless through the expanding area between the broken door and the jamb.

"We can't hold it!" Donna cried. "Run to the back and get up the stairs!"

The rickety door slammed into the metal desk with a thud, Donna in the triangle between the edge of the failed door and the desk. Abbey appeared out of nowhere.

"I'll hold it, you go," she said calmly.

"But they'll—"

Abbey held up her bleeding arm, "They already did."

Abbey pushed against the door trying to stem the tide of infected while Donna skirted the desk and two reaching hands. She fled to the rear of the room. The walls were concrete block, but the floor above had been made of wood, and most of it had long since collapsed into the room below. The room had been cleared of the wreckage and designated as safe to use as long as nobody went up the spiral metal staircase in the corner. The ten-foot ceilings between the floors now gave way to a twenty-foot tall room.

Donna was incredulous. "What are you doing? Up the stairs!"

"Those aren't stairs!" one of the newer women countered, "Those are pre-Columbian art!"

Abbey started screaming and the other six ladies spun to see.

The dead had her. She was fighting valiantly but was already bitten in a few places. She hacked and slashed with her hatchet, cleaving wrists and not a few heads, but the number of infected was such that she was overwhelmed in moments and she went down screaming.

"No!" screamed Ali and she tried to run to help her friend.

Both Donna and Juanita grabbed Ali. "It's too late! She's gone!" Juanita screamed. Several of the dead broke off from the group tearing at Abbey to hunt the rest of the living in the room.

Donna tentatively put her foot on the lowest meatal tread, then realized that she needed to speed things up if she wanted to live. She rushed up the stairs, the metal creaking beneath her feet. "Come on!"

Her friends also sprinted up the spiral, the ancient metal holding the weight of them all. What greeted them at the top was an uneven catwalk made up of three feet of broken and rotting floor that ran the length of the west wall. At the far end, a larger piece of floor jutted into space. Eight or nine feet of floor with a door in the wall called to them.

The dead had begun to meander up the stairs or reach for them from below before Donna was halfway across the makeshift catwalk.

"Can we just kill them as they come up the stairs?"

Donna didn't know who had asked that, but Ali answered for her. "Didn't work out so well at the door."

The girls had reached the far side of the rotten wood before the first dead man put his foot on it. Donna threw the ramshackle door open, ready to run through, then pinwheeled her arms so she wouldn't fall twenty feet to the concrete on the other side. Juanita grabbed her and they both stared into the next room. It too had no second floor, but this time there was nothing to walk on.

The bit of floor remaining between the women and the stairs creaked as the dead started across.

Donna aimed her sidearm at the oncoming dead. "Cover your ears," she said aloud. She fired and missed the first target's head, but in hitting the second in the shoulder, it spun and took two others off the thin bridge where they plummeted to the concrete twenty feet below. Ali fired her bow as well. Between them, they were able to knock nine of the things down before they ran out of ammo.

There were no more dead entering the room from outside, but at least a dozen of the things were clambering to get up the stairs and a baker's dozen more stood reaching for the stranded group from below.

One of the women passed a table leg to Ali whom the dead would be the first to reach. She brought the leg up high over her head and brought it down on the decaying thing in front of her. The wooden weapon thumped the skull of the first attacker, and it slumped to the wooden catwalk before it too fell into the room. A dead woman in what used to be blue scrubs snarled, took a step forward to reach for Ali and was blasted off the broken floor from below.

Rick and Pitt stood side by side, aiming their rifles at the invaders. Pitt fired at the ones on the ground, Rick at the things closest to the women. The gunshots made everyone's ears ring and concrete chips flew. The dead toppled to the floor below destroyed or broken. Two began to crawl toward Pitt, but he continued to fire at the remaining infected shuffling his way.

"I need to reload!" Rick exclaimed. He slid a fresh magazine into his M4, discarding the old one and charging the first round.

One of the things had maneuvered in to grab Ali's table leg. It latched on and wouldn't let go. She used leverage to push and pull the creature out into space and it reached a filthy claw toward her before it spilled from the ledge and crashed to the concrete.

She prepared for the next dead thing, but they had almost run out. Two more made the top of the stairs, but Rick finished them off with his rifle.

"Get back down, we need to get to the sub!" Rick yelled to the ladies.

"That's a bad plan, Rick," a familiar voice said from behind he and Pitt.

Both spun to see a younger guy, blond, with a scar on his jaw. His fist was closed around the hilt of a Samurai sword dripping with the vile fluids of the dead. Pitt raised his rifle because he didn't know the man.

The man cocked an eyebrow. "Seriously?

Rick smiled. "Billy. Glad to have you."

Billy nodded toward Pitt. "He isn't. Gonna lower your weapon, Sarge, or do we fight it out?"

"This is Billy?" Pitt asked.

"This *is* Billy," the young man echoed. He glanced at Rick, genuine concern on his face. "Where's Sam?"

"She's up on the water tower with some of our snipers. She's safe."

The women clanked down the spiral staircase, Billy glancing in their direction. A huge smile split his face. "Hey, Ali!" He waved at her, and all Pitt could think was that this guy was nuts.

Pitt moved past Rick and Billy to secure the door behind them. Ali sprinted to Billy and embraced him in a huge hug. Billy hugged back, the hand with the katana stuck out to one side.

She began to sniffle. "Where have you been? Why didn't you come back? It's been so long! Did you find another group? Tony said he saw you!"

Billy blinked. "Wow. Um..." He began to tick off items on his fingers, "San Francisco. I don't like jail. It has been long! Nope! Yeah, I saw him too. There were rockets and stuff." He held up one finger. "Scuse me. One sec." He darted back through the door he had entered. "Watashi no hobākurafuto wa unagi de ippai desu!" they heard him yell. "Hi-YAH! YAH! YAH!"

A dead woman strode into the room, hissing. Both the Lt. Commander and Rick brought their rifles up quickly, but before they could fire, ten inches of Japanese folded steel protruded from between the creature's eyes. It was withdrawn just as quickly, the undead thing collapsing.

Billy put his hand on the door frame, breathing heavily, "I really... gotta start... working out more." He looked up at Rick. "Ya know?"

"Is it clear out there?" Pitt asked the new guy.

Billy scrunched up his face and wiggled his hand; *mezza mezza*. "You're ok up here for now, but this place still crawls. I had to take a Coke break after just a couple minutes of ninja-ing when I got off the boat." His eyes lit up. "Oh! Chris and Anna are on the boat with some soldier dudes, that special guy, and the Gossamer-Bigfoot. It was good to see them all again." He smiled. "They're moving around to the other dock, this one was occupied."

Pitt switched radio frequencies. "Sabre, this is Rock, how copy?"

"Rock, Sabre. Tying up to the back dock now. We're heavy some civvies and picked up some friendly hitters as well. Going to muster at Rally Point B and pick up ammo. This place crawls."

Pitt looked at Billy but spoke into the radio, "Rally point B confirmed. Ammo up and head to the Lighthouse. We'll meet you there."

"Sabre copies all."

Ali nocked another arrow onto her bow. She stood staring silently at the pile of bloody rags that used to be her friend.

"I'm so sorry we weren't in time," Pitt said. Rick put a hand on her shoulder.

Ali sighed, too angry for grief yet. "She saved us all."

"I thought *I* saved us all?" Billy said confused. He glanced at the shreds of flesh and pints of blood on the concrete floor.

"That was Abbey," Ali told him. She strode to the eviscerated corpse, knelt, and drove her knife into the thing's eye just as it started to stir.

"No," Billy breathed. "No!" he grabbed Rick by the shoulder and Pitt tensed, lifting his rifle slightly. "Where's Sam?" Billy shouted at Rick.

"Still on the water tower, Billy. She's safe."

Billy sprinted back out the door he had come in. Ali ran after him.

SHE WEARS THE PANTS
JOURNAL ENTRY 9

"How we looking?" Remo asked me as he slid a full magazine into his rifle.

I couldn't see any infected. "I got nothing." Remo took our place on overwatch as Ship and I grabbed two full magazines and the big guy took a full MOLLE pack from Kev.

Seyfert did a quick check of his rifle, then started barking orders, "We stay quiet until we can't, then kill as many Limas as possible. We have plenty of ammo and we're going to be carrying more to anyone who needs it." He glanced at Gary and Steve. They had been designated the ammo carriers, and both bristled with MOLLE packs. Steve, a bigger dude, also carried two ammo cans full of loose 5.56 rounds.

We moved as a tactical unit up the hill toward the lighthouse. We saw our first group of infected feasting on something that had been wearing jeans. There were six of them, and they didn't even turn to look at us until we were almost on them.

Lynda made to drill one with her newly loaded sidearm, but Alvarez put a hand out to stop her. Ship strode up to the scene, the things unaware of him. He lashed out with a canoe-sized boot and three of the six toppled over. Alvarez, Remo, Seyfert, Buttons, Danny, and I were there with knives and rifle butts to help finish what Ship started. We straight up wrecked those dead assholes without ever firing a shot.

"Do you know him?" I asked Seyfert in reference to the person that had been dined upon.

"Can't tell."

The SEAL didn't stick around to identify this person. He started back up the path and soon the shadow of the lighthouse engulfed us. Seyfert pointed to my group, then to the right of the structure. His group would take the civvies and go left, and we would meet in the middle on the other side.

Twenty feet into our trek, we noticed a lone infected gazing out into San Francisco Bay. He just stood there, so Alvarez smoked it with his blade. It was only another minute or so before we met Seyfert's group at the door to the lighthouse. He tried it and it was unlocked. He and Danny burst through the door when they opened it, the SEAL moving left and the Army guy moving right. Remo and Alvarez followed, and soon we were all inside.

"Drop the ammo here, we'll use this as a fallback point. Danny, get the civvies up top. Lock the door and stay with them. Teems, you and your group stay here too and cover the door. Anna, set up a triage and check everybody for scratches."

"Copy," Danny said as Steve and Gary put the ammo on the floor by the stairs. The big biker just nodded.

"I can stay down here and h—" Steve began, but Lynda cut him off.

"The hell you can. You're coming up those stairs with me. Now." I turned away to hide my smile. Seems I wasn't the only one with a bossy apocalypse wife.

I watched Danny escort the remaining civilians (including Steve) up the renovated spiral staircase. There were four of them left and one was likely infected. We had started off with ten and were down to four. I had to wonder if the rest of them would have survived without us, then remembered their situation. No chance, they had been doomed. I suppose that guy who ran off back into the building could have made it, but for how long? They had been down to nothing in the supplies department and the structure had been crawling with the dead.

Gunfire from close by brought me out of my shitty thoughts into all new prospects.

"Stay close," Seyfert told us. "If we need to fall back, get back in here and lock the door. Nobody gets left behind."

He and Buttons copied the entrance move on the exit, and soon we were all flashing the business ends of our guns toward the sound of chaos. Sustained shots came from down the hill in front of us, but I couldn't see shit. We moved forward as a unit, coming to the edge of the concrete base of the lighthouse. Peering over the red railing, which looked brand new, I could see a group of eight people making their way up the hill with the dead on their heels. One of them was Donna.

The hill was steep, but the dead had them surrounded on three sides with the only clear way being forward.

"Kev and Remo," Seyfert shouted, "with me. The rest of you, light 'em up!"

"No!" I countermanded. "Remo is a better shot than I am, I'll come!"

I felt Ship swipe at me, trying to keep me with him, but he missed. The SEAL and I dropped the five feet from the concrete abutment and began moving quickly down the steep hill. That buzzcut commander dude was with the group below and he was bellowing orders while firing his M4 into a crowd of pus bags off to his right. I heard shots from behind me and noticed the closer of the infected drop and roll back into their brethren.

"Come on!" Seyfert screamed at them. We were two-thirds of the way down the hill when I realized we weren't going to get to them in time.

The dead on the right and left of the group were having trouble negotiating the incline, but the ones giving chase were mostly on all fours clawing at the hill to gain purchase. One of the women in the group stumbled, then slid maybe ten feet back toward the horde. Another of the girls, this one with auburn hair and tattoos on her left leg reached back to help, but one of the dead vanguard latched a filthy paw onto the ankle of the girl who had fallen. It leaned in to tear into the unfortunate girl but collapsed when it took a bullet to the noggin.

"Get them up!" I heard Kat scream through the radio, and another monstrosity dropped like a sack of rotting potatoes. The tattooed chick yanked her friend up and they sprinted as well as they could up the steep hill.

Lead was flying down range from multiple directions and the dead were dropping like flies, but they just kept coming. I was close enough that I could see the fear in my girl's eyes and that shit was enough for me. I rushed forward and slid down the hill on my right hip, firing. I could feel the skin burning through my jeans, but I would deal with that later. Stupidly, I had lost track of my shot count, and my rifle clicked empty as I reached the little group of meat.

"Are you fucking crazy?" Donna screamed.

I didn't even glance at her as I slid almost past. "Yes!"

I slid into the hands of one of the things scrabbling up on all fours behind my girl and it fell on its face. Pity its face landed right in my crotch. Thank all that is holy this particular infected lifted its head to stare right into my eyes for a moment before trying to bite me. I swung my rifle butt at it hitting it in the face. Vile shit rained from its ruined mouth as the jaw came away on its left side, hanging like some perverse denture. I swung the rifle again, knocking the thing away, but another was there to join the fun. I smacked that dead asshole in the face too, the cheekbone sinking into its skull with a crunch. I knocked two more down before a stinking hand reached around my head from behind and the filthy nails of the thing gouged furrows into my face. The fucker had gotten me in the right nostril, upper lip, and for fucks sake my mouth. It tore a nasty gouge in my upper gum and that shit fucking hurt. Spitting blood, I tried to round on it, but another grabbed my T-shirt and another my rifle. The bastards took me off balance and I fell into the crowd.

I've gotta tell you, face shredded, prostrate on my back, I felt like I was the Roadrunner and a bunch of coyotes were looking down at me. It was not a wonderful experience. Not only was it shitty, but it was brief, because they wasted no time in trying to eat me.

My head was pointed down-hill, which means my feet were above me on the incline, so getting up was going to be tricky. What made it downright impossible were the cold, slimy hands that grabbed my ankles and right arm. I was able to get my rifle between my face and the face of the dead girl who had grabbed my gun. She wanted to make out, but I felt one of them bite me in the right leg, and I let out a yell. It didn't hurt as much as I thought it would and remember; I had been bitten before.

The leg thing continued to gnaw, and I both considered my imminent demise and continued to wonder why it didn't hurt, when the kissy thing reached around the rifle and tried to claw through my T-shirt. Her head popped like a bubble full of stinky shit, her goo flying all over, and suddenly, Seyfert, Buzz Cut, the little girl's dad, and pretty much everybody else was there to assist. Those who hadn't waded into the dead were shooting them and soon, the little girl's (I couldn't remember her name at the time) dad was extending a much-wanted hand down to help me up. I thanked him and he nodded in response.

Another contingent of infected was scrambling up the hill, but we fired into them as we retreated to the light house.

"Jesus!" Donna said as she saw what used to be my pretty face. "You're bleeding!"

I spat blood. "Tends to happen with they grab you by the face."

"Assholes!" she screamed at the dead. A ridiculous gesture, but I fucking loved it. She began to cry.

"Whoa! What the hell are you on about? I'm fine."

I grabbed her by the paw and we ran up the hill together. "But you could be infected!"

"Yeah, but for how long? I'm more concerned with my face than my life. I'm fuckin' pretty!"

"What the hell do you need a face for, anyway?" demanded Buzz Cut with a yell.

I yelled back, "I dunno! Face things?"

Seyfert shrugged. "Chicks dig scars."

"No, we fucking don't!" Donna screamed and Seyfert demonstrated his vast intelligence by shutting the fuck up.

The whole group of us made it to the light house pretty much at the same time. The only casualty seemed to be my beautiful countenance. We skirted the concrete abutment the light house sat on and soon people were filing through the door.

So, I don't know much about light houses, but aren't they supposed to be round? I grew up in New England, and we have lighthouses aplenty. They're round, I shit you not. This one was square as fuck, and as I looked at the concrete angles, I realized that no dead people were going to be able to get into this structure unless they were invited. The door was steel, and it had a double slide lock on the inside.

Unfortunately, there wasn't a lot of space to shoot down into a crowd of dead surrounding the tall building, so all I could think of was there were about to be thirty people trapped in a building made for five.

Fuck that.

I tried to call to Seyfert, but Donna almost tackled me. "Oh shit..." She kind of let that hang when she looked at me. She pointed at me, "They got you." She immediately began to rummage through her pack.

"Flesh wound," I said and spit a half gallon of blood onto the concrete. The fucker had stuck his nasty fingers in my mouth and up my nose. Prick. Normally you would think the nostril would be the painful part, but it was my mouth that hurt like hell. Anybody who had known me less than a month backed away a step.

"Seyfert," I began as Donna dabbed my face with a gauze pad.

He had been barking orders to his crew, but he spun to speak to me, "What do... Holy fuck!" He pointed at me. "You're bleeding!"

"Flesh wound," repeated my apocalypse wife as she pushed a bandage up my nose. "Loog, I dode wad do day id here," I said through the gauze as Donna tried to choke me with it. I glanced around at the people checking their weapons and feeling the concrete walls.

"Don't worry, we're safe in here," Seyfert told me. "Somebody will come get us. We have ammo and supplies—"

I spit out the cloth and cut him off, "*We're* the somebody. *We're* supposed to get people. If we stay here, we're trapped just like everybody else."

He seemed to ponder that for a moment. I gently pushed Donna's hand from me. "Where are the kids?"

She looked at me and made a face. I couldn't wait to see myself in a mirror. "Richy is on the water tower and Chloe is safe in the sub."

"Right. Fuck this." I pointed at her. "You're staying here." She made to object, but I pointed at Anna, who was helping a woman with an injured knee. "Anna needs help and you're the best medic around. I'm going to go thin the herd."

I made to yell for Ship and Remo, but when I turned, they were flanking me on each side. It scared me a little as I wasn't prepared for it. Ship was projecting a stink eye that could melt most people. As I had received this look on countless occasions, I would survive. Probably.

Remo was Remo.

"We're leaving," I told them.

Remo raised an eyebrow. "Oh?" Ship, shockingly, said nothing.

"Now," I said and made for the door. They followed me. I radioed to Kev, "Buttons! How are we looking outside?"

His reply was instantaneous, almost like he was waiting for someone to ask. *"Decent size contingent coming up the hill. They'll be banging on the door in two minutes."*

"Is the door clear?"

"I can't see it from here. Nothing else is clear though. Dead assholes are all over the island."

I felt a hand on my shoulde; it was Seyfert. "You don't have to —"

"Yeah, I do. My kids are out there. Not to mention a few others I know." Danny had been standing in front of the door, and honestly, I didn't want to have to fight him to get out, but I know he never would have let me go without an ok from the SEAL. He would have stood there until Ship ate him.

"Danny, let 'em out."

Danny immediately threw the latch and a million guns were pointed at the door. Nothing was outside of it, so I bolted through it. I could hear Donna yelling behind me and I knew I was in for a ration of shit later, but I could do more good out here than in there.

Remo's voice came from behind me, "What now, genius?"

"Well, I'll remain the comedian, Ship can continue to be large, and you just fucking kill everything."

He jutted out his lower lip, "Good enough." He pulled his sidearm and drilled a wayward infected whose head came into view past the abutment.

I could hear shots all over the place and knew that others were fighting their own battles the length and breadth of the Rock.

Fucking zombies.

"What do you fellas think about sweeping the area on the way to the water tower, and then heading to the sub?"

Ship snapped his fingers twice, pointed at me, then gave a thumbs up.

Remo nodded.

We checked the group of dead that had been climbing the steep hill. Two had made it almost to the top, but the rest were only about halfway. I saw why in a moment. The things were on all fours trying to climb, but when one of the things saw us, it stood. The angle on the embankment was steep enough that gravity did some astounding work. The stupid infected douche fell backwards and slid to a stop fifteen feet further down the hill. As it was getting up, a second of the things followed suit and took out the first one, both now ten feet lower on the hill than before.

At this rate I could bust out some margaritas and a sun umbrella, point, and laugh. Unfortunately, I was shit out of booze and umbrellas.

Remo took down both the industrious ones near the abutment with casual sidearm shots. Ship and I took aim at the ones on the hill and soon instead of living dead they were just dead.

I radioed to Seyfert that the lighthouse was clear, and he told me he would get the civvies settled and come out to help.

The three of us moved off toward the water tower. A giant building stood in our way, so we had to skirt it. The tower came into view when we rounded the corner of the building. I could see three figures up there, two with rifles and one of them quite small. Checking several frequencies, I finally got through on channel nine.

"Hey, Richy, how many did you get today?"

I saw the boy sling his rifle and pull something off his belt. *"Hey! Where are you?"* came over the radio.

"About a quarter way between you and the lighthouse. Top of the hill to your…" I had to think about it for a sec, "left."

He pointed the rifle in our direction, panning it until he found us. "Got you!" I could tell he was smiling into the radio.

"How are we looking from us to you? Any infected?"

"Shitloads. There's fifty or so maybe a hundred feet in front of you and around the corner of that building."

"Might want to rethink that language, kid. Donna might have her radio on."

Ship raised an eyebrow and Remo huffed.

I didn't get it. "What?"

"You're chiding the kid for language? *You?*"

"Back off, Jarhead. I don't give a rat's ass what the kid says. But Donna—"

An infected came around the corner and latched a filthy paw onto my rifle sling. Once again, I had become complacent. Ship grabbed the thing by the shoulder and pitched it against the cinderblock wall of the building before it could even go for a bite. The creature's head broke open like a dropped egg. The brain must have come off the stem, because what looked like the whole damn thing slipped out of the shattered noggin and fell to the ground with a wet thud. I looked up at Ship to nod thanks as I pried the dead fingers off me, but all I got was the stinkeye.

"You still there?" Richy's disembodied voice asked. *"They're moving to you now! You got about twenty seconds and they'll be on you!"*

"The dead must not like you chiding the boy either," Remo snarked.

I heard rifle fire and peeked the corner to see the incoming horde. My kid was firing at the dead and he was doing damn well. There were already two on the ground. Several of the things kept coming in our direction, but most turned back to investigate the shots.

Remo was impassive when he said aloud, "There's a lot."

"They're between us and where we have to go."

"That's a lotta ammo," MARSOC told me.

I drew my SOG from its shoulder sheath. Ship already had the airplane wing he called a machete in his fist.

"Cover us?" I asked Remo.

The three of us stepped around the corner. The small horde had split in two, with about fifteen of the things coming our way. There was, maybe, a fifty-foot gap between the two groups of them. When the first of the things was within reach, it did that lunge that they do, and I intercepted it with a hand on its chest. My knife slid into the side of its dome with practiced ease and it dropped like a hot rock. I heard a wet thump next to me that sounded exactly like a cantaloupe hitting the pavement. It was a different type of melon, and it was still snapping, Ship's machete having done its work.

We backed up as they shuffled forward, but they were spread out and easy to take. Remo covered us with his rifle as Ship and I dealt re-death to these assholes. Unfortunately, the group who had gone back to check out the gunshots was now wise to us, and they had started their arduous journey in our direction. Seems we were popular because another cluster was headed our way from down the hill.

I could hear the rifle fire from the water tower, and now there was fire coming from the guard tower. We were thinning the hell out of this herd. I took a glance at the base of the guard tower and noticed that the folks up there had problems of their own. Maybe twenty of the things were on the steps up, with another twenty milling about below.

"Change of plans!" I yelled as I stuck a rotten woman in scrubs in the eye. "We get the guys in the tower, then get the kids, then clear the fuck out of this place."

I felt heat and wind next to my right ear, the dome of one of those rotten fuckers who had gotten to close snapping to the side. I glanced back at Remo with a *what the fuck, dude?* look on my face, but he just shrugged, sighted and blew another thing away.

Ship picked up one of the desiccated bastards he had destroyed and threw it into an oncoming crowd to the right. Strike! He got all three of them on the ground. One was dropped as it tried to stand, I don't know if the round came from Richy, or the guys on the tower. Ship kicked another in the face, teeth and shit flying to the side. I didn't get to see what happened to the last one as I had two in front of me. I wrecked both with the SOG and suddenly we were devoid of monsters. I mean they were coming, but nothing was close.

"Richy," I heard Remo speak into his radio, "We're going to get the men in the tower on the ground to help us, then we're coming for you. You ok up there for a bit longer?"

"Are you kidding?" was the boy's immediate reply. *"This is the most fun I've had since Ratchet and Clank on Atlantis."*

I had no idea what the kid was fucking saying. No clue. None. What the hell did he mean? I'm shaking my head now as I write this because I still don't know and forgot to ask him.

"Shoot the dead people, Rich, and watch the sass."

There was no reply from the boy, but I could hear his big rifle. I could hear a bunch of rifles, actually.

The dead might not be fast, but they're persistent as hell. They began to make for our corner of the building, and I still wanted to avenge my face. I touched the bandage there and wondered if I would have to deal with another night like I'd had in the Airstream trailer. This was fingernails and that had been teeth, but who's to say?

Something occurred to me right then; each subsequent bite had gone better for me insofar as getting sick and then telling the disease to take a hike, but I also felt more of this shit in me if that makes any sense. I could feel it building up. What would happen to me when my storage capacity was reached? Is that even a thing? I mean I know I'm a special case, but—

Remo tapped me on the shoulder and passed me a black baseball. "You know," he said, looking at me like I was an idiot, "when you have the time."

I peeked the corner and was surprised to see the crowd of pus bags was significantly closer. Maybe forty feet away. I looked at the baseball and smiled.

Now, I've chucked a couple of grenades since the dead started to snack. I wouldn't say I'm an expert, but think about it: Pull pin, throw at bad guys. I mean, that's it, right?

Wrong.

I did just that, I pulled the pin, stepped around the corner of the building, and pointed at a gray thing in stained and rotten scrubs. "Hey fuck knuckles! How about some of this?"

I threw the 'nade, then stood there smiling because I knew what was coming. I hit that former nurse or doctor right in the damn chest.

"Not too close to the building!" Remo uncharacteristically yelled as the weapon flew from my fingers.

I'm cool. You guys know this because you've read my journals. I don't lie or embellish, it wouldn't make sense to do so. I tell you what happened in my own way, both the good and the bad. When I'm the hero, I'm proud AF, and I tell you so. When I screw up, I tell you that too.

This was a screw up. A big one. I'm no soldier, I've said that a hundred times, but I am learning. One thing I never really did learn was how to throw a grenade. I did learn a few things when I threw this one though. Firstly: Tell your buddies you are about to throw a grenade, even if one of them just passed it to you. Secondly: You really have no idea how big the boom from a grenade is until you've thrown one yourself. Movies do not do that shit justice. Thirdly, and most importantly: My grenade throwing aim needs work.

You would think that me hitting my intended target would be exactly what we needed. It probably would have been, but my intended target was somewhere in the midst of the group of the things. I had hit the closest one of the crowd, the little explosive knocking it back a step before the 'nade rolled against the cinder blocks of the side of the building. My smile turned to a frown as I stood there with my hands on my hips looking tremendously awesome in my head, but a complete moron in everybody else's.

I was yanked off my feet like a child by the Yeti and unceremoniously thrown to the ground. Both he and Remo were already down with their hands on their ears when I tried to gripe about my recent treatment, so I thought it best to emulate them.

I was about to remove my palms from the side of my head and ask some incredibly stupid questions when the earth shook like a ten-point-five on the Richter scale.

Fucking boom.

"Holy shit!" came through the radio. It was Richy, and when Donna chided him later, I would own up to the boy's swearing as my fault.

Dust, rocks, concrete, sticks, and gooey shit flew by where I had been stupidly standing, then I heard a secondary commotion around the corner. It sounded like someone had dumped a ton of bricks on the walkway.

The three of us got up quickly, me trying to peek the corner again but Remo putting a hand on my chest. He stuck his mirror around the corner then nodded for us to follow him. We came out weapons at the ready and I had to admire what was in front of us.

Three tons. Three tons of bricks were on the walkway. Bits and pieces of the building I had just blown up were interspersed with bits and pieces of the zombies I had just blown up. It was nothing short of a mess. The good news was that there were no undead standing. The bad news was that whatever building this was, we were going to need a new one.

"Was that a grenade?" Seyfert asked through the radio.

Remo and Ship, who always seemed to know what each other was thinking, rushed forward, me following a couple steps back. Some of the dead were starting to stand and we plugged them before they could. Most of them anyway. Some got up and came for us as we tried to finish the ones on the ground. Others would never walk again, with one or both legs blown either to useless shit or completely off. They could crawl though, and they did.

Another contingent of the dead began to come around the far corner of the building, too. A whole bunch of them. I looked at the damage the grenade had done and sighed. I had destroyed maybe six of the things with another five or so crippled. We had shot another ten before the rest were plodding at us.

Remo looked at the hole in the wall and shrugged, wiggling his finger in his ear. "Free air conditioning."

Undesirability
EAST DOCK, ALCATRAZ

Billy moved with the herd. There were a lot of dead folks. He slowed down a bit and they passed him on both sides until he was at the back of the pack. His sword was sticky with the viscous fluids of the ones he had killed, and he wasn't sure if the stink would ever come off of his newest toy.

"They do stink," he thought aloud, drawing his forearm across his nose. Instantly, those undead nearest him turned to see if they could eat what had spoken. They slogged off, following the herd, when they couldn't find food.

Billy shook his head. They still didn't want him. *Undesirable*, he thought.

He passed by a bench with a dead man sitting on it and sat next to him. The thing held a bloody brick in its hand and stared at Billy.

It blinked hard a few times before asking, "Are you alive?"

"I think so," Billy replied. "I mean, nobody's told me I'm not."

"Why didn't they eat you?"

"I'm undesirable." He raised his eyebrows questioningly, "You?"

"No idea. They just never wanted to bite. Ate everybody else, just not me."

The man was covered in gore, his shirt and clothes saturated with the fluids of the dead. He stank.

Billy wrinkled his nose. "You stink."

"It's them. I mean I have them all over me." The guy wrinkled his own nose. "It's icky."

Billy smiled and pointed at the brick. "You've been braining them with *that*?"

"S'all I had. Name's Bob." Bob stuck his hand out for Billy to shake. Billy made a face and shook his head.

"After we clean them off you, yeah, we'll shake there, Bobby Boy. *It's icky*," he copied. "I'm Billy."

Bob smiled and drew his arm across his brow leaving a brown smear. "It's hot."

"I hear you. Plus smacking that brick into the domes of these things must have made you pretty tired."

"Thirsty too."

Billy reached into his bag and pulled out a Pepsi. "Here."

"Wow, thanks!" Bob accepted the drink, popped the tab, and drank greedily. "Thanks," he repeated.

Bob glanced forward as he took another pull on the soda. "Uhhh…"

Billy tracked his gaze. "Oh."

A contingent of dead had them surrounded in a semi-circle. The things were staring and not moving away as they normally did.

One of the male creatures took a step forward and growled. It couldn't possibly have seen the two humans as both of its eyes hung from their sockets by the optic nerves. Billy pulled his baseball bat from his pack and handed it to Bob. "Stings the paws a little, but it's better than a brick."

The dead started toward them as a group when Billy spoke. Bob stood and hurled his brick at the thing with the weird eyes. He missed, but hit a female infected directly in the forehead. The thing collapsed instantly, and Bob pumped his fist. Billy leapt to his feet and began slashing and stabbing with his sword. The creatures didn't seem to want to eat the two men, but still pushed en-masse to get near them, at which point they would try to walk off, but the group pushed steadily forward. Billy's weapon made whooshing sounds as he slashed and sucking sounds as he pulled his blade from skulls. Bob's bat made slight pinging noises when he connected with a cranium.

"Ow," said Billy's new friend. "Ow. Ow. Ow." Each whack of the bat was accompanied by a quick exclamation from Bob. Billy knew exactly how Bob's hands must feel, Billy having used the weapon a few hundred times.

They were able to stay together for a moment, but the surge of the crowd separated them. Billy was able to make out Bob wringing his hands from thumping heads with the aluminum sports equipment. His new friend faded into the crowd and was lost from view in seconds. Billy was able to see the bat rise and fall but couldn't make out Bob in the throng.

It was getting difficult to swing the blade in the confines of fifty infected. Inevitably, after he skewered a brain, the sword got stuck in an infected skull. The creature crumpled and Billy had to put his foot on the body to extricate his weapon. He overcompensated, stepped back too far, and lost his balance. The sword went clanging away, and even though he was amid half a hundred dead things that ate people, all he could think was that he was going to be angry if his blade got scratched.

He latched onto the long skirt of a dead thing, trying to pull himself up, but all he succeeded in doing was tearing the clothing off.

"Excuse me!" he blurted while averting his eyes. He grabbed hold of a pair of jeans and used momentum to help him to his feet. He searched frantically for his sword but could only hear it being kicked around as he pushed at the bodies around him.

Something put a hand on his shoulder, and he spun to face it. He had thought it would be Bob, but it was a dead man with half a face. The other half was dull yellow bone.

"Skulls are great!" Billy told it. "You don't need no body!"

The thing just stared at him.

"Ba dum tssst?" Billy asked and it lunged.

The thing grabbed him by the shirt and tried to bite his face. Billy kept it at arm's length as best he could, but the creature fought for purchase. They both tripped over the feet and legs of the other undead in the crowd and toppled to the ground.

"Scrappy... critter," breathed Billy as he pushed while it pulled. "No sense of humor." Billy couldn't help but think that a baseball bat would not have gone amiss right then. He rolled on top of the thing and put an arm across its throat. The man reached down to pull his knife from his hip only to realize it wasn't there.

"No bat, no knife, no cool sword, shotgun out of ammo... not one of my better days." He was going to use his shotgun as a bludgeon when the thing twisted and he fell to the side. "Ow!" he said as he hit something hard. He struggled with both the dead thing and the inanimate thing for a moment until he was able to roll to his right a bit, the undead man still attached to him like a leech.

"Figures," Billy said aloud. Bob's broken brick was right next to him. He rolled again and re-straddled the dead man. He held the thing by the throat with his left hand, the skin sloughing off under his fingers. "One sec," he told the creature, grabbed the brick, and brought it down on the thing's forehead. The skull gave way instantly as did the creature's zeal. Its arms fell to its sides and Billy took a deep breath.

"Still stinks," he said to no one as the dead milled about him. He stood to survey his surroundings. He had gotten all the way to the dock in his fight with the dead man. Bob was nowhere to be seen, but he could see dead people streaming out of the water onto the cut-stone embankment.

He moved through the mobile bodies and took a seat on the bench to the right side of the wide concrete pier. His battle with the dead man hadn't gone unnoticed by the other dead, but they didn't seem to care. A half dozen or so shuffled in front of him and he pulled his shotgun from his pack. He would have a bruise where he landed on the weapon when the thing had grabbed him.

But why had it grabbed him? He couldn't figure it out. Every now and then, one or two of the nasties would decide he needed chewing on, but he didn't know why. His clozapine, a drug that was supposed to turn *him* into a zombie but had the adverse effect, only seemed to make the things want to dine on him, but as soon as the stuff wore off, they didn't seem to care anymore.

"Weird," he said and stood. The things in front of him stared. One of them, a younger girl in what used to be a blue dress, stepped toward him. It reached out a hand and Billy slapped it away with the shotgun. It repeated the reaching and Billy let her touch him. She latched onto his pack strap, grabbed his shoulder with her second hand and seemed to look him over.

Her red eyes rested on his and she stared. Billy was about to push her away when a taller dead man put a hand on his shoulder. The other four creatures began to come his way and he didn't like it. He pushed the girl on the chest, but she held firm. The taller man growled, and Billy realized that he didn't like this at all. He began to fight with the girl, the taller thing reaching for him as well. Another thing swiped at him, and he shuffled to his right.

He pushed the girl, who still wasn't trying to bite him, as hard as he could. He took a step back and was suddenly fighting gravity as there was no dock behind him. He began to fall backward, the dead girl moving forward and adding to his weight. The tall thing reached a hand out, almost like it wanted to prevent them from falling, and in a grand moment of panic, Billy accepted the hand, latching on with his own.

The three of them plummeted five feet into the water below, several other undead walking off the pier after them.

FRIENDS WITH HOLES.
JOURNAL ENTRY 10

You know when you've got something in your mouth that isn't supposed to be there, like a canker sore or stitches or a broken tooth, you just can't stop touching it with your tongue? Yeah, that was me with the furrow that dead fucker had dug into my gum. It hurt like hell, and I was pissed, but I couldn't stop playing with it.

"Good one," I said to Remo about his air conditioning joke and felt instantly bad about it. He didn't need my bullshit.

"Bunch coming from behind you," Richy told us. *"You don't have a lot of time before you'll get pinched between groups."*

Remo hastened over my handiwork of broken cinderblocks and ducked into the hole in the wall. He panned his light around as I followed him in, and Ship brought up the rear.

Technically, the no-legged crawler that had latched onto Ship's boot was really last into the breach. Ship figured out he had a hitchhiker and glanced down at it. This one had been dead a while, its gray skin mottled with black and stinking. He dragged it in a bit further, trying to shake it loose, but its nasty digits were dug in like a tick. The sasquatch used his machete to de-hand the thing and I've got to tell you, that was cool as hell. Ship still had two hands attached to his pants when he kicked the nasty bastard in the face and one of the coolest things I had ever seen transpired. Ship's boot went through the facial bones of the dead thing like tissue paper, the head coming clean off and taking a bit of spine with it.

Picture this: a giant yeti looking motherfucker with a couple of severed hands attached to his left leg and a human skull stuck to his right foot dancing around trying to get everything off.

Now, that shit is funny.

I laughed and my mouth hurt. Not allowed two seconds of uninterrupted joy.

Remo toppled over a metal shelving unit into the hole in the wall, then another. It might slow the dead bastards down, but it wouldn't stop them.

Ship pointed to his skull-foot and signed to me, *"Remove it."*

I blinked, then raised my eyebrows in surprise.

"You mean take it off you?" I asked.

He nodded vehemently, standing on one leg that had two hands attached to it.

It was my turn for stinkeye. "Hard pass," I told him. "You're the biggest guy on planet Earth, just stomp your hundred-pound foot."

He did, and the concrete floor was showered in skull fragments and not a little bit of black goo. He was blissfully unaware of the hands still on him. I thought about letting him walk around with zombie fingers but decided that could be an infection risk and told him.

The big bastard actually jumped a little when he saw them. He reminded me of an elephant who was afraid of a mouse.

Moans, rasps, and that gurgling hack came from just outside the hole in the wall and we decided to vamoose. Arms reached through the shelving and grabbed for us, but we were well away from them.

The building we were in was old and definitely off-limits to the general public from a safety standpoint. The small storage room we were in opened up into a larger area where the ceiling was about twenty feet from the floor. We hurried through this area and saw light streaming through an open door in the back. The area was clear, so we moved toward the door.

A dead guy ambled past the door outside looking like he was out for a noonday stroll. He glanced into the building and looked right at us. He either wasn't hungry or didn't see us, because the dead bastard just kept on going.

Remo used his mirror to clear the area outside and we skulked through and into the sunlight. Other than the sounds and stink of the dead, it was a really nice day.

We were about fifty yards from the guard tower, moving quickly between the decrepit building we had just left and a larger structure when half the city of San Francisco turned the corner in front of us. I know this sounds like one of those tropes used by lame authors to cement a scary situation in the reader's mind, but it actually happened. What would further the trope is if the other half of the city stumbled and shuffled out of the doorway we had just left. I guess I'm a troper, because that's exactly what happened.

Ship tapped me on the shoulder and began moving up a small walkway to the door in the building next to us. Fresh human remains were puddled on and in front of the ancient steel door. Somebody had been trapped here and had paid the ultimate price. There was no body, just some torn clothes and blood. The fuckers had either eaten the whole dude, or he had gotten up to join their party.

The door was locked, so Ship used his size huge foot to persuade it. This was a strong door because it took three kicks from King Kong to open it. "Open" is probably not the best terminology here as the heavy thing bent the metal jamb and the top hinge came away.

Like everything else today, that door was just going to slightly slow down the dead that were hot on our heels. Ship dragged it closed and tried to lock it, but as previously mentioned, the jamb was all kinds of fucked.

I swiveled my bleeding face to see Remo looking up.

An ancient, metal, spiral staircase ascended into the floor above us. I thought we were going to bypass it and search for another way out, but we heard things moving around in the darkness in front of us.

Remo started up the stairs, tactical light panning everywhere, and we followed. The three of us reached the next floor, the stairway creaking under Ship's four hundred pounds, and Remo shined his light into each of a bunch of small rooms. He whistled, but nothing came for us.

I heard the door crash to the concrete below, the last hinge quitting on us like a little bitch and knew more of the things were inside. It wouldn't take them long to investigate what was going on upstairs and then we would be in for another gun battle. We could probably hold them on the stairs as only one could come up at a time, but for how long?

I got the stairs, I signed to Ship and stood guard. He nodded in the semi-darkness and I was thrilled with myself that I was able to sign correctly. I mean, I might have just told him I needed to pee, but I was confident I had signed the proper words. What I really wanted was the unspoken communication that Remo and Ship had. Chloe and Richy could do it too.

I could see figures illuminated by the light below moving past the base of the spiral staircase. It was much darker up here, but if I could see them, they could probably see me, and all they had to do was look up. None of the stupid sons of bitches did. Every one of them just kept ambling on past us fifteen feet below. There were a lot.

I just stated a few paragraphs ago that Ship weighs in at a comfortable four hundred. Remo is about six feet tall and weighs, maybe, a hundred and sixty. That's almost six hundred pounds of tough guy, and they didn't make a friggin sound as they cleared this level.

What did make a sound was the gunshot that echoed and reverberated through every cubic inch of the building.

The dead scare me. You know this. It doesn't do anybody any good to live in constant fear, so I've toned it down to constant wariness. There have been times during my travels where I could have used a cork to save my skivvies, but for the most part I think I do ok.

When that gunshot went off, and every single one of those dead fuckers looked up at me, I wasn't the least bit scared. I noticed an enormous, mostly naked dude, wondered why he was only wearing the top half of a pair of socks, and our eyes locked. He put his foot on the bottom step of the spiral and all I could think was that Ship and Remo were supposed to be professionals. What the hell were they doing popping off rounds when we were trying to go quiet?

Then it dawned on me that they both had suppressed sidearms and the gunshot I had heard was from an unsuppressed weapon. It hadn't been Remo's HK, nor Ship's shotgun, so what had made the sound?

I glanced over my shoulder but couldn't see the boys. Looking back down, I could see that the entire continent of North American dead was coming up the stairs. Socks was first and he got stuck. He was so fat, he jammed up in the spiral railing on the third step or so and was stuck fast. I laughed out loud, and I don't think the dead liked it. I wasn't fat shaming, it was just funny, I swear.

They all started those awful noises. You know, the ones that shrink your nuts even when you just told everyone who would listen that you weren't scared?

I plugged the big dude and he just sort of stopped moving, his freshly punctured melon lolling to the side. He couldn't collapse because the railings held him in place. The dead behind him were having a really difficult time pushing his enormity out of the way and I thought that this could very well be the most effective way to stop the onslaught of an oncoming horde in a tight space.

I shot a few more, who did collapse, and the rest just tried to climb over them. The entirety of Operation Plug the Hole had taken about thirty seconds, and when it was over, I could see Ship dragging two people down the short corridor. One I knew, the other was a stranger. The one I knew was bleeding.

Ship abruptly tossed the stranger at my feet. He was a shorter guy with glasses. I had seen him before but didn't know his name. Ship wouldn't have chucked the guy if he didn't have a reason, so I dared a glance at the dead below us, then pointed my weapon at the head of the little dude on the floor.

He shrieked and threw his hands up in front of his face like they would stop bullets. No, Dear Reader, I didn't riddle this guy with lead. I had no idea what was going on and there was a still a bit of stuff on my plate to deal with.

"Ship, report!" I said in an authoritative tone. It was totally ridiculous too, because if Ship tried to sign to me what had happened, we would die of old age before I got it all in this low light. Remo might die a bit sooner, as his red stuff was leaking from a hole beneath his plate carrier.

"What happened?" I asked over the din of the dead from below.

Ship broke out his medical equipment and began to peel Remo's stuff off him.

"What *happened?*" I demanded of everyone.

"I'm sorry!" shrieked the little guy. "I thought you were one of them!"

I rounded on him, what had transpired finally dawning on me, but still not able to believe it.

"You... you shot him?"

"I thought he was one of them!" the little prick repeated.

That was about all I was going to take. "Flashing a light around and being sneaky? Are you an idiot? Stand up and turn around." I glanced at the log jam on the spiral staircase. We had a couple of minutes as the dead were piled up around the big guy, but if they crawled over or ate through him, they'd be on us quickly unless I took some more out.

"A... are you going to kill me?" I know this sounds ridiculous, but this guy was all body with a fat neck. He reminded me of the Abominable Snowman from the Rudolph the Red Nosed Reindeer Claymation cartoon. Bumbles.

I shook my head. Another futile gesture as he couldn't see me. "Jury's out." I zip-tied his hands behind his back and stole another glance downward. One of the things had managed to climb onto the back of Hefty Smurf, so I gave him a subsonic round to the back of the noggin.

I dared a glance at Remo. Ship had MARSOC's shirt off, and there was a neat hole in his abdomen about two inches above his left hip. I absentmindedly rubbed my scar, which was in exactly the same spot but on my right side. Our eyes met and he looked nervous. Remember how I said up above that the dead scare me? Well, nothing scares this man. I truly believe this guy is never afraid because he doesn't know how to be. He did know what was coming next, though, and I felt for him.

Ship was already tearing the little silver package of Celox open. Celox was originally fabricated in Hell by Satan himself in order to torment already wounded and terrified combat specialists. But it did stop the bleeding.

Ship passed Remo an Israeli bandage, pointed at Remo's mouth, and hovered the open package over the bleeding hole. Remo put the bandage in his mouth and nodded once to Ship, who immediately dumped the entire package of anguish directly onto the wound. Remo made a couple of undignified sounds, and it was over. Well, half over. Ship pulled the jarhead forward by his left shoulder, a move Remo didn't care for, and looked for an exit wound. He searched long and hard, but in the end, glanced at me and shook his head in the negative.

Fuck. That meant the bullet was still in my buddy.

Ship grabbed the bandage from Remo's face, tore off the plastic covering with his teeth, wrapped it around his middle, and fed it through the smiley face looking thing. He then wrapped it back the other way and secured it with the plastic piece. He hauled Remo to his feet, and to my utter surprise, slapped him across the face.

"I'm good," Remo told us.

I peered down the stairs and shot another industrious undead who had made it over the stuck dude.

It was proving to be an interesting day.

DEATH SOUP
SLIGHTLY OFF THE COAST OF ALCATRAZ

Billy had never drowned before. Really, it wasn't all that bad. It had been hot out in the sun, but down here under the waves it was nice. Considerably colder than he had thought it would be, but nice, nonetheless. Two of the infected had latched onto him on the dock above and wouldn't let go even when they plunged into the water. They didn't try to bite him, they almost never did, but still, they weighed him down. He sank into the darkness as he fought the dead things that were attached to him.

The three of them hit the bottom quickly. Billy, with not an ounce of fat on him, sunk like a stone in the water anyway, but when combined with two dead things it was like he was holding onto an anchor.

Sediments from the bay floor puffed into the water and hung suspended, partially obscuring the other dozen or so dead that had walked off the pier. Billy pushed on his attackers, not in a panic, but because he knew his clothes would stink like dead people later.

But were they attackers? Billy thought. *Grabbers for sure, but they aren't really trying to hurt me. Did they need something? Like a massage or maybe a pet duck?* Several other thoughts flitted across Billy's mind before he came to a realization.

Ummm... I need to breathe. Yeah, I need to breathe real soon.

Drowning had gone from not so bad to *Holy Shit!* at light speed. Billy looked at all the infected around him and suddenly didn't want to be at the bottom of this death soup. The undead girl who had hold of him was strong, but he was able to grab her wrists and bend them outward. Her hands came away, he shrugged out of his pack, which was what the other infected was hanging on to and kicked for the surface. He almost made it too, when the tall, infected man grabbed his ankle.

His lungs burning, he kicked furiously and was able to free himself. He broke the surface of the water and took in huge, gulping lungfuls of air. The dock was too high to climb, so he swam to the embankment and walked onto the Rock just like the undead had.

Unpleasant, he thought as sea water dripped from his clothes. He climbed up the cut-stone embankment and hopped the short fence. Undead bodies lay everywhere, skulls dented, crushed, or outright missing. Billy jutted his lower lip forward and nodded in appreciation.

"Not bad," he said aloud. A couple of the dead things reached over the fence behind him when he spoke.

Billy moved to his left, stepping between the fallen bodies, searching for his sword. He searched for a few moments before a glint of sun hit him in the eyes. He strode to the glint, smiled, and picked up his weapon.

His smile vanished. The tsuba on his sword was bent. The tsuba, or handguard, on his sword was bent. It was bent. Bent.

Billy hadn't been this angry since he found out Abbey had died. That was like, an hour ago, but still, before today, he hadn't been mad in months. Stupid dead things.

One such thing shuffled up to him. He glanced from his damaged weapon to the dead woman. He could only think of a singular word. "DIPLODOCUS!" he screamed at it and decapitated the creature with his best single-handed reverse swing to date. The head fell to the cement walkway with a wet squelch, but that wasn't good enough. He gingerly placed his sword at his feet, grabbed the head and spun it so he could look it in the eyes. The jaw moved and the eyes focused on his.

"Wrong!"

He slammed the face of the creature into the pavement until what was in his hand was unrecognizable. He would stink as much as Bob had when this ordeal was done, as he was now covered in everything a smashed head contained.

Billy let the tattered scalp drop to the blood-spattered concrete as he stood. He grabbed his sword with his left hand and absentmindedly wiped his palm on his jeans.

"Ew," came a voice from behind him.

Billy sighed and glanced sideways. Bob leaned against the chain link fence, the baseball bat sitting idly against his leg.

"You did all of this?" Billy asked, giving a wave to the truly dead people on the ground with crushed skulls.

"Yeah. Well, no. We both did. I saw you Excaliburing the deaders with your sword earlier."

Billy presented the sword. "Broken," he said, defeated. In half a second, totally in contrast to his last expression, his face lit up. "Excalibur?" Do you think you can name a ninja sword Excalibur?"

Bob pointed to the blade. "That's modeled after a Muramasa."

"What's a Muramasa?"

"He was a who not a what. Japanese sword maker. It was said that his swords were cursed." Bob shrugged, "I'm a sword guy."

Billy swallowed hard, pushing the weapon ever so slightly away from him. "I'm holding a cursed sword?"

"Nah. It's unlikely that's a real Muramasa. It would be worth ridiculous money if it were real."

"I pulled it out of a dead guy." Billy creased his eyebrows. "Come to think of it, he wasn't very lucky. Are you sure this isn't cursed?"

"Nope."

Scrapes on the concrete alerted them to a few meandering undead.

Bob pointed at the sword, then made *pass it to me* motions with his hand.

Billy obliged. Bob turned the blade over in his hands a few times, uttered a brief, "Hmm." and pulled a pair of Vice Grips from his back pocket. He adjusted the bolt, clamped the tool onto the tsuba, and released it. The tsuba was mostly straightened.

"Sword guy and a mechanic," Bob told him and handed the sword back.

Joy. Pure, unadulterated joy spread across Billy's face. He moved in too quickly for Bob to do anything and caught him in an embrace.

"Thank you!"

"Hey, you let me borrow your bat. I was doing brick-smacks all morning."

Billy marveled at his mostly-fixed weapon. "Keep it. The bat, I mean. Until we can find you one of these." Billy lunged and skewered the skull of a dead woman in an apron.

"Still works!"

Bob raised his eyebrows. "You good?"

"So good!"

Three more of the ambulatory deceased were making their way past the dock and Bob pointed at them. "You wanna?"

Billy smiled and nodded.

TWO LITTLE LADIES AND A MAN
USS FLORIDA

"The box! The long green one with the metal clasps!" Moe screamed as he pushed against the hatch. Hands and fingers scratched and pushed at the steel from the other side. Two arms had made it through the opening and reached for he and Chloe, who also had both hands on the metal. One of the arms oozed blood from a savage bite mark. Moe recognized the watch on the infected wrist.

"It won't open!" Vanessa screamed back.

Frustrated, Moe whispered to Chloe, "Help her!"

"Can you hold the door if I let go?"

Hatch, he thought to himself. *Skip would own her for that one.* "We need the box open as much as we need the hatch closed!"

She pulled her hands from the door and suddenly it got significantly heavier.

Chloe ran to assist Vanessa. The two of them fought with the clasps on the Pelican case and when they were unlatched, the case still wouldn't open. Using her knife, Chloe got the blade between the case halves and pried it up. The black box opened a bit, and the girls got their fingers into the gap.

"That's the shit!" Chloe said when the case opened wide.

She reached into the box and pulled out a black MP5-SD. A wicked looking sub-machine gun with an integrated suppressor. A dozen magazines were placed neatly on a green blanket to the left side of the big case.

"I don't know how to use it!" cried Vanessa.

Moe began to yell.

Chloe grabbed a magazine full of subsonic 9mm rounds. "Take this thing, stick it in here hard, make sure it's facing like this." She jammed the magazine into the receiver. "Pull back this thing," she yanked the charging handle, "and flick this switchy thingie so it points to the red bullet! Don't point it at anything you don't want to shoot!" She passed the charged weapon to her friend but kept it on safe. "Give that one to Moe when he gets back to us. Pick up the mags, those things," she pointed to the spare magazines, "and stick 'em in your pockets."

Vanessa put the charged weapon down while Chloe repeated her actions on the second weapon. Vanessa began shoving magazines into her pockets.

Moe pushed for all he was worth, which was damn little if he let these girls die. The weight on the other side of the steel was far superior to his though, and the hatch began to inch toward him. It was then he realized he was going to die. More than that, the girls would be torn apart by dead things. If he could buy them some time by bull rushing into the crowd, he would do it. His mind made up, he became serene. Fuck these dead things.

The torso of a gray-faced woman poked through the opening. The creature was close enough that it wasted no time in grabbing his arm. He pulled away and the hatch opened wide with a squeal. *XO would lose his shit if he heard that hatch*, Moe thought. Dead people spilled through the portal onto the deck in front of him. The dead woman pulled his hand to her mouth and her head snapped back, her grip loosening immediately as the air filled with the sound of a suppressed gunshot.

"Get back here!" Chloe shrieked and Moe didn't need to be told twice. Several gunshots rent the air while he scrabbled toward the girls.

"Locked and loaded," the blonde one told him. "Safety's on!" She plugged another two infected climbing through the open hatchway and a third trying to stand on this side of the portal. Moe grabbed the loaded weapon, flipped the safety off and joined the gun battle.

"Magazine!" Chloe shouted and Vanessa passed her a fresh one.

Where the fuck did these kids come from? BUD/S? wondered the sailor.

"Moving forward," the girl shouted over the gunfire, and she strode toward the oncoming dead, firing as she did so.

The things were plugging the open hatchway with their bodies as they attempted to crawl over each other and between the sailor and the teenager, they destroyed all the dead in the immediate vicinity. More were coming down the corridor and Moe slung his weapon.

"Cover!" he yelled and began dragging bodies into the room. Several of his shipmates and a dozen or so civilians shuffled toward them over the deck grating. Chloe fired once more at a huge, bald infected that was ten feet away, then Moe was able to push the hatch closed. He flipped the handles to lock it from the undead and put his hands on his knees, heaving.

He glanced sideways. "Where'd you learn to shoot like that?"

Chloe slapped in a fresh magazine. "Internet." She spun and sighted down the weapon moving in the opposite direction.

Moe surveyed his surroundings. They were in a small antechamber with another hatch ten feet away. This hatch had key card access. A three-foot corridor ran the length of the room toward the back of the sub. Everything was painted a dull green.

"Stop," he told Chloe.

She glanced back at him but kept her weapon facing the corridor.

Moe swallowed. "Jesus fuck, we were shooting in here."

"Yeah, there were zombies. So?"

He pointed at the hatch. "That's the reactor room."

"So?" both girls asked

He passed a granola bar to each girl.

"So, a stray bullet might have killed not only us, but everybody near the sub. The whole island would be a radioactive mess for a long time."

"Right," Chloe said, charging a round into her MP5, "bullets, bad. I suggest mean faces. A stern talking to. That will chase off the dead things for sure."

"Just don't shoot in here."

"No plans to. Ya know, unless there's a zombie. Hey, maybe the dead guy will be up for a game of parcheesi. Otherwise..." She held up the sub-machine gun and wagged it a little.

Moe shook his head. He nodded down the long, skinny corridor, "Let's go."

They inched down the corridor slowly, fists banging on the hatch behind them. No open doorways with who-knows-what inside existed to frighten them, so they sped up. At the far end, a black steel ladder ascended to another hatch, but this one was round and sealed them off from the deck above. Moe climbed the few rungs and tapped the hatch with his weapon.

He slid back down the ladder, the three of them waiting to see what happened.

"Here we go," Vanessa told everyone as the hatch wheel began to turn. Several firearms were pointed in both directions as the hatch was pulled up and away from the three survivors.

"Moe!" a sailor exclaimed and passed his shotgun out of sight. The man smiled and stuck his head through the hatch. "And company," he said, staring at the two girls.

Moe sighed. "Never thought I'd see your ugly mug again, Hart. Kinda glad to see you."

Hart made a *come here* gesture with his hand.

"You first, kid," Moe told Vanessa. She climbed the ladder and accepted Hart's hand. Chloe went next, sliding her weapon to her back. Hart looked like he was about to have a coronary when he saw the young girl with the weapon. When Moe was standing on the deck above staring at six of his uninfected shipmates, Hart grabbed his hand.

"Good to see you, buddy."

"You too," he glanced around, "all of you. What's going on?"

"The dead hold everything forward of the galley. We don't know how many of our guys bought it, but only a few of the civvies got out. The skipper is in the Conn, he's giving orders from there." Hart looked at his shoes for a moment, "Nobody is picking up phones when we call."

"Get me to the skip. I have intel."

One of the sailors pointed to Chloe's MP5. "I'm going to need that weapon, little lady."

Chloe creased her brow and took a step back. A difficult task in itself as there was little real estate in the room they were in.

"Seriously, that thing is dangerous." He took a step toward her, and she flipped the safety off.

"So am I."

The sailor glared at Moe. "You gave the kid a friggin' machine gun?"

"No, DeRuzzo, she gave one to me. She killed a shit-ton of those things and honestly, she has better weapon discipline than you do, you Wop douchebag. She saved my life," he pointed at Vanessa, "her life, and likely yours too when we go to clear the boat. I vouch for her, and I'll talk to the captain about it."

Chloe didn't smile, but her opinion of her new sailor friend skyrocketed. She flipped the safety back on her weapon and nodded to Moe.

***

Moe sighed and nodded. "Aye, sir. At least ten that I saw."

"Ten!" McInerney almost shouted. He rubbed both palms over the stubble on his head.

"Aye, sir. We took out several of the civvies as well. I lost count, but—"

"Nineteen total," interrupted Chloe. "There were two other sub-guys in the kitchen that got killed too. One had red hair and the other guy had dark hair and glasses." She glanced sheepishly at Moe. "Sorry. Been doing this a while."

"Talbot and Ricks," a sailor told his captain.

"The guy with the glasses saved our lives," Vanessa said through tears.

The captain nodded. "Thank you." He looked at Chloe's weapon then glanced at Moe who stood tall. McInerney raised an eyebrow.

Moe did not smile. "I would venture a guess that she's destroyed more of those things than any sailor on board, sir."

McInerney's face was unreadable. "Chloe, we discussed firearms, didn't we?"

"Yes, sir. That was before our house was infested with dead people. I believe the term you used when my brother asked you about us having guns was 'not yet'. Is now yet?" She thumbed at the sailor who had tried to take her weapon earlier. "How old is he?"

McInerney loved these kids. They weren't part of his crew and so didn't need to speak to him with respect, yet they did. They were also experts in hand-to-hand combat and clearly proficient with firearms. The brother was on one of the towers making shots on moving targets that an expert marksman would call tricky. The sister had defended herself and others when most of his sailors were shitting their pants with fear. He wished he had ten more like them.

But he couldn't let an armed child run around his boat.

The captain looked at the sailor Chloe had indicated and raised his eyebrows.

"Twenty-two, sir."

McInerney shifted his gaze back to the kids. "You've more than proved your worth, young lady, but I will not put you in harm's way. I'm so very sorry, but you need to give up the gun."

Chloe checked the safety on the MP5, removed the sling from her shoulder and held the weapon at arm's length. Vanessa started removing magazines from her pockets.

Every sailor, including McInerny was smiling.

Chloe failed to tell any of them that she had a fully loaded sidearm with an extra magazine tucked into the waistband of her jeans. She rubbed her wrist across her shirt to ensure the 1911 was still there.

Moe, smiling at her, was also curiously silent about her weapon.

LIKE, WTF?
JOURNAL ENTRY 11

"Down there?" the shithead asked.

Four of us stared down something that would have been called stairs in the 1930s. They were broken and jagged concrete steps that jutted out from the side of the building into the dark space of the area we were in.

"Yeah, if you don't like it, we can leave you here. The creak of the ancient floor a room and a half behind us told me that the dead had gotten up the equally as old spiral stairs.

"I need my hands!" Bumbles exclaimed so loudly that the dead answered.

He was right, though. There was no way I would let the guy try to negotiate this deathtrap with his hands behind his back. We'd just end up with another zombie to fight. I flipped open my folder, keeping my SOG on my chest harness, and he was free.

He wrung his hands across his wrists like a little bitch and I hated him even more. Until I remembered I had done the exact same thing on several occasions. Either neither of us were bitches, or we both were.

Shit.

Ship started down the decrepit thing in front of us, the treads protesting almost as loudly as this asshole we had come across.

I considered the steps. I'm too young to know what Shinola looks like, but I know what shit is, and those steps weren't Shinola.

The sounds of the dead were getting closer.

"How do you know what's down there?" He strained to look past Ship, which was like trying to peek past a small town. "I can't see!"

"I don't know what's down there, but I sure as shit know what's up here! Move!"

"Can I have a gun?"

"No, you can't have a gun, but I promise you, I'll give you a bullet if you don't shut the fuck *up*!"

I pointed my Sig at his face. His eyes grew wide, and he swallowed hard, nodding. The guy had just shot my friend, he was annoyingly whiney, and fucking *loud* when etiquette demanded silence. I am not ashamed to say I was not ashamed to point my gun at his noggin. Stupid sentence there, but screw you, I like it.

He started down after Ship and Remo. The combined weight on this archaic stairway was mindboggling with just Ship on them but add the three of us, and it was terrifying. We made it, though, and quickly.

My rods and cones had to adjust to the illumination as we made our way into the sunlight. I didn't like it and neither did my eyes, so I put my palm above them to act as a shield. I heard dull thuds with a side order of splash behind us and knew the stupid dead assholes were just walking off the floor above and impacting the one below.

Complacency. I'm a soldier now. I've had some training, but nothing like Remo or Seyfert or Alvarez. These guys simply don't get surprised. They don't get surprised because they are always on alert. When they're sleeping, walking through the woods, or taking a dump, they're paying more attention than I ever could at my best. I'm always thinking about the next witty thing to say or the ass on the chick in front of me, and that's bad. It was just such a complacent moment when a dead thing wound its decaying fingers around my tactical webbing and leaned in for a nibble. Now, Ship, Remo, and our new douchesickle had walked past this concrete column not one second before, and nothing. Me? Shit magnet. Second time this had happened in less than twenty-four hours.

It pulled itself toward me and got within biting distance before I even knew what was happening. I had no chance to defend myself or stop the attack in any way. The smell of it permeated everything, a palpable wave of rot that saturated my senses enough to make my eyes water. I felt its teeth on my throat and knew I was dead.

But it didn't bite me. Stupid of it, really, because in the time it took to not do what zombies do, I did what I do, jammed my Sig under its chin, and sent chunks of infected cranium skyward.

Now, I just said up above that Remo and his ilk don't get surprised, remember? Remo, leaning on Ship, just turned to make sure I hadn't shot myself. Ship didn't even turn at all. The little peckerwood cock-cabinet that we had just picked up jumped like he had a spider crawling on his neck. I'm surprised he didn't bump his head on the ceiling.

I threw the dead thing to the floor and made my way to the boys. We were outside and in the clear in just a moment, me slamming the rickety door on anything behind us.

"You're bleeding!" the little shit-mongering cheese-weasel said.

I looked down his extended, accusatory finger to his face and said, "This is from hours ago. I'm fine." It still hurt like hell, but hey, I wasn't telling him that.

How many times in our travels together, Dear Reader, have I told you that someone *had done the stupidest thing ever*? Answer: a lot.

This guy tried to snatch my gun. He was three feet away and he made a grab for it. It was a weak attempt that was both woefully short and pathetically inaccurate. Had his grab succeeded, I would have had to give him a tip for a rub n tug.

Unfortunately for both of us, he's an idiot. The only things he accomplished were putting his face closer to me and pissing me off to the almost-breaking point.

So, I thumped him across the face with my sidearm. He dropped to the ground fast, screaming and holding his assaulted nose. Oh, it hadn't been a Superman punch. It was a little tap. I mean, yeah, he was gonna be sore for a bit, but there were no fatalities.

"He'd bleedig!" he shouted to Ship and Remo, the finger still pointing. "He'd godduh bide ud!" He was holding his nose like I had already bitten it off and let me tell you, it crossed my mind.

Ship had his arms full of Remo and he wasn't about to assist this shitsickle, so I extended a paw down to him and gave him a digit wag. Clearly my hand was fabricated out of lava as the guy yelped and inched away on his ass.

"Suit yourself," I told him with an eye-roll and sauntered past. The thing that was supposed to be a door ten feet behind us shuddered from the impact of something on the other side. "Enjoy the day," I said over my shoulder.

Normally I wouldn't turn my back on a guy who just made a grab for my weapon, but this dude scared me less than not at all.

"You're going to leave me?" I heard him ask. His schnoz must have made a miraculous recovery because his question had been crystal clear, although twinged with terror.

"Not if you keep up. Besides, I'm one of them now, remember? You sure you want to stick with us?"

He didn't answer.

We were running out of real estate on this island, and more than that, ammo was getting scarce. I had nineteen rounds in my rifle with one extra magazine, my sidearm had two full mags and I was happy about that. Cursing myself a fool, I switched out rifle mags so the full one was, ya know, in the rifle.

I caught up with the fellas and noticed that Ship wasn't assisting Remo anymore, he was carrying him. The jarhead had passed out.

That was bad. Not only was Remo our resident expert at killing everything, Ship was laden with our former-marine's unconscious body. I have no doubts that Ship could carry Remo's 170 pounds until doomsday, (I mean a different doomsday), but that means both of them were out of the shooting business and this was a day for bullets.

Remo's rifle barrel began to drag on the ground, and I stopped Ship to take the weapon. I slung his and kept mine at the ready.

The dead began to show up and I knew we were going to have to run. "Get in front of me," I told the douche-crust. "Follow the big guy and do what he does. Do not make a sound."

He pushed up and I realized this was a bad plan. I needed to be first because Ship was full of Remo. I let the Yeti know, and it looked like he was going to bitch about my proposal, but after likely a quadrillion calculations fired off in his noggin, he acquiesced and I moved to the point position. I didn't like the shithead behind me, but what could I do?

A steady stream of stinkers behind us made me decide that this mission was FUBAR. "We're heading to the sub," I told Ship.

"Yeah!" the other conscious guy who could speak almost shouted, "Let's get to the submarine!"

Sound discipline. Right.

There was no point chastising the guy, especially since my soldiering skills were not at the level I wanted them to be. We moved as a unit up to the corner of a building and I peeked the corner. Eight or nine of the things were coming straight for us from the right, but behind them it was a straight shot to the Florida. There were fifty behind us and even more to the left. They'd be on us in seconds.

We wouldn't make it. I might be able to get through, but Ship would get taken down while he had his arms full.

"We need to leave him and run!" Bumbles exclaimed. He had been talking about Remo.

Right then I knew that this is the kind of elitist, dirt-bag, asshole who puts ketchup directly on his fries. I'm ashamed to say I briefly considered plugging the prick in the knee and leaving him so me and my buddies could escape while the dead munched on him. In the end I just did me. Which is, as you know, always something monumentally stupid.

"Ship, get Remo and this whiney douche to the sub." I peeled around the corner and fired into the first of the dead. There were way more than I had initially thought, my peeking skills not on a MARSOC degree.

Ship and his packages followed me, but so did the small army of dead that had been to our left. I was pondering where the ones in front could have come from when I saw a few of them stumble from a hole in the building on our right.

"I'm right behind you!" I yelled. "Run!"

He did. For a big guy he was damn fast.

Decisions, decisions. If I fired into the ones in front, my buddies would get away, but the ones in the back would get me. If I only shot the ones in the back, my pals might not make it. I saw Ship throw Remo into a fireman's carry and swing the jarhead's feet into the shoulder of an oncoming infected. The short dude was hiding in Ship's shadow, waiting for a gap so he could sprint for the sub. He was wringing his hands and I could see a growing wetness on his crotch.

I fired my weapon at the ones near Ship. I dropped quite a few before a big group got between us. He had a clear path and sprinted toward safety. Even carrying Remo, he outdistanced the little pudgy dude, but they would all make it.

I wouldn't.

Resigned, I turned to fire on the crowd behind me. I never got the chance as they were a tad closer than I had thought. About a foot away. They plowed into me, grabbing, and my rifle went off. I only had four shots left but the rifle became a moot point as the barrel was pushed skyward. Three of them had me with more on the way. I let the rifle go and tried to reach for my sidearm, but cold fingers wrapped around my wrist.

And that was when Jackie Chan showed up. Some tall guy in a black T shirt leapt into the fray and punished the fuck out of a bunch of dead people. He grabbed the arm of the thing who had my wrist, lifted it straight up into the air and lunge-punched the forearm of the dead guy. The thing's arm bent ninety degrees and it let go of me. I wasted no time and drilled it in the face with my Sig, but ninja-dude had moved on and was twisting and bending the dead until they snapped. The guy didn't have a weapon because he was a weapon. It looked like the dead were ignoring him, but it may have been because he was so damn fast.

My weapon went dry, and I performed a tactical magazine switch that would have made Remo show emotion. I emptied the Sig quickly, but they were still coming. One walked right past Jackie, then right past me.

WTF? In case you don't know what WTF means, it is an abbreviation of What The Fuck? Because, what the fuck!

Another walked past, then another. I was just starting to think I had turned into a super hero and I would be able to Billy my way through hordes of undead, when one of them grabbed me and tried to see what my carotid artery tasted like. I like my arteries. I like them enough that I wanted to keep them where they were, so I got my forearm between the dead guy and my important bits. Hands reached around the thing's face, latched onto its jaw, and viciously jerked it to the left. I saw its spine pop out the side of its neck and some black shit squirted on my face before it collapsed.

Karate man briefly looked me in the face and for the first time in the apocalypse, I actually pissed myself. Alright, so it hadn't been the first time, but this one was full on code yellow. It was more than leakage, there was flow.

The person saving my life wasn't a person at all. It was the infected kid I had seen on the boat. His eyes were red as blood, he looked feverish and twitchy, but his face was devoid of the one emotion a Runner possesses: Hate. This wasn't something I could comprehend, so my synapses overloaded, and I checked out for a sec.

He grabbed me by the wrist, exactly where the dead guy had grabbed me not two minutes before, and I knew I was dead. He was going to break me into little pieces and play tiddlywinks with my vertebrae. He was... He was... He was shaking his head *no* and proceeded to pull me away from danger. I ran with him, my empty Sig clutched so hard in my paw there might be blood later.

We ran about fifty steps, and he let me go, but we kept running. I ran with him because I had no idea what else to do. He had saved my life. He had cleared a path through the dead, but was I really going to follow a Runner? Was I going to go with this thing so it could have its way with me in some quiet corner?

Yes. That decision had been made in a microsecond, and as you are reading this journal right now, you can probably figure out that I'm still alive, so it had been a good decision.

But, as you know, I'm still a shit magnet.

A lone undead stumbled out of an open doorway next to the building we were running past and slammed right into us. The thing wasted no time in latching onto me and then he did what, up until recently, all undead do: he bit me.

Dear Reader, I know what you're thinking: *"Yeah, but you're like, immune and stuff. You won't get infected, you'll just shake it off and be home in time for waffles."*

Well, that's just stupid. Where the hell would I get waffles in the apocalypse? More importantly, you have never been bitten. You would be dead if you had. Me? Yeah, I've survived bites, but they're *bites*.

Something has bitten me. Take away the fact that the biters are infected with the worst shit in history, and I still have a hole in me. It *hurts*. More than that, at some point, I'm going to bleed out or parts of me won't work right because of all the missing pieces.

This thing, a younger zombie, maybe late teens, got me on the right arm between the shoulder and bicep before I was able to push it away. It still had a hold of me, but its teeth were no longer embedded. It tried to bite me again, which was good because that means it wasn't chewing. If it wasn't chewing, at least most of me was still part of me. Blood dribbled down its chin and that pissed me off. We struggled and went down in a heap.

A shadow loomed, but before infected ninja boy could save me, I saved myself. I thumped the thing on the side of the head with my pistol until it let go, then smashed the weapon down until its melon resembled an abstract art piece.

I snarled. I heard it. It hadn't come from the dead or the kid, it had come out of me. I was getting mad and when two more dead assholes decided they wanted to nibble, I had had enough. I screamed at the one coming in for you know what and launched myself at it. It was kind of like an out of body experience. I knew what I was doing, but had no control and more than that, I didn't care. The only thing I wanted was to tear this thing limb from limb.

So, I did. I grabbed it by the face as it attempted to bite and sunk my thumbs into its eyes with a couple of squishes. I hooked the thumbs outward and dragged the thing to the ground. Straddling this dead son of a bitch would only make me stink later, but again, caring about anything other than destroying this thing had left the building. I smashed and punched and gouged. I swear to all that is holy I thumped its head into the concrete walkway until I heard a crack and just kept going. A few cracks more and I reached into its busted head, ripped stuff out and held my prize high, screaming. I had heard that brains sort of melt into a yogurt-like substance after death. Either that is horse shit, or it didn't happen to infected, because I was not holding yogurt.

I heard a noise beside me and glared up at it with hatred. It was the kid. He was absolutely a Runner and he was scared shitless of me. He took a step back with a *you have got to be fucking kidding me* look on his face.

I was certainly *not* kidding and let him know it. I stood, chucked some brain to the ground, and stared the kid down. He held his hands up in red-eyed supplication and I launched at another undead with a scream. The scream was decidedly inhuman, and again, it had come from me. Whatever the fuck this shit inside me is pushed me aside and I was no longer driving.

TIME TO GO
WATER TOWER, ALCATRAZ

Richy yawned as he aimed the rifle. He blinked a couple of times to clear his vision after the yawn. The boy glanced at his friend, who had tugged on his T shirt sleeve.

Kyle frowned. "I can't get Remo on the radio."

"How about my dad?" Sam asked in a frightened voice.

Kyle passed her the radio. "Daddy? Dad are you there?"

"What is it, honey?" Rick answered immediately. *"Everything all right?"*

Relief flooded the girl. "Yeah," she sighed. We're good up here. Where are you?"

"We're by the lighthouse. We're going to link up with Seyfert and run some sweeps. You gonna be ok up there for a few hours?"

"Yeah, we'll be fine. We're all clipped in and safe."

"Let me talk to him," Richy asked, sticking his hand out for the radio.

"Mr. Barnes? I'm looking at the east dock now. There's tons of them still coming out of the water."

"How many?"

"I don't know, but it's going to be really hard for you to kill them all. We've been shooting them all day, but this feels like a band aid solution."

"Are there any fast ones?"

"No, sir. We saw Billy and some other guy killing lots of them earlier, but I lost sight of them."

Kyle pointed at the sub. "Look!"

Richy passed the radio back to Sam, who began to speak to her father again. Richy put the rifle to his shoulder to get a better look at what was going on near the Florida. "That's Ship. He's carrying somebody, but I can't tell if it's Remo or... Holy shit!"

"What? What is it?"

"Ship just used whoever he was carrying as a club to knock down two dead ones!" Richy lifted the rifle barrel up slightly to see how far Ship was from the submarine. He was about twenty yards away, but the people on the foredeck of the sub were struggling to get the gangway from the sub to the rocks on Alcatraz. The dead had surrounded Ship and whoever he was trying to save. The boy saw a man jumping up and down, pleading to be let aboard the submarine.

Richy noticed it would take at least thirty seconds for the sailors on the sub to get the gangway situated. "They aren't going to make it," he said softly.

Our position is precarious, Ship thought as he surveyed his surroundings. *Our situation, dire. I have not made it this far because I am willing to give up.* Ship jogged another six steps and fired into the face of a dead nine-year-old. He shot a woman in a tattered green evening gown with a few sequins still attached. He ended the misery of a thing in torn blue scrubs. He dispatched three more and the slide on his sidearm stayed back. A thing in a frayed Celtics jersey tried to grab him but it had no hands.

I miss the Celtics, the big man thought. *But a Celtics fan in San Francisco? I would think that would be gauche to say the least and completely unacceptable to some. Perhaps this poor man was not a Celtics fan but received the jersey as a gift and did not want to offend the giver. Perhaps...* Ship dropped his pistol and reached for his machete, but it was too large to get off his back while he carried Remo. Ship could hear the smaller man that had shot Remo screaming for the sailors to help. He had sprinted far ahead and was now begging to be let aboard the sub.

I am sorry, my friend, Ship thought as he swung Remo's legs into the side of an enterprising undead who had gotten too close, *but we will not survive this.* Ship knew if he dropped Remo, he would be able to make it to the safety of the submarine. He knew that a decision like that would be beneficial to the most amount of people. It made sense to drop his friend and make a leap to the men struggling to stretch the gangway to the island. Even if it meant the death of his friend, it made sense for him to survive.

Fuck sense, he thought and smiled. He put Remo down gently and drew his massive blade. He swung at the nearest undead, its rotten face sloughing off when its severed head hit the pavement. He swung three more times destroying three more of the things before they had him.

The arc of his machete was rendered ineffective when one of the things shuffled in close enough to impact his swinging arm. His blade clattered away when he dropped it. One of the things came at him with a toothy snarl, but its head popped like an over ripe melon, and suddenly the sound of automatic weapons fire shattered the air.

"Don't hit the live ones!" came a scream from the sub. "Focus fire to the front and let them get aboard!"

He took a step back under the onslaught and to his horror, felt Remo's arm under his boot. He lifted his foot and four of the things hit him at a slow charge. He started to fall backwards but shifted his momentum and threw two of the creatures away. One of the things began to crawl toward the unconscious Remo, but its head also imploded and then Kat was in amongst the dead.

The girl swung her rifle by the barrel and nearly decapitated a thing in shorts with the impact, its head now tilted at an impossible angle. She shifted stance and brought the rifle down on the top of a dead thing's shoulder, the collar bone snapping.

She stood over Remo heaving while Ship picked up a dead thing by the throat and tore its arm completely off. Ship threw the arm into the faces of a few more of the things.

"Pick him up!" Kat screamed as she swung the rifle again. One of the dead grabbed it and she let it go, drawing her knife.

The big man gave a mighty shove and pushed four of the dead away. He used the split second of time he had to grab Remo and throw him into a fireman's carry. He heard the aluminum gangway clang onto the rocks and sailors flooded across, shooting.

"Run!" one of them screamed. "Now! Run now!"

They did. They sprinted up the gangway, the sailors following them. The dead reached the aluminum before they could draw it back, but a few dozen rounds took them out and they collapsed. The gangway was reeled in, and Ship placed Remo on the deck, kneeling next to him.

Kat stood next to him, hunched over, hands on her knees, heaving. "You're the smartest guy on the fucking planet. You're so God damned big you outweigh the needs of the many, and you didn't think to just fucking throw him to these assholes?" She meant the sailors who had come down the gangway. "It was five feet for fuck's sake!"

She stared back at the dead, who had begun to shuffle off the rocks and disappear into the dark water between the sub and the island. She gave a defiant middle finger to the oncoming dead, "And they got my fuckin' gun!"

Ship made to explain to her that not only would it have been folly to throw an unconscious man into the arms of other men who were in the midst of using firearms, but the distance was far greater than she had surmised. He started to sign to her, but Kat cut him off.

She pointed up at him, one hand on her hip, "Don't wave hands at me, motherfucker! You should have chucked him like Gimli." She turned on the sailors who were still pulling the gangway aboard or shooting any undead futilely attempting to climb aboard from the water. "Somebody gimme a clip for my gun! I'm out!" She held out her sidearm as the wide-eyed sailors backed away from her fury.

Richy had packed up whatever stuff he thought he would need. He couldn't see his apocalypse-dad from his vantage, but he definitely saw that Ship and Remo needed help. He had identified Remo as the one being carried by his clothing. The boy had no illusions about the danger he was about to face when trying to save the endangered men, but they were his family.

He and his sister had sat in an attic for a year, freezing, roasting, and shitting in a bucket while the dead killed every living thing in his town. His parents and his brother included. He would not lose another family member and the two guys down there were family. He checked the load on the sidearm he had pulled from the footlocker. He took an additional four of the ten magazines. He checked himself over and was ready to descend the ladder into Hell.

"They made it!" Kyle yelled.

Richy whipped his head up so hard he hurt his neck. "Let me see!" Sam gave him the binoculars as Kyle was looking through the scoped rifle. Richy smiled. "Kat."

The boy shook his head and immediately regretted it as he had just injured his neck. He absentmindedly scratched at his left bicep. Kat, Ship, and Remo were on the sub, men were attending to Remo as he lay stretched out, apparently unconscious. The other man was Mr. Martingale. Richy glanced at his arm where the dead thing had scratched him. It stung just a bit and had already stopped bleeding.

"Kyle."

The taller boy glanced at him. "May I have the rifle please?" The boys traded weapon for optic and soon Richy had the rifle scope to his eye. He put the crosshairs on Martingale's head. It was a very long shot for an inexperienced shooter, so he lowered the barrel until the man's ample belly was in the sight picture. Richy pulled his eye from the scope long enough to look once more at the twin furrows in his arm, then re-sighted.

There would be no coming back from this. The word *murder* flitted across his mind. This was a different world now, though. While this man had not directly tried to kill them, he had put Richy, his friends, and his sister in a position where they could be killed, and then had left them to die.

Richy let out half a breath, tightened his finger on the trigger, and felt a small hand on his arm. The boy glanced down at Sam. She didn't say a word. Didn't even nod, but he knew what she was about.

"You know what he did," Richy told her. "What will he do next time, and to who?"

"I didn't stop you for him," she answered.

Richy lowered the rifle and sighed. He smiled at Sam. "Did you just save two lives?"

Sam shrugged.

"Alright," Richy sighed again. He shifted the end of the rifle barrel to the dock and shook his head. "They're still pouring onto the island. How did they know we're here?" He stuck his hand out to Sam, who read his mind and passed him the radio.

"Mr. Barnes?"

"*I'm here; who is this?*"

"It's Richy on the water tower. The dead are still coming ashore by the dock. I'm looking at the rest of the island and it's crawling with dead people."

"*Just hang on, we'll be there in about an hour.*"

Richy looked Sam in the eyes. She stared back and nodded.

"Sir, in an hour there will be more zombies on this island than bullets. If we wait for you, you'll never get to us. We—"

"*Richy, we have a lot of ammo.*" It was Commander Pitt on the radio now. "*I need you to stay up there and we'll get to you as soon as we can.*"

"Sir, if we stay here for ten more minutes, we're dead. You're dead too if you try to get to us. There's a thousand of them now. There's an opening I can see if we go soon, but it will close as soon as the dead pinch it. That's in ten minutes or so and then nobody is ever getting to us without a tank."

"*Son, if you come down from there, you'll be—*"

"If we stay, we're dead. We're heading for the sub now. Don't come for us or you'll find an empty water tower."

"*Richy, don't leave that—*"

Richy switched the radio off. "He sounded pissed. We go or we die, look." He pointed to the dead that were moving steadily toward them from the east. "There's only a few below us. We smoke them and run for the sub."

It was Kyle's turn to point. "But, look, There's a ton of them by the sub, too."

"Most of them went into the water. There are about fifteen or twenty walking around right where we need to go." Richy switched the radio on and called out, "Can anybody on the submarine hear me?"

"*This is the Florida, identify yourself. Please give your location and a SITREP. The Florida is—*"

"Yeah, I don't have a lot of time for your cool military talk. I'm fifteen-years-old and I'm coming fast with two other kids to the sub. If you aren't ready for us, we're dead. We'll be there in five minutes. Also, one of the kids is Rick Barnes' daughter, so don't be late with the bullets and stuff."

"*Listen, kid—*"

"Five minutes!" Richy shouted into the radio and switched it off again.

"You ok with this, Sam?"

"Do I have a choice?"

"Of course, you do. If you want to stay, we'll stay. I promise you this, though; we're going to die if we stay here. One of them is going to see us or hear us and then there will be a thousand of them clawing at the bottom of the water tower."

"I don't want to go either," Kyle admitted, "but he's right. There are too many of them."

Sam unclipped herself from the railing. "Then let's go."

Richy dug through the footlocker. He passed Kyle a 9mm Beretta taking one for himself as well. "Sorry, Sam, there are only two." He passed her an old K-Bar style knife and she accepted it with her thanks. "There's eight extra clips." He passed four magazines to Kyle.

Richy moved to the ladder and peered over the edge. "I can't see them below, but I know they're there. Me first, then Sam, then you." He eyed Kyle, "Don't miss."

The tall kid smiled, "You don't miss."

Richy climbed over the edge onto the ladder. He swallowed hard. It was a long way down. Six or seven rungs down and he could see them. There were only two dead under the tower, the rest having meandered off. He glanced upward to make sure his friends were following, then proceeded down. Neither of the dead saw the living and when Richy was fifteen feet from the ground, he hooked his arm through one of the rungs, drew his Beretta, and promptly dropped it. He fumbled with it for a moment before it plummeted earthward. It struck the second to last rung with a clang that would have roused the dead.

It did. Both turned slowly and saw the kids. They started toward the children and Richy began climbing down as fast as he was able. He made it to the weapon just as the dead made it to him. He rolled left, grabbed the gun, and shot the first creature in the shoulder. He readjusted, fired, and the thing crumpled. He changed his aim so that the second thing's nasal cavity was in the sight picture and squeezed the trigger. Nothing happened and in the boy's moment of confusion, the thing was on him. It grabbed him by the shirt and his weapon hand and wasted no time in trying to bite his face off. He fought it as best he could, but it was almost twice his size. The boy gagged as the stench was overpowering. It snapped at his face as he retched, but he ducked to the side and one of its teeth flew from its mouth. With a mighty shove he pushed it back and his shirt ripped. Losing one hand hold, it slammed into the ladder. Two loud reports later and the kid was toppling over with the thing as it fell. Confused, he looked up at his friends. With his arm hooked through a rung, Kyle nodded to Richy, wisps of smoke coming from the barrel of the tall boy's sidearm.

"You don't miss," Kyle repeated with some snark.

Richy cleared his misfire with a rack of the slide, the useless round flew off to his right. The other two were on the ground in short order and the three of them fled. They moved to the right of the tower and noticed that a huge contingent of dead had heard their shots and were on the way.

"We have about two minutes before they're eating us!" Kyle told him. "Follow me!"

The kids ran toward the hill they had climbed earlier. They scooted down on their butts until they hit the cement walkway. Richy fired into the head of a single undead woman in a black apron. Dead people began to make their way toward them from both directions. Dozens came from behind and several from the front. The ones that hadn't reached the sub yet turned and began their arduous trek toward the kids.

"Don't like this!" admitted Kyle.

Richy grabbed Sam's hand. "Stay here, then!" They ran down the walkway toward the submarine. Richy could see sailors on the foredeck scrambling to get the gangway back to the island. This time Ship was assisting, and he was able to bring great strength. Both boys fired into the oncoming mini-horde, selectively picking targets. They did well but couldn't get all of the dead. They thinned out the herd enough that they were able to skirt past the reaching hands. Incoming rounds from the sailors helped as well and soon the kids were through the gap and sprinting for the safety of the sailors and their sub-machine guns.

Two of the men were using hand signals and yelling for the children to *Come on!*

They raced up the gangway followed by the armed sailors, Kat and Ship grabbing Richy. Kat gave him a high-five. "That was all kinds of ballsy, kid!"

"We're good like that," he answered her.

Several of the sailors and Kyle pointed at the hill between them and the water tower, "Look!"

Dozens of undead walked headlong off the top of the hill and tumbled to the walkway beneath.

Kat folded her arms, "Looks like a fuk'n Slip n Slide."

"The agony of defeat," added one of the sailors.

NO FRIGGIN' WAY
JOURNAL ENTRY 12

My head hurts. That was the first thing that came to me; pain. I opened my eyes but couldn't see much, it was pretty dark. I tried to survey my surroundings. Thin corridor, maybe five feet high, damp brick, ancient pipes overhead. I rubbed my eyes in a futile attempt to both alleviate the pain and allow me to see. Neither happened.

I sucked in a lungful of air and smelled something horrible. Then I realized the smell was coming from something in my mouth, so I spat it out immediately. I smacked my lips together and scrunched my eyes like you do when there's some revolting shit in your mouth. I spat and spat until my spitter was sore, but that taste wouldn't go away. I was wondering if a couple tubes of Crest would do it when I heard movement in the semi-darkness.

I reached for my sidearm only to realize it wasn't there. My SOG was missing from its chest sheath as well, and my rifle, if it was near me, was hidden in the darkness. My knife being gone was tantrum worthy, and I would have had a self-pity party right then and there if not for what happened next.

Something put its hand on my shoulder, and I shot to my feet. A stupid action, because if you remember, there were pipes up there.

I woke back up an indeterminate amount of time later. Could have been ten seconds or this whole apocalypse thingie could be over. I dunno. I *do* know that my head hurt ten times worse than it had before I had launched it at some cast iron pipes.

Fucking ouch. Neck hurt too, but I would survive.

I still had that nasty taste in my mouth, so I tried to spit, but had no saliva. I reached for my canteen, but like my weapons, it was gone. Something gently nudged me, and I swear to Christ I almost got reacquainted with those damn pipes. I shot a look toward the nudger and noticed my canteen. I followed the extended arm back to the person it was attached to and lo and behold it was ninja-boy.

He nodded at me and pushed the canteen a little harder. I accepted and took a swig, rinsing and spitting.

It was delicious and I instantly felt better. Not good, but better. Another swig, this one accompanied by a swallow, and I was right as

182

rain. All we needed was hookers and tequila and this would be the perfect Saturday night out.

Except it was Monday, I think, and I was in some kind of access tunnel with a screaming headache in the middle of the zombie apocalypse with one of those almost-zombies handing me water.

Now *that*, Dear Reader, is a sentence you are unlikely to read again.

As my eyes began to penetrate the gloom, I noticed that ninja-boy was feverish and twitchy, just like any other Runner. The difference with this Runner, I mean other than the obvious fact that he wasn't trying to use my skull as a beer stein, was that he appeared... *focused*.

Runners couldn't stand for five seconds without screaming or attacking the nearest moving thing, including other Runners and the dead. It was rare, but Runners could fight each other. This kid didn't do any of that. Infected? Sure. Dangerous to me? I wasn't getting that off him, and that was new. More than that, he seemed to understand his environment. He looked around just like I did, but he didn't whip his head back and forth and have his red eyes search in all directions the way I had seen Runners do.

Then I had an epiphany. It actually made my head hurt worse. This kid was infected with whatever shit this is. He wasn't attacking me because I was also infected.

I was infected. I could say it a hundred times and it still probably wouldn't compute. Up until now, I had known this shit swimming around inside me couldn't be passed from yours truly to someone else, but I hadn't ever bitten anybody. Well, nobody except a prick Sheriff in Utah, but he totally deserved it. He never got the chance to turn though, as his buddy popped him in the dome with a rifle that would have made Tom Horn proud.

So, could I infect others? I didn't think so as I had engaged in many fluid transfers with my apocalypse wife, and she hadn't gotten infected. I remembered something Ship had said... I mean wrote down. What if I reached my threshold with this virus thing and I go feral? Would I then want to use eyeballs as marbles too?

I couldn't have that, but I also didn't want to give myself a 9mm face-enema if I was fine.

I took another swig and fought the revolting taste in my mouth. It tasted like... I looked at the kid. "Shitty taste in my mouth."

He glanced at me briefly then pointed toward the floor of the little tunnel five feet away. A former ambulatory deceased man lay in a crumpled heap, his back in the corner of the tunnel, his face mercilessly looking right at me. Most of his face had been torn away, and that was nothing new, but the bites didn't look old. They looked like someone had…

No.

I looked at my chest. What I saw there made me pull my shirt out a bit so I could study it. The vile black shit that the dead have for blood coated my shirt. My hand shot like a striking rattlesnake to my face and I felt that sticky, gooey shit there too.

I turned over and puked my guts out. I don't know what was in the vomit because I couldn't see the puddle in the darkness but let me clue you in to something: I wasn't fucking hungry. I was quite happy not seeing.

My head hurt worse when I was done, and I could hear the noises of the dead. They were outside of whatever we were in. I was going to jump to my feet, but the kid stopped me and pointed up.

I nodded, a really dumb thing to do as everything from the nipples up was in agony. I stood and so did he. He jerked his twitchy head toward wherever the tunnel went, and he began to move in that direction. I followed him.

In a few minutes we came to a room with big machines. I had no idea what they were, but they hadn't been used in decades. It was significantly darker in the room than in the tunnel, but for some reason I could see much better. I know that doesn't make sense, but I really could see better. Until a flashlight shined right in my face.

I threw my arm up to protect my eyes and the beam lowered. I dropped my arm and three figures stepped out from between the rusty, antiquated machines.

They glanced at each other, then back at me. They were all shaky and feverish, with sweaty faces. The blood-red eyes gave them away first though.

Infected. Runners.

They did not try to kill me.

I went into sensory overload for a moment and checked out. I may not have come back from this one except I heard something that I couldn't possibly hear.

"You should come with us," the one with the light said.

Said is probably the wrong term because the voice was not human. If you picture a person gargling with broken glass, then swallowing some gasoline followed by a lit match, the resulting fuckery that is expelled from that person's mouth still couldn't sum up what that voice sounded like. It tore long shreds from my sanity curtain because *no*. Just, *no*.

"With us," repeated the woman to the right of the light-bringer.

I took an involuntary step back. An action that did not go unnoticed and the two flankers looked like they were about to jump me.

The dude with the flashlight growled, "*Leave it!*" His people glanced at him and stopped.

I needed to know a few things before I retreated into an impenetrable terror shell or just outright dropped dead, so I managed a quick, "Who are you?"

"Not bad," the thing said, then thought better of it. It looked angry when it said, "Not... *evil*." Granted, these fucking things always looked mad. "This place, the island," It looked around for a moment, "not safe for you."

I wanted to tell him *No shit, the place crawls with infected*, but then realized that he and his buddies were cousins to the things that were eating people and had likely murdered some folks prior to now themselves. Then I thought maybe the guy was saying I wasn't safe because my friends might shoot me when they saw my red eyes.

"I... I can't come with you," I told it, shaking my damaged noggin.

It grunted, nodded to its companions, and they disappeared in between the machines.

I looked to Ninja, but he wasn't behind me anymore.

Did that just fucking happen? Did infected just converse with me?

My dome was threatening succession from the Union, so I decided to make myself scarce. I stepped on something and looked down to see my Sig and my SOG wrapped neatly together on the machine-room floor.

I would need them in a moment. The rifles, both mine and Remo's, were not present.

The sounds of the dead floated into the tunnel as I followed the pipes back to the entrance. An ancient steel door greeted me, and this door had a little hatch in it that looked like a mail slot but was at eye-level. A peephole.

I shrugged and pulled the steel peephole cover open. It made a screech the likes of which had likely never been heard before. Honestly, it sounded like the rending of metal from when I was on a container ship in a hurricane.

Every single dead eye outside that fucking peephole peeped back. Both of them, because there was only one dead woman. I had to work a little to get the door open. Hey, it was rusty, and my head hurt. By the time it was open, the woman was reaching for me. Part of me wanted to let her grab me to see if I was still unsavory toward the undead. The *Fuck That* portion of my brain won though, and I brought my blade down in an overhead arc onto her dome.

The knife skidded off and down the side of her face, carving a fillet off that looked like a slice of Thanksgiving turkey. Ya know, except for all the nasty shit.

A flap of zombie face fell down over her eye, but she still latched onto me. I went for the eye-poke and twisted the blade when it hit home. My SOG came out with a sucking sound and that was when I noticed that I had been noticed. They were probably angry that I had wiped my blade on this nice dead lady's shirt. They were coming and I didn't want to play with them. I wanted to take my knife and go home. The noise of them was getting to me, that hacking rasp and those mournful wails scratching fingernails down the chalkboard of my mind.

My mag pouch was gone. No idea where it had gotten to, but I hoped whoever had it was putting it to good use. Likely it was being trod upon somewhere by undead shoes. I ejected the mag on my Sig. For those of you who haven't used a Sig Sauer pistol in the apocalypse, you need to find one. I'm no gun expert but I can tell you, this one is nice. It's a P229, the shorter version of the P226. The action is great, and I can hit a zombie dome at fifty feet most of the time. The magazines have these little holes near the primers for each round in the mag so you can count your rounds without unloading. I fucking love that, and next to the cool iridium sights, it is the best part of the weapon.

I had eight shots left. Eight shots to get me from wherever I was to either the sub or back to the lighthouse. Both had their pros and cons. The sub had Ship, if he made it, but the lighthouse had Donna. I really wanted some play time with the wife, but I wouldn't get the princess if I didn't slay the dragons.

The sub it was then. I took stock of my bearings and realized I couldn't see much from where I was. The dead were coming, but maybe they didn't want to eat me anymore. The thing is, that's a bitch to test and I was unwilling. I jogged forward and looked up. I could see the top of the water tower over the building next to me. That meant the sub was to the east. I jogged that way and sure enough, I could see water. Granted, I was on a friggin Island, so any direction I looked meant water, but I could also see the mainland, so I knew I was on the right track.

I rounded the corner of the building and could see the black tube in the less-black water. The only thing between me and the sub was... my finger started bobbing up and down as I counted. Carry the two… about eighty undead.

Pity I had also lost my radio. Ship and Remo would have a hemorrhage over that one.

The dead behind me were closing, but they were three minutes out at least. I made it to the hill overlooking the bay and there was a lone undead dude considering the drop. He stood there with his back to me, either not seeing the meat popsicles crawling all over the sub or not giving a shit about them.

I didn't ask him. I just lashed out with my boot and kicked him in the back. He went ass over teakettle, flopping down the hill all rag-doll like. The landing was unkind, and he looked a bit on the broken side, but that was totally ok with me. Now he saw the sub, or decided to give a shit, but his right leg was at an angle that would have made Joe Theismann puke. There were bones sticking out as well. These things are both extremely durable, but brittle as fuck at the same time.

I waved my arms around like I was doing jumping jacks and eventually somebody saw me. The only person I knew for sure that was on the boat was Ship.

I began to hear gunfire and the dead started to drop. Judging the distance between the sub and the rocks, there was no way I could jump it. I also watched half a dozen of the things slip between the rocks and the metal, so who knows how many submerged dead were waiting to grab at my ankles.

Fuck that noise. Been there, done that. It ain't fun.

A quick glance behind me showed that the dead had been doing some gaining. They were about fifty feet away and would be on me in thirty seconds.

Eight shots. I would make them count before I had to go to the knife. I slid down the hill on my butt. My BDUs would be filthy, but I would rather have a dirty ass than have it bitten off.

I could see some sailors messing with a bridge thingie from the sub to the rocks. It was a long way, so it must have been heavy. Ship helped and soon two undead were making their way up the aluminum. The sailors plugged them and then fanned out across the rocks, eliminating threats. I used all eight rounds and the slide stayed back on my Sig. By the time I got to the gangway, the ground was littered with stinking bodies.

I was expecting the stinkeye from the Yeti, but he smiled and grabbed me in a bear hug. My feet came off the ground in an undignified manner but asking him to stop was impossible as all the air had been crushed out of my lungs.

He put me down, grabbed my shoulders and looked me in the eye.

"I love you too," I said, and he started with that stupid shaking thing he does when he begins his silent guffaws.

"'Bout fuck'n time," I heard over the commotion and spun to see Kat. I made to hug her, and she backed up. "I'm not huggin' you until you take a shower." She waved a hand in front of her nose, "Nasty ass."

We all moved back to the submarine, and I realized that with everything that had happened since I showed up, this was the first time I had been on it. Her? Is a sub a her? All the sailors but the two kneelers and two guys with submachine guns stayed out with us. The rest of the sailors scrambled up a ladder into the thing that sticks out of the middle of the sub and disappeared.

I was all smiles until I saw two guys working on someone on the deck. They had an IV and looked to be hurrying. Richy was on his knees next to the person on the ground holding his hand.

I tried to get to them, knowing who was on their back, but the little douche who had shot Remo was suddenly in my face. "You made it! Listen, I just want to thank—"

"Save it," I told him and brushed past. I didn't mean to be a dick, but I wanted to check on my bullet ridden buddy.

I squatted down. "How is he?" I asked the medics. I would find out later that they were called corpsmen, but I didn't care at that time.

"Stable," one of them said without looking up, "but we'll know more when we get in there. He's going to need surgery to remove the bullet."

I looked at a smiling Richy. "S'up, kid."

"'Nother day in paradise."

"Where's your sister?"

"She's in this tin can with Dallas, I hope."

Now the medics did look up. Both had looks of dread.

I did not fail to notice. "What?"

"We have infected on board," sighed one of them. "We've been fighting them all day."

That did it. Remo sat up and grimaced. One of the medics laughably tried to hold him down but ended up rubbing his wrist as my MARSOC buddy almost twisted it off. I stuck out a hand to Remo.

"Whoa! He needs to put his ass back on the deck until—"

I pulled the jarhead to his feet.

"Ow."

I raised an eyebrow. "Pussy."

He must have been in agony, but he smiled just the same. He pulled his sidearm and counted his load.

We made to get into the sub through that hatch in the tower, but the tall kid stopped us.

"He needs help. He's been scratched," he said.

I was dumbfounded. "What? He who?"

The kid lowered his eyes and pointed at Richy.

"Rich?" I asked, my mouth suddenly dry again. My headache had been forgotten, but it made an astonishing reappearance.

Two of the sailors began to raise their weapons to point at my kid. One of them went flying across the top of the sub, his weapon clattering to the steel as he put a hand out to stop from going over the side. The other had Kat's forearm across his throat from behind and her sidearm to his head.

"You fuck'n think so, huh?" she asked him with such menace that I have no doubt the sailor kid was full code brown.

Richy shrugged. "Doesn't even hurt."

The medic with two good wrists rushed to Richy to check him out. He moved Richy's left arm around for a sec checking stuff, then reached in his pack, pulled out a bottle of clear liquid, and dumped half of it all over the kid's arm.

"Fucking hurts now!" the kid squealed, then hissed in pain.

The medic dude stood. "Superficial, but there's broken skin. We won't know anything for a few hours, but he needs to be isolated."

"Richy, when did this happen?" demanded Remo, who was looking more like the killer he was by the second. I'm actually shocked the fucking bullet that's in him didn't veer off course out of pure fright when it saw where it was going.

"Ask him!" Sam screamed almost in tears. Everybody followed the tip of her finger. It was pointing directly at the little shit who had shot Remo. Sam buried her face in Kat's side and did begin to cry. Kat let the sailor go when she realized the guy wasn't going to shoot Richy.

The accused was darting his eyes back and forth to everyone on the deck of the submarine. He saw the looks he was receiving and pointed his finger at Sam. "That little brat is a liar! Everybody knows she has it in for me!"

"He locked us in one of the tunnels," Kyle said softly. "When the dead came out of a hole behind us, he just ran away when he saw them. He left us."

"I had to save the island!" the guy shrieked, eyes still flying every which way. If he had said anything else, anything at all, he would probably be sitting in a cell right now.

Kat held Sam's face in her side as she had surmised what was about to happen. "Don't watch this," she told Sam.

I pulled my pistol, but Remo put his hand on my hand. It would have done me no good anyway because the Sig was empty. I started toward him, but the guy tried to escape. He turned and sprinted four inches into Ship, and short of using a lightsaber, the little prick was going nowhere. With a single tear in his eye, Ship reached down, picked the thrashing douche up over his seven-foot head, and slammed him down face first into the steel of the submarine.

Bumbles did not bounce.

Pretty much everything inside the guy broke and I both heard and saw his neck snap from ten feet away. The backs of his shoes went way past the top of his head as his spine splintered. Like everything Ship did, it was quick, painless, and efficient.

"Dammit, Ship," Remo said quietly as he knew what this meant. Our group had just murdered one of the Alcatraz group. No matter how shitty of a person or how much he needed murdering, or the fact that shit was different in the apocalypse, this wasn't going to fly.

The medic, looking at the jelly-thing that had been Bumbles, redirected his eyes first to the other medic, then to Richy, then to me. "I didn't see shit."

"Holy fuck!" yelled the sailor that had been kicked in the ass by Kat. "You... you killed him?"

"A little!" I yelled back.

The medic stood and pointed at the sailor. "I didn't see shit, Squid, and neither did you! Guy left kids to die. Fuck him."

The look the medic gave me told me that he didn't know if this sailor would report what had happened to his superiors. That meant we needed to get our people and find a new place to live. I mean why not? That's the way shit goes with me. But this time it had been Ship that fucked shit up.

"Where's my rifle?" asked Remo as he searched the gleaming black deck of the submarine. Everybody looked at me.

"Uhhh..."

BILLY BOB
SOMEWHERE ON ALCATRAZ

"Takes… takes a lot out of you… you know?" Bob heaved as he leaned against a metal railing next to the cement walkway.

Billy, too tired to answer, held up one finger and heaved as well. He stood and looked behind them. Both the walkway and the surrounding grounds were littered with bodies. He smiled a tired smile, then froze. "I… I lost count!"

"Let's call it a hundred a piece, yeah?"

Billy pointed at his friend. "I like it!" He regarded his sword. Other than the scratches put on it by the dead stepping on it, it appeared brand new. "Cursed?"

"S'what the legend says. Like I said though, it might be a rip off."

Billy frowned. "I didn't steal it! I mean, I took it out of a dead guy, that's not stealing, right?"

"Nah, it's yours. You took it from a conquered foe. It's what the Samurai did on the reg. And I meant a fake, not that you stole it."

"Oh," Billy said, turning the gleaming blade over in his hand. "I kinda liked the idea of a cursed sword, I'm not gonna lie."

Bob shrugged. "That's what everybody says until the curse gets them." He pointed behind Billy. "No rest for the wicked. Or maybe the cursed?"

Billy glanced behind him. He rolled his eyes and stared at the sky. "Ohhhhh! Come on! I want to sit for a spell. Huh. I sound like Pittsburgh."

"Huh?"

"Nothing." He reached into his right hip pocket, pulled out a Pepsi, popped the top and took a huge pull. He let out a dainty burp and passed the can to Bob, who took a sip and tried to pass it back. "Finish it," Billy told him with another burp.

Several of the dead moved perpendicular to them, all but one looking like the grey things they usually do. Billy sighed when he saw a freshly dead thing. It was infected, but its face was hardly touched. "Martin."

"You know him?"

"Yeah, he was a good guy. I can't leave him like this." Billy moved toward the man he had once known. The man had gone from college professor to homeless, to undead slayer, to Alcatraz resident, to undead. The needlessness of it made Billy sad.

"I'll come with," Bob told him.

The two strode tiredly up to the small group of infected and Billy raised his sword. "Sorry, Martin, I—" The dead thing spun quickly and launched itself at Billy, hitting him at chest level and making it impossible for Billy to make his weapon effective. The Martin-thing began to scream as it pushed and they both went down, Billy landing hard on his tailbone.

"Ow!" he yelled at his infected friend's face. "You're not dead! Where are your glasses?" The thing wasn't trying to bite him but instead was throwing haymakers that pounded on Billy's forearms. It lasted about five seconds before a baseball bat connected with the side of Martin's head and he went sprawling. The infected wasn't dead, but it was messed up. Bob strode forward and brought his bat down on the infected once on its shoulder, once into its ribs, and the third struck the thing's head again.

Martin mercifully stopped moving. Billy, on his back, let out a big breath and looked sideways at his now dead friend. He let out a long sigh, "Owwwwww."

Bob held a hand down to him. Billy blinked and stared at the offered hand. "I might just lay here for a sec. Collect my thoughts, ya know?"

"Not too long." Bob pointed at the other dead who were almost upon them. Billy grabbed the hand and Bob pulled him to his feet. "Ready?"

"No, I'm tired."

"They don't..." THUMP! "...care." Bob told him as he whacked a dead woman in the side of the head.

Billy slashed at a dead thing's neck and poked his blade through the eye of another. He was getting better with the sword. "You would think, what with this being an island and all, plus the fact that it is supposed to be really difficult to swim to the mainland because of the current, that these dead things would not be able to get here."

THUMP! Bob wrung out his hands They were starting to get numb from the constant vibration of bat vs. skull. "But they didn't swim. They must walk from the mainland under the water. If they swam, they would be dragged out to sea. The current is..." THUMP! "way worse on the surface."

"Sure, smarty pants. I mean, it doesn't really matter, they're here."

"But not *here*," Bob smirked. They both looked around at the carnage they had wrought. Bodies lay everywhere, the undead destroyed by the two of them. Nothing moved except Bob's fingers as he tried to flex the pain away. "Hurts, you know?"

Billy nodded as he sat on a stone bench. "Been there. You gotta get a Muramasa. Way easier on the old digits. Wanna have a quick sit-down? Pretty sure I was supposed to be doing something, but I can't remember what it was."

"I hate that!" agreed Bob as he pushed a truly dead man off a stone bench. He was going to sit but thought better of it when he noticed the fluids the dead thing had left behind on the cement. "Ew. You'd think these things would be all dried up and stuff after all this time, but they're still all…"

"Gooey," they both said at the same time.

"We should try for the sub," Bob said suddenly.

"What does that mean?"

"Go to the sub. The submarine? The big black death tube that sinks boats. It's anchored over there," Bob pointed. "Or maybe there?" he pointed in a different direction.

"Nah, it's to the south of the island," Billy told him, pointing east. "That way."

Billy brightened. "Wait! That's what I was supposed to do! Get to the sub to make sure Sam is ok!"

"I thought Sam was on the water tower?"

"Nah, sub. Let's go."

Billy stood up from the bench and both men turned in different directions. Bob about faced and moved quickly to catch up with Billy. They strode east, talking about swords and Pepsi.

FOREDECK
USS FLORIDA

Dallas shook his head. "Nope."

Clyde stared at him. The smell of all the humans in this tiny room couldn't overpower the stink of the metal and electrical components. He didn't like it. He did like the scent emanating from the big guy's pocket. He whined.

"Said no, dog. I'm try'na listen."

Dallas turned to face McInerney as he doled out orders. Three kids; the two girls and the boy Caleb, were also in the room. The older girl was listening, but the younger two were fiddling with their clothing. It was hot and cramped in this room, and nobody hated it more than Clyde.

The dog put his paw on Dallas' leg.

"Ow! Gotta get them nails trimmed, ya leg humpin' flea-farm," Dallas told him and ripped a piece of pepper jerky in half. He tossed the pooch a big piece. "Now, hush." The big Texan began to chew on his half of the snack.

"Report in every five minutes and stay alive," McInerney finished.

"Aye, sir!" eight men and one woman replied. They filed out of the conning tower checking weapons and gear.

The captain moved past a sailor staring into the feed of one of the periscopes. He paused and put a hand on the man's shoulder. "Anything?"

"Negative, sir. No seaward targets and the island still crawls with dead people."

"Anything from SONAR yet?"

"Negative." The crew member picked up a wired microphone. "SONAR, Conn. Respond." He repeated the command and glanced at his captain, shaking his head.

"Keep trying."

"Aye, sir."

McInerney glanced at the girls before he crossed the deck to them. "You provided us with excellent intel. I wanted to thank you for that."

"He helped," Chloe said with a chin wag toward Moe's back. The sailor would be the last of the undead hunters through the hatch. He checked the load on the MP5 that he and the kids had taken from the footlocker. Before he stepped through the hatch, he glanced back at his captain and nodded. He glanced at Chloe and Vanessa. Vanessa saluted him, and he chucked the girls a huge smile.

"I know," replied the sub commander. "I asked him how he kept the two of you safe and he told me he didn't. He said it was the other way around." He raised an eyebrow, "Is there truth to that?"

Chloe shrugged. "Anybody not doing everything they can to fight these things is likely one of them by now. We would have been dead without him."

McInerney smiled. "He said that too."

The submariner didn't know how many of the dead were aboard his boat. They multiply like rabbits, but worse, for every one of us lost, there's one of them gained. A two-fold increase in their numbers. He was thinking about the dangers he had sent his men and women into in the tight quarters of the Florida when the sound of gunshots echoed off the guarded hatch in the conn.

"Thinning the herd?" he asked the sailor on the periscope.

"Aye, sir. We're also heavy a few more civvies. One of them is that enormous guy that came in the other day. He seems to be with his friends and there are some kids with them too. One looks wounded."

"What?" Chloe demanded, "Who?"

"I don't know their names. Can you—"

"Let me see!" She tugged on the sailor's shirt.

Before he could even look to his captain, McInerney told him she could use the periscope.

"Richy!" she shouted when she looked at the screen. "And Ship, and Kat, and… Oh no. Remo's hurt. Wait a minute… Oh shit!"

The sailor and McInerney looked concerned. "What is it?" the sailor asked hurriedly.

Chloe stepped away from the periscope and looked absolutely everywhere but at the captain. "Nothing. It's all good."

The sailor moved to the secondary periscope, but McInerney went for the hatch ladder.

"One of the civvies is down, sir. He's not moving."

The captain moved to the exit hatch and spun quickly. He pointed at Dallas, "My dog does *not* have fleas, Texas!" He spun back and hurried down the corridor to the top hatch access with Chloe and Vanessa in tow.

The two hatch guards glanced at each other with raised eyebrows. Both toted sub machine guns with cold-loaded rounds, but neither brought the barrels up when they saw the big guy throw the little guy.

"I mean you saw that, right?"

"Depends. If you're asking me if I saw that prick get what was coming to him, yeah, for sure I saw it." The guard made a disgusted face. "That shit will stick with me too. But if you're asking me if I saw *how* it happened..." his face hardened, and he looked out into the bay. He jutted his lower lip out and shook his head, "...nah, missed it."

"Report!" they both heard and almost shit themselves.

McInerney and the girls both climbed out onto the steaming hot, black foredeck of the Florida.

"Mostly quiet up here, sir. I mean, other than that." The guard pointed at a non-moving Martingale.

"A few dead tried to get up the gangway when we were getting civvies on board, but the deck crew took care of it. Nothing got close."

"And what happened to him?"

"Didn't see anything..." both guards said in unison and glared at each other.

McInerney strode toward the crowd encircling the dead man. His boots thundered across the steel. "Report!" he bellowed a second time.

"Aye, sir!" the kneeling medic retorted as he stood. "The kids told us that this asshole left them for the dead. That guy, (he pointed at the guy with the torn face) drew his sidearm to apprehend the asshole, who then made a run for it. The asshole collided with the big dude, then drew a firearm, at which point the big dude disarmed him and turned him into pulp."

"He murdered him?"

Ship put his hand on his sidearm and Kat raised the barrel of her rifle up almost imperceptibly.

"Negative, sir. It was justifiable. The guy was off his rocker and left kids to die."

"That is not your decision to make!" McInerney was incensed. "That's up to Detective Meara! He's in charge of civilian justice, not any of you!"

"He wasn't here," the guy with the ripped lip said. "Neither were you. I would have plugged him myself, but I'm shit out of ammo." He glanced at McInerney and quickly added, "Sir."

"He shot me," Remo said, his IV bag attached to his shoulder strap with medical tape. He looked both woozy and strong at the same time.

"Help him," the captain told the medic. He ran a tired palm over his buzz-cut, then sighed a weary sigh. "We'll deal with this later. Right now, we have dead inside my boat, dead all over the island, and the group is spread out. First, we need to clear my boat. Then, we get all the living people to safety. Then, we clear the island."

DEATH TUBE
USS FLORIDA

The captain reminded me of the captain of a Destroyer I know. Is there a mold where they make these dudes who just seep authority out of their pores? Where the last guy and I didn't hit it off until a mutual respect had been achieved, this guy was just a straight up douche. What with his telling us what to do and how to do it. Prominently displaying his pointing and demanding demeanor.

I liked him immediately. I had gone out of my way to be a dick to Schumitz, the last captain, and it had been a mistake because he turned out to be someone that I could not only trust, but that had saved my bacon. I would not make that mistake again. I still wasn't enthused about authority figures, and this dude positively radiated authority, but I would give him the benefit of the doubt until he pulled some monkey shit.

"Captain, my team will help clear the sub."

I actually looked around for a sec to see which of the dickheads in my crew would utter such nonsense, then had to scrunch my eyes closed hard because I realized it had been me.

The captain gave a curt nod and I noticed Ship, Kat, and Remo began checking their gear.

"Whoa!" I blurted and everybody looked at me. I pointed at Remo, "You're broken." I kept my finger up but shifted it to Ship, "You won't fit through the front door let alone keep your noggin un-lacerated from the hatches inside this thing. And you…" My finger had moved of its own accord toward Kat and we both stared at each other over it. Where my glare was all puppies and kittens, hers was the temperature of an airburst nuclear device at ground zero. I swallowed so hard it echoed off the sub. "Are coming with me," I finished.

She shook her head like I was a moron, so I spun to face the boss.

"Uhh, Captain? You got any ammo?"

***

It's really easy to be all brave and show how cool you are when you're standing on the deck of a submarine with the waning sun on your back and a cool breeze in the apocalyptic California air. It is a completely

198

different thing to be standing inside said submarine, the smells of the unwashed and metal constricting you almost as tightly as the quarters of whatever room we were standing in. I had left Richy, Chloe, Remo, and an incensed Ship on the deck above us. Remo was fucked up. He would never admit it and could still probably kill everyone on this steel beast blindfolded, but he had a bullet in him and wasn't 100%.

Richy and Remo were being tended to by the medic. Ship on the other hand was going to kill me, of that I had no doubts. He was constantly telling me that I shouldn't do exactly what I was about to do. Moreover, he couldn't come with me on this one. It wasn't that he didn't try, but McInerney put the kibosh on that.

I'm a big dude. Six-two and about one eighty. My shoulders barely fit through the hatches down here and I still turn sideways to go through them. Ship? He's *twice* as big as me. He pushed four hundred pounds and is just shy of seven foot five. It was physically impossible for him to be effective in this environment. He knew it, I knew it, and he knew I knew he knew it. I think that was the thing that pissed him off the most.

He was just too fucking big. The captain had told him as much and right then I was pretty happy Ship couldn't talk. I also knew, beyond a shadow of a doubt, that if Ship wanted to chew through the hull of this thing, nothing would stop him.

Remo put up no stink at all, and that scared me. He knew he would be a liability down here. Kat was chomping at the bit to kill something, and that *terrified* me. Kat was absolutely, utterly fearless, but she was also stubborn AF. She was good taking orders to a point, but once that point was reached, anything could happen. I couldn't have her being bitten in here where there was no room to evade a mosquito let alone a hundred-fifty-pound dead thing that wanted to bite her.

So, I stuck her in the middle. There were four of us. Two sailors, Kat and me. One of them was an ensign and I dunno what the fuck the other dude was. I don't even know what an ensign is. Their names were Tom and Harry. No shit.

We weren't even short a Dick, because I was there. There were so many dead on this submarine, we might come up with one more of each anyway.

Two teams were already sweeping the sub, but they had encountered such heavy resistance that they had been forced into retreat several times.

I had wanted to use my Sig, but was told no. They issued me a Remington shotgun. It was a short, stubby thing, but I liked the feel of it. I'm sure Ship, Remo, and every other military dude on this boat would be able to say, "Oh that's a (insert model name here)." but I had no idea what it was.

"My dad had an 87P," Kat said aloud, marveling at the shotgun, "how about you?"

Well, that was fucking humiliating.

"Yeah. Yeah, it's great. Kicks a bit much, but…"

All three of them stared at me for a second. I couldn't help but think I had committed some breach of etiquette or had said something ridiculous. As luck would have it, I didn't have time to find out which.

Harry made a fist. He chin-wagged toward a blood smear on the wall of the sub. It was a sliding hand-print, and when we looked more closely, the whole area was bloody.

"Don't get any on you," I told them under my breath.

The hatch in front of us was open, but we couldn't hear anything in the room in front of us. Harry made to step through, but I halted him and pulled out my inspection mirror. It had been bequeathed to me by a good friend and I experienced a brief moment of sadness. I poked the little mirror through the hatch and almost shit. Two feet to the right of the other side of the hatch was an infected. He was all twitchy and shit, but totally silent. He also had his back to the mirror but jerked around as I withdrew it. The room was a cafeteria, not sure what they call that on a sub. I know it's a galley on a boat. There were several bodies on the floor in addition to the asshole Runner.

My finger shot to my mouth in a *shhhh*-ing motion. They all got it, not that we had be squawking anyway. I drew my SOG from its well-used sheath. Kat put her hand on my arm and vehemently shook her head *No!* She held out her shotgun and it was my turn to shake my head in the negative. I held the knife in my fist and stepped through the hatch as quietly as possible.

The fucking thing was looking right at me. Its eyebrows shot to the sky and it leapt.

My head always seems to hurt in the apocalypse. I'm always bumping it, or somebody is thumping it, or I haven't had water in a day or two. Regardless, my head was killing me as this creature, a submariner with a bite mark and a bullet hole in his side, came shrieking at me. He managed to get his nasty paws on me before I was able to twist and throw him into the bulkhead. I heard the air get pushed out of his lungs and it was my turn to leap.

I landed on him hard and drove the knife into his throat to the hilt. He made a quick gagging noise until I turned the blade, then his eyes rolled back into his noggin and he was gone. He didn't take any time bleeding out, he just up and died. I used my blade to make sure he wouldn't get up again. I wiped my hands on his pants and stood, glancing around the room. My eyes landed on my crew of fighters and all three had wide eyes.

I waved them into the room as quietly as possible, even though the inhuman shriek of the Runner was likely heard in Nebraska. Hey, they fuckin' yell. Maybe the dead wouldn't give a shit for once. One of the bodies on the floor stirred and began to stand and two more came through an open hatch on the far side of the room. So much for that.

"Shit!" Tom yelled and fired his shotgun into the one standing up.

I told you they had issued us shotguns. I didn't say they issued us hearing protection. Because they didn't. What you can't understand from movies, TV, or books about discharging a firearm in close quarters is how fucking loud it is. It's loud. It *hurts* it's so loud.

The good news was that the thing attempting to stand would never do that or anything else again. Its head evaporated in pink splash, and I immediately thought that intent to chastise young Tom for both deafening us and telling the entire planet where we were may have been unwarranted.

Oh, there was bad news too, I didn't forget that shit. The two dead who had stepped through the hatch across the room had brought friends. Three more from that door and two from another began to shuffle toward us. We could either retreat or end these assholes. We opted for pellets, and four shotguns barked twelve-gauge death. Another dead thing tried to make its way through the same hatch the first ones had come through, but I blew it out of its shoes, and it disappeared back down the corridor. I weaved through the bodies and tables in an attempt to shut the hatch while Harry did the same to the other one. I didn't see anything else coming, but Harry made an undignified squeak before he was able to pull his hatch closed.

I glanced around the metal room. We had succeeded in ridding the sub and the world of a few more infected and had gained one room back. Blood and goo covered everything. I wasn't sure how the sub dudes would ever get this room usable again. Enough bleach to fill the bay, maybe? Whatever had happened in here had been bad.

How had it started? Either somebody had hid a bite, and I have no idea how that wouldn't be caught, or someone had died, turned, and started some shit. That shit had turned into a storm. There were at least four infected or dead in civilian clothes and the other four were wearing uniforms or part of a uniform.

What a waste.

I shook my head and got a bit dizzy. I realized that I had accepted a mission to kill human beings the day before yesterday, had never gotten the chance, and had been running for my life ever since. Karma? That shit didn't make me woozy, it was lack of sleep and safety that grated on me. I blinked a couple of times and heard Harry on the radio.

"Copy that, sir. There are eleven bodies in here. We've secured the Galley and the port and aft hatches. There were several Limas on the other side of the port hatch and they're itching to get in." Thumps on the steel made me believe him.

"How about the aft hatch?"

Harry looked to me, and I shrugged. "Looked clear before I closed it."

"Did you get that, sir?"

"Roger. How many of ours are down?"

"Five of ours, six civvies."

"Copy," the weary voice replied. *"Is it safe to continue?"*

My eyebrows shot skyward. "Is he fucking kidding?" I whispered.

Kid chucked me a side-eye. He needed lessons from Ship if he wanted that shit to stick. "Affirmative, sir. We'll sweep aft and clear as we go. We'll make sure to close and lock all port and starboard hatches and doors along the way and fall back to the galley if we feel we may get overrun. Bravo out."

I looked at Kat and we shrugged to each other.

"I love your plan," I told Harry as he switched his radio off and clipped it to his belt.

He nodded. "Let's go."

"Yeah, about that. We need somebody to keep this room secure so we can fall back to it like you outlined in your master scheme. It would really suck if our fallback area was full of pus bags if we, ya know, actually had to fall back?"

"Yeah. Yeah, that's a good idea." He looked at Kat.

So, I'm pretty sure I've introduced you to Kat, Dear Reader. By now you should have gleaned that this particular almost-twenty-year-old young lady can melt eyeballs with a glare. She was denied that portion of DNA that allows one to exhibit both tact and self-control.

She pointed at us. "Fuck *ALL* of you!" Rude, really, as Tom had said nothing.

"I'm not staying here!"

"Not alone," I added. She shifted her eyes to mine, and I shit you not my eye juice started to boil.

"What the fuck does that mean?"

"It means that Tom is staying with you. Nobody on this death-filled contraption should ever be alone."

"So then why can't I come with you?" I could see her ire rising.

"Because I need somebody I can trust back here." I glanced at Tom, "No offense, kid, but I don't know you."

Kat made the face. It was only a matter of time before she went off like Krakatoa, so I needed a placation tactic quickly.

"Then why don't you just stay here with me?" That question had the slightest hint of a scream to it.

"Same reason. You and I are way better at dealing with the dead than these two guys." Harry began to protest, but *my* eyeball melting glare kicked in and he shut up most Ricky Tick.

"We've been out there, Kat. These assholes have been stuck in here all safe and sound since the beginning. Couple of rotations on Alcatraz, maybe some soup, or a shower, and then right back here surrounded by steel walls."

Both Tom and Harry made the agreement nod, and I knew I had won.

"I need you to keep this room safe in case the shit hits when we go deeper into this thing." I pointed at the aft hatch. "You're the best at doing that. We need your aim."

She smiled. "Then I'll go, and you stay."

Fuck.

"Nope. I know you're ferocious as hell, but I'm bigger and stronger than you. If we get surprised, I definitely have the advantage. Also, one of us could get bitten." I let that hang. "If we were long range shooting, who do you think would have the best gun, you or me? Besides, you think I want to go down there?" I pointed at the hatch again. "I'd rather do butt-stuff with a walrus."

She steamed but saw my logic. "Alright." She pointed that finger at me again. "But if you get into it, you call, and we'll come."

"Not only can you not do that, but if I call back and tell you to, or worse, if you get no contact at all, you need to shut and lock this hatch and get more people to come get us." She began to go super nova, but I held up a hand. "Think about it. If it gets bad in there, you wouldn't be able to help. It will already be too late, and we need this portion of the sub as an FOB."

"What the fuck is an FOB?"

I smiled. "A forward operating base. You have to defend this area. There are only three entrances; the one we came from, the one currently being banged on by dead people, and the aft hatch. Keep us safe."

I spun around as she said, "I will."

I took a breath and faced the hatch. A quick glance at a stainless table showed me what looked like a grilled cheese sandwich sitting on a plastic tray. There were red drops spattered across the bread that were likely not sriracha sauce. I was both repulsed and oddly famished at the same time.

LOSS
ALCATRAZ

"Most of the dead have focused on the Florida," Seyfert told the group. "There are groups clustered throughout the island and they're still coming ashore slowly." The SEAL pointed to a laminated map card, "Many of the Limas are clustered here and here." He raised his eyes to search the faces of the group, then shook his head. "Nobody's coming for us. We have to either get back to the boat or make our way to the Florida." He sighed, "Alcatraz is lost."

"Well shit," lamented Steve. "We just got here."

Danny hiked up his rifle and leaned in. "What's the plan, boss?"

"It's going to be dark soon. We go quiet and exfil to the boat we came in on. It's closer than the Florida and we can see the dead below us as we move down the hill. We just did a recon from the catwalk above and the area around us and all the way to the boat is relatively clear. We'll do it the same way we did it on the way here. Civvies in the middle, anybody with a gun on the outside of the group. Kev, you take point with Danny, and I'll take rear with Alvarez. Questions?"

"I ain't goin' nowhere," said one of the bikers. He had been sitting on one of the metal stairs and now stood. "I'm fucked." He held up his bandaged forearm. "They got me when I was trying to help with the ammo. Scratched, but I can feel that shit in me."

"Me too," Kayla agreed. "Might just stay here for a bit."

Donna and Anna looked helpless.

There was some argument from Chris and Teems about their friend staying behind to die, but when the white of his right eye flooded with red, everybody knew it was over for the biker. Kayla also felt sick, and after being scratched the way she was, it was likely a death sentence.

In the end, the group left two behind in the lighthouse as they made their way back to the boat.

They moved in absolute silence, the civilians in the center with the operators on the outside of the group. Steve and Lynda were the only civilians with firearms. A small outcropping of stone and topiary blocked

Danny's view to the right. Kev could see to the left, and he gave a two-tap to Danny's leg which was the sign to proceed. They took the corner at speed and ran into a large contingent of infected.

The dead, who had also been silent, plowed into the small group of the living and attacked immediately. There was nothing for it, so Danny fired into the crowed for a moment before he was overwhelmed. His rifle was pinned to his chest as he fell backwards, half a dozen dead on top of him.

Kev had had his back to the right as he was still clearing the left and was grabbed from behind. Teems and the bikers began firing, Seyfert and Alvarez joined in, but the dead were in amongst the living, biting and tearing.

Steve fired his weapon dry in moments, Lynda following suit quickly after.

Chris and Anna were fighting hand to hand, blades vs. teeth. Anna was bitten almost immediately but fought like a cornered tigress. Chris fired once with his rifle, realized he would never be able to bolt in another round and swung the weapon like a club.

Gary had no weapon and tried to bolt, but he had been close enough to the mini horde that he was grabbed and taken down. He never made a sound.

One of the bikers fired his shotgun point blank into the face of a dead woman in a hospital johnny, her head vaporizing in a disgusting mist. He jacked another round into the chamber but never got the chance to fire it as the infected tore his throat out.

Donna lashed out with a kick that staggered a hefty infected.

"Run!" Seyfert bellowed to the civilians, and they did.

Seyfert tried to move into the crowd, the screams of his friends urging him to help, but Alvarez grabbed him by the vest.

"No! No, they're gone!"

Seyfert spun to face him, murder in his eyes as he struggled to free himself.

"They're gone!" Alvarez screamed. "We need to move!"

The SEAL came to his senses, and he fired selectively into the crowd as he retreated. Donna pulled a sidearm from Alvarez' holster and began firing as well.

The dead had begun to feed on the fallen and Alvarez pulled a grenade. He waited until the survivors were a decent distance away and lobbed it over the heads of the few oncoming dead. The device hit the concrete with a *tink* and rolled into the feeders, but he had already sprinted after his friends.

Even at about fifty meters away the *whump* of the grenade was felt on the asphalt as they ran. Chris and Anna were both bleeding, Anna limping badly. Teems, also bleeding, fired his rifle into the crowd once more before he clicked empty. All their biker friends had been savaged and were lost. Steve and Lynda were unharmed and the only ones left from their high rise haven.

"Come on!" Alvarez screamed at Chris and Anna, as he fired his suppressed rifle. Anna fell to one knee, Chris stopping with her as they held hands. The horde, which seemed to have grown despite the bodies on the ground, staggered toward them at fifteen feet away.

"Go," she told him.

He pulled her to her feet and turned his head. A circular bite mark dribbled blood from the tooth holes in his neck under his right ear. She started to cry.

"Don't," he said and produced his own grenade. They both smiled and pulled each other close.

"No!" both Teems and Alvarez screamed as the dead reached their friends. The explosion was muffled, but it still knocked the vanguard of the horde down.

"Fuck!" Teems yelled, running his fingers over his bald head. The big biker wiped at his eyes as he fled. "Fuck!"

Steve frantically searched himself for extra rounds. "I'm out."

"Me too!" agreed Lynda.

Dead people ambled at them from the direction they had come. They were spread out, but there were too many to dodge.

"This way," urged the SEAL. The group, now down to six, had lost more than half their number in moments. "You bitten?" he asked Teems.

The biker glanced at his friend. "Huh? Who, me?"

"Yeah, you have blood on your arm."

Teems pulled his T-shirt sleeve up a bit and looked but couldn't see the source of the blood. "Dunno, am I?" He flashed his arm to Seyfert.

"Nope, but you've got a cut on your shoulder."

"Let me see!" Donna demanded.

The grizzled biker shook his head. "When we get a sec."

The SEAL pulled his magazine as he ran; he could tell by the weight he had half a mag.

Alvarez drew his wrist across his brow. "The whole island is going to be on us in a minute after the rounds we just threw. We'll never make it to the boat. I dunno how to sail it anyway."

"I know. We need to get to the Florida, but it means going through that." He pointed to the crowd in front of them. All were plodding their way toward an early dinner.

The crowd behind was closer and significantly larger. To the left of their position, infected stumbled down the hill, most losing their balance and ending up rolling into the tube steel railing. Arms reached through to grasp at the survivors jogging past on the asphalt walkway.

Alvarez put his palm on Seyfert's chest, and they stopped as a unit.

"What do we do?" demanded Lynda, fear evident in her voice.

Alvarez pointed to the right into the bay.

"Can you swim?" Seyfert answered, slinging his rifle. He moved to the other side of the walkway and leaned over the corresponding tube steel railing. A fifteen-foot slanted drop would bring them to a short beach and then into the water. No dead could be seen below them.

"Yeah," Steve said, "but I'm fifty-seven years old! I can't swim half a mile to the frikkin sub!"

"Yes, you can," Seyfert told him as he tied a quick line onto the rail. Alvarez was over the railing, down the line, and on the beach in five seconds. He cleared the small area and waved everyone else down. Seyfert helped Lynda over the barrier followed by Steve, Donna, Teems, then himself. A mottled hand grabbed his helmet, and he was forced to jerk away from the accompanying growl. He rappelled down the rope quickly, smacking into Teems before the biker could move away.

"Rock, this is Sabre, we are entering the water south southwest of the parade grounds to evade hostiles. Need watercraft for exfil, Sabre out!" Seyfert didn't wait for a reply, gently pushing Steve and Lynda toward the water.

In seconds the entire railing from east to west held back reaching arms from the hungry dead. Red eyes glared down at the survivors and the more industrious of the dead figured out how to get over the rail and plummeted to the beach.

Alvarez waded into the water and on the fourth step went under. "It gets deep fast!" he shouted.

"Shit we're really doing this?" Teems asked, nervous.

Seyfert thumbed behind him. "Better than that!"

The six of them entered the water and swam out a few meters. The dead who had tumbled down the short cliff were beginning to stand.

Lynda coughed. "I dunno how long I can swim for!"

"There's a boat coming!" Seyfert yelled as he swam out further.

Alvarez spat out sea water and said under his breath, "Unless there isn't."

The SEAL breast stroked to Steve and Lynda. "Float on your backs and I'll pull you. Teems, can you..." Seyfert spun around in the water, looking for his friend. The big biker was nowhere to be seen.

"I'll go, you stay with them!" Alvarez shouted. Before Seyfert could object, his new Army buddy disappeared beneath the waves.

Alvarez swam toward the last place he had seen Teems. The biker had only been a few feet away, but in the waning light and murkiness of the bay, Alvarez couldn't see anything. A flash of white through the darkness startled him, but he swam toward it anyway. The tall biker came into view as Alvarez swam in his direction.

Teems was frantically battling the grasping hands of half a dozen of the undead. They were standing on a rock, pipe, or sandbar that gave them the elevation in the deeper water to grab Teems. Alvarez swam in behind the first infected, thinking for a moment that he would cut the throat of his enemy, then realizing that would only alert it to his presence. It was still difficult to remember that these creatures wouldn't succumb to injuries a human adversary would.

He jammed his knife into the base of the skull of the thing in front of him. It instantly went limp and slowly collapsed. Alvarez yanked another thing away from his struggling friend and the creature immediately latched onto his tactical vest. Alvarez wasted no time in pushing his blade into its eye. He needed to breathe, but his friend likely needed it more, so he jammed the blade into the skull of another of the things.

Teems was kicking and pushing for all he was worth, but he couldn't shake loose the iron grip that held him firm. The big man put both feet on one of the things and pushed hard, rotten fingers and an entire hand tearing free of their owner. Handless, the creature couldn't grab him again.

Alvarez destroyed another of the creatures but the thing batted his knife away as it fell. He made a grab for it, but it sank into the darkness. *Please don't let me put my hand in it's friggin mouth*, he begged as he reached his hand around to the last thing's lower jaw. He put his other hand on the cap of the thing's head and gave a vicious twist. The thing's neck gave an audible snap, just as the fight left Teems. The army corporal grabbed the biker and swam the short distance to the surface but not before he felt his friend shudder several times. *Did he just fucking drown?* thought the soldier as he kicked to the surface.

Sputtering and coughing when they broke the surface, Alvarez gave a watery shout to his friends, "Pick your feet up! There's dead below us!"

Alvarez attempted CPR in the water. He held one arm out so Teems could float on his back and pressed hard on his chest. "One, two, three…"

Donna swam up to them and put her arms under his friend's back. "I'll hold, you press!"

"Four, five, six, seven…"

"Is he dead?" demanded Lynda, her voice just under a scream.

"Eighteen, nineteen, twenty…"

Teems' eyes opened, and Alvarez let loose a sigh of relief and ceased his compressions. The whites of Teems' eyes exploded into red at the same time their focus snapped toward the corporal. Teems lunged, but everything was more awkward in the water. The dead man latched onto the living man, and though Alvarez made noises that were undignified, he fought the thing off well. The thing that had been Teems clamped down on Alvarez' tactical glove. A tooth snapped off as it bit down on the Kevlar knuckle guard.

Alvarez let loose a yell, trying to wrench free his hand when the dead biker suddenly went slack and its bleeding eyes lost focus. The soldier pulled his hand free and swam back a bit before Teems body slid beneath the waves.

Donna trod water, her combat knife in her fist. "You bitten?"

"Yeah, he got me. Dunno if it broke the skin through the glove. We'll have to worry about that later." He spun to face Seyfert, Steve, and Lynda. "You guys ok?"

"No!" yelled Steve. "We are *not* fucking ok!"

"Let's swim out a bit further," the SEAL suggested. The five of them back stroked out another fifteen meters or so before they heard an engine.

Alvarez pointed northwest. "RHIB incoming,"

"It's a CRRC, Army," corrected Seyfert.

"Douche squid," said Alvarez with a huge half-smile.

HOBO WITH A SHOTGUN

I don't like shotguns. They're pretty to look at and I like the weight of them, but I like my rifle better.

I was told that firing rifle rounds inside a submarine was a bad idea. I get it, I do, but I have previously fired my rifle inside a container ship which was densely packed with the living dead. Nothing bad ever happened to me in that ship.

I mean other than a former friend of mine taking an enormous chunk out of my arm and a current friend shooting me in the side. I suppose I should be happy the round that hit me wasn't fired from a shotgun.

The point is, I like my rifle much better. I'm a decent shot now, but still no sniper. I miss and another round is chambered semi-automatically. I fire again and hopefully I drop a dead guy. I can do that thirty times before I need to switch magazines. Switching magazines takes me five seconds but only because I'm not good at it. Watch Remo switch out a mag. He can do it in less than a second. This stubby little shotgun holds eight shells. Eight. It takes forever to reload, too. One shell at a time.

We are firing number one buckshot as well. That's like a bunch of small steel balls a third of an inch in diameter coming out the business end of the gun. Aren't they gonna fucking bounce all over the place? Why would they want that in here? Inside a steel tube?

I found out ten seconds after that thought had pervaded my noggin. A lone infected stumbled into view in front of us. It didn't see us as it was curiously focused on a bulkhead. I drew my knife and summoned all the menace I could.

Harry didn't see it, either, as he had been pulling closed the door of the tiny room he had just cleared. I tapped him on the shoulder, pointed, and he gasped, "Shit!"

Now the friggin' thing knew we were there. It started toward us, that rasping hack echoing across the steel. I was going to smoke it with my knife and save both ammo and sound, but Captain Noise Discipline brought his weapon to bear, and we were subjected to screaming ears in a moment.

The thing's head just went away. Everything from the chin up simply ceased to exist. I mean, it was all over the vertical pipes and shit, but it sure as hell wasn't attached anymore, nor was it recognizable.

The kid was wiggling his pinkie in his ear. "Fuckin' asked for Salvos, but they said no."

I had no idea what he meant. I would have to ask Remo or Alvarez later. I liked that the kid was already loading another shell into his shotgun. I didn't like that a bunch more infected had decided to join the party.

I couldn't hear a god damned thing when it was over. It was like I had spent the entire night next to the amplifier at a Metallica concert. It actually hurt, and remember, I had stood up under a pipe a few hours ago.

I had no idea the length of this submarine, but it felt like we had snuck around in here for a mile or two. My head was pounding, and we had just dealt with another six infected. One may have been a Runner, but I had beheaded it with my 12 gauge before it could even fully turn in our direction.

Harry turned to me and said something. I really wish I had been able to hear it because it was the last thing he said to me. An infected grabbed him from the door we had both failed to clear, pulled him back and took an enormous hunk out of his trapezius and neck. Blood sprayed all over my face and I was temporarily blinded. I quickly dragged my forearm across my eyes and was able to see the thing, a ravaged sailor, swallowing the kid's important bits down before it went in for bite number two. I jabbed my SOG at the thing but missed the eye. I hit it in the mouth and the tip of the blade broke a tooth and went deep. Not deep enough though as the thing chomped down on the blade.

I punched forward with a palm strike, driving the steel into spine and the thing was spent. Both sailors collapsed to the deck. Both were still moving. I kicked the dead man until he was done moving, then tried to help Harry.

The poor kid was trying to hold in his red stuff and was failing miserably, his left hand over the right side of his neck. He coughed and blood dribbled from the corner of his mouth. Then he really coughed and expectorated more than I thought possible.

"Let me see it," I told him, but he didn't move his hand. "Let me see it!"

His hand came away and I knew this poor boy had moments left. He reached for his shotgun and fumbled with it. He was trying to get the barrel toward his face, but strength was leaving him quickly.

The gun clattered to the deck and his young eyes, so full of terror, locked onto mine.

"You won't turn. I promise. I also promise to kill every one of these fuckers."

The kid smiled, nodded, and died.

I could hear the dead coming for me from someplace forward, but I didn't turn to face them. This kid would stand up and try to kill me in the very near future. I had promised him I wouldn't let him turn.

The captain had one of the sailors give me thirty rounds of 9mm for my Sig. I had loaded them into my magazines on the way down to the galley. I drew my sidearm and pointed it at the boy's head. I thanked him and squeezed the trigger.

It is amazing how so many things can happen at once. Truly miraculous. When it's good stuff, it tends to lighten moods and can even save lives. When it's bad stuff, people die. This was bad. The kid's head snapped back as the bullet passed through his brain, hit the bulkhead, ricocheted, and hit me in the shin. I yelled like a bitch and dropped to the deck clutching my leg as I held my foot up. That was when the dead found me. It was also when someone of greater importance than I decided they needed a SITREP and my radio started asking pointed questions.

I had neither the time to bitch and whine about my leg nor to answer the phone. The dead were coming through a hatch fifteen feet in front of me. They sounded like they always sound: hungry.

With my ass on the deck, I took down two with my sidearm before I switched to the big guns. I angled the shotgun up at their nasty faces. The resulting mayhem is worthy of note, and also cemented the clear and certain fact that shotguns are fucking devastating. Three of the things collapsed from extreme pellet damage. I thought it odd that there weren't a few dozen pellets ricocheting all over the inside of this tin can, but hey, I'll take it. It's almost as if the people who had issued me this stubby cannon had thought things through.

A few more of the things stumbled over their dead brethren and I used that short space of time to drag my sissy ass up and shoot them. I jacked shells and fired them until the gun was empty. Rather than reload for the last few assholes, I picked up Harry's boom stick and boomed the last three dead away.

I stared at the carnage for a moment, my ears screaming as loudly as the agony in my noggin. I blinked, watching some black gooey shit drip down the bulkhead. I could feel more than hear a sound far off. It sounded like voices, yet I knew this portion of the sub was just dead things and me.

Military people are all about callsigns. It can't be, *Hey Bob, how's it going?* It has to be, Orca Seven, you take point, or in this case *Moray, SITREP! Moray, come in! Report Moray!* I was Moray Two and the sound I had heard was my radio demanding to know what was happening.

"Moray One is down," I told the radio. "Moray Two is proceeding with the mission. Nine tangos also down.

"Moray One, what is—"

I cut his ass off. He could stuff his questions. "My head hurts and the radio is drawing the dead to me. Kindly shut the fuck up. I'll turn the radio back on when I'm done with these dead dipshits."

"Moray One! That is not—"

He could suck it. I switched off the radio. Remo will be pissed when he reads this and I'm sure the captain would fume, but I was done being someone else's bitch. I was going to be my own bitch. I tried to roll my pant leg up, but it hurt too much when it started to roll by my boo boo. I used my knife to cut the pants and was surprised to see very little blood. The bullet hadn't penetrated my leg but it sure as shit had opened me up a bit. It looked like... well, it looked like a fucking bullet hole, but I could see it didn't get into my leg. Must have had just enough oomph to dig a little hole in me but not enough to warrant surgery.

Whatever.

The ringing in my dome was better, but I still couldn't hear my feet on the deck. I felt thumps from in front of me and knew I was not as devoid of the living dead as I had hoped. I reloaded the kid's shotgun and then mine. Sixteen shots with eighteen loose.

Picture this, Dear Reader: My bad ass limping down the corridor, a stubby shotgun in each hand, clearing doors and closing hatches behind me. I was tired of being cool. Now I just wanted to kill dead people.

One such thing in a flannel shirt moved past the hatch in front of me. I had seen him when he was alive but didn't know his name. It hit me then that all these dead people were fresh. Whatever had happened, it hadn't been an infected who had gotten aboard, it must have been someone who had died here. Bites couldn't be hidden as everyone underwent a thorough exam before being let into the sub.

I pondered that as he did a Crazy Ivan and looked right at me. The thing bared its teeth, growling and I moved forward. My shotgun was on a sling, but the kid's had been devoid of one, so I let mine dangle and opted for the blade. Flannel shirt did that cheetah thing when it got close, but I dodged and stuck the metal in the back of its head when it went past.

The guy was fresh, but his head was soft if that makes sense. My knife went into Flannel's noggin deep He didn't give a shit.

As he was pushing himself up to eat me, I couldn't help but ponder the situation. While not commonplace, I had certainly been witness to this phenomenon before, and like then, it was unnerving. He was getting up with four inches of polymer handle sticking out of his dome at a bit of an angle like a pencil stuck in an apple. He had an equal length of steel inside his head but for whatever reason, the brain damage he most certainly was suffering wasn't enough to destroy him.

I kicked his back and he fell face down. Of course, he immediately wanted to stand, so I stomped my size twelves on his dome until he stopped moving. I'm a righty and so used my right foot, but this was also my boo boo leg, so it hurt. A lot. I didn't like it.

Retrieving the knife took a sec, but it came out with a sucking sound after a few tugs. I wiped the blade on the dead thing and moved on. I cleared another four small rooms and came to a dead end. There was a round, blue hatch in front of me, but it was sealed and there was something on the other side of it banging to get through. Sounded like a few somethings.

Whereas the other hatches that I had come through had clearly been installed to keep water from flooding multiple compartments, this one screamed go away, with a side order of fuck you.

Both the FU and the go away spoke to me, so I did. I turned around and switched on my radio. "Command, this is Moray-two."

"Moray-Two! SITREP!"

"Yeah, what the hell did you think I was calling for? A Pizza?" This last was met with a disdain I could clearly hear in the voice on the other side of the radio, but I was in no mood for shit and let him know it and cut him off. "I came to a big blue hatch that I am not too keen on opening. We eliminated all hostiles and closed all other hatches and doors all the way down here, but there are definitely bad guys on the other side of this blue hatch. I also feel compelled to express that they may be upset at being shut in there."

"Command copies all, Moray-Two. Sending a team to assist. Sit tight."

The radio went silent and all I could think was *sit tight?* I started re-thinking the pizza ask. I glanced at my surroundings and realized that while I've written down quite a bit about shotguns and zombies, I haven't regaled you guys about submarines.

The corridors can be any color and are not smooth. They are jam packed with all kinds of shit on the walls and ceilings. Pipes and dials and boxy stuff that's probably super important. But the thing is, with all the stuff, there is zero clutter, and everything is spotlessly clean. It isn't like you're stepping over a pair of boots, but you do sometimes have to step around a red box with a diagram, or thread yourself through a tight squeeze. There are no fat guys on subs.

I would describe it as purposeful. I knew everything was there for a reason even if I didn't know what it was or the reason for it.

Another thing is the sound. There's none. If not for the continued pounding of the shitheads on the other side of this blue hatch, I would be able to hear a pin drop. Also, this thing is a boat, right? The captain calls it "his boat". Well, it's floating in the water, but it's solid as fuck. It doesn't move like a boat on the surface would. Like, with the waves and stuff? It just sits here all heavy and deadly.

While I was pondering what to tell you about submarines, some things pushed their way into my brain. Remo being shot. Alvarez and Donna not being accounted for. Richy being scratched. That last one was making me sweat. At the end of the day, there wasn't a lot I could do about it but worry. I loved this kid. The prick who had caused him to be scratched was gone and that could end up being a shit-show, but hopefully the captain would see things our way. If not, we would have to run. I wasn't about to have Ship or any of us be subjected to Navy frontier justice.

I absentmindedly rubbed the back of one leg over the shin of the other and the fact that I had shot myself took the driver's seat of my thinking. Ow. I looked at the wound through the slice I had made in my BDUs. It was very angry with me. Already yellow and purple with a single thin rivulet of blood running toward my sock, the little hole hurt.

I heard sounds back the way I had come. It was either the guys on the way to help me, or I had missed some dead people.

"Moray-two, this is Barracuda squad. Hold your fire!" came echoing through the steel corridor.

Morays, barracudas, sharks. WTF? Sub dudes are weird.

"Relax," I yelled back. "I'm not going to shoot you unless you try to eat me. Or prefer ranch dressing."

A guy I hadn't met stepped through the open hatch with a suppressed MP5 and a smile. "Ranch sucks."

Three other guys and wielding the same stubby shotgun I had and a woman stepped through next. The woman was Kat. She looked right at me. "I wasn't stayin' again. There's two idiots back there guarding the FOB now, so shut it."

These boys looked like they had been through the ringer. They all had blood on their clothes, and I knew immediately they had been fighting the dead on board just as I had. I had to admire their lack of fear. Or maybe they were just too tired to be scared because they looked exhausted, too.

"This is it," the lead dude said. We've cleared the entire boat except for this corridor." He leaned against the red, boxy thing that was sticking out from the wall. I have no idea what it was, but there were a bunch of them in this corridor and they would be great for hiding an infected or two. "There are six crew unaccounted for, but we're not sure on the civvies. We've got three different tallies that give us between nine and sixteen. That plus the six crew means this could get dicey fast."

I loved this kid's math. Instant worst case scenario. His head was in a good place.

"Yeah, but we have these," I added, jacking a shell into my shotgun for emphasis. I had just reloaded, so what I actually did was jack a shell out of the shotty and it clattered to the floor, rolling under the red thing.

Idiot.

When I was done picking up my shotgun shell I stared at the kid, my face burning. He had an eyebrow raised and I wanted to kill him for it. "So, twenty-two possible infected an inch away through this round steel door? If we don't plug the hatch with them or if there are any fast ones, we're dead."

"We have another team on the other side of the corridor waiting for us behind a hatch just like this one. We'll breach at the same time and catch the dead in a cross-fire."

I furrowed my brow. "Is this a straight corridor?"

"Yeah, we're at the back of the boat."

"So, won't we be shooting at each other?"

The kid blinked. "Acceptable risk. The dead will be between us."

My look went from concerned to surprised. There was still concern, but surprise was winning facial cues at the moment. Kat and I exchanged glances.

"Kid," I started, and that was a huge mistake because I could tell he didn't like being called kid. "I've done this before." I pointed at the hatch. "You hear that?"

"Yeah."

Everybody could hear the shitheads pounding their fists to stumps on the other side of the steel.

"Let's join the band and start banging this drum from this side. Every dead fucker in the corridor should come to try and eat the noise. Call your buddies on the far side, they open their hatch and start blasting. If the dead start to get too close to them, they shut their hatch, call us, and we open ours and shoot." I shook my head and shrugged. "Rinse and repeat until we run outta dead guys."

Not a lot of things to tell after that. The kid jutted his lower lip out in consideration, then made a call. "Lamprey, this is Barracuda One."

Now we had lampreys. All I know about lampreys is I don't want to meet one. The kid told the other kids the plan, we executed it, and in about eight minutes, we were inside the corridor, a bunch of bodies on the deck, staring at our lamprey counterparts across the gooey carnage. We had never even opened our hatch.

The Barracuda kid called the captain and began to report. "You guys have any beer on board?" I asked one of the sailors. The captain must have heard me because he said out loud that he had a case of Scotch in his quarters and everybody on the fish teams was getting two fingers.

Usually, the hardest stuff I drank was Bud Light, but I would swallow every drop of that Scotch today no matter how much like lighter fluid it tasted.

TAKEN

Ship knelt on the deck and tapped Remo on the shoulder. Remo, in quite a bit of pain, glanced up at his enormous friend. Ship chin wagged toward Alcatraz. Two guys were wading through the dead, one with a sword and one with a bat. Remo put his head back on his makeshift pillow.

"Billy," was all he said and closed his eyes. The corpsman holding the IV bag squinted toward shore as did the one working on Remo's side. "Mmm," the Marine added as the corpsman shoved a needle into the bullet hole.

It didn't take long for Billy and his comrade to dispatch the dead, after which they took a brief respite against a stone retaining wall which held back shrubbery and a portion of the hill.

The quiet engine of a Zodiac style boat drifted to Ship's ears, and he stole a sideways glimpse to the left. A small black boat, the same one which had been dispatched from the Florida a few minutes ago was zipping across the waves. Ship brought his binoculars to his eyes and was happy to see Alvarez and Donna bumping up and down in the boat. The big man smiled and was about to tell his friend that the last of their rag-tag group was about to come aboard but thought better of it and didn't disturb the wounded Marine.

He had to admit that every one of the people in his group was top of their game. Ten years ago, he had realized that society was no place for him, and he had moved to the wilds of New Hampshire to escape it. He had still had ties to the world, but none he couldn't sever had he needed. The dead had taken care of that for him. He shook his head. His father had always told him that everything was a miracle. Ship had to admit that the dead coming back to life had been somewhat miraculous, even if the miracle hadn't been what was expected.

Ship redirected his gaze and saw another miracle. Billy and the guy he was with were sharing a can of something, passing it back and forth and guzzling. The guy with Billy drew his forearm across his lips then began spitting and wiping his mouth with his hand. Both this guy and Billy were oblivious to what was coming at them from both sides. Ship squinted, then brought the binoculars to his eyes again.

He blinked, then rubbed his eyes and peered through the field glasses once more. There appeared to be two groups of three people sneaking up on the two men. They twitched like Runners, but not nearly as fervently. The shakes were considerably weaker. Both groups of three cast furtive glances at the sub as if they were afraid of it. All six exhibited the red eyes of infected.

Ship stomped over to a group of two sailors with rifles. He pointed at Billy and his friend sixty meters or so away leaning on a rock wall. One of the sailors held his own pair of binoculars to his eyes. "Yeah? It's that guy that the dead don't give a shit about. He just killed a bunch of them."

Ship rolled his eyes and pulled the binoculars a bit to the left. "Who the hell are they?" the sailor asked.

Ship grabbed the man's rifle. The sailor put up a brief struggle and everyone started yelling, but Ship ended up with the weapon. He put optic to eye and sighted on the closest infected to Billy. It had been a larger man and wore clothes that were not as ragged as most of the infected. He pulled the trigger just as one of the sailors grabbed the barrel of the rifle and the shot went wide. The round hit the rock wall and the three infected on the left first ducked, then scrambled up the wall and disappeared into the foliage. Billy became aware of people shooting at him and searched for the source. He waved at the men and women on the deck of the sub. They appeared to be fighting.

"What are they doin'?" asked Bob.

"I dunno. I mean they wouldn't shoot at us, right?"

Billy and Bob turned their heads slowly and stared at each other. Billy raised his eyebrows. "Right?"

"Oh shit!" stammered Bob and brought his bat up. Three infected sprinted at them from the right.

Billy put his Pepsi can on the rock wall and waited for the Runners to come. "Easy peasy."

The things sprinted directly at Bob and when he swung in anticipation of their attack, they halted their run. Bob overswung and one of the creatures grabbed the bat, pulling it out of unsuspecting hands after a very brief struggle. The three things backed up a step as Billy charged, sword held high.

The infected in front put its hand forward and growled, "Stop!"

Billy did. He looked the things up and down. They were feverish and twitchy, definitely infected, but they didn't attack and did one of them just talk?

He made to swing the sword again because he had clearly just made the leap from crazy to bat-shit crazy and couldn't have heard what he had heard.

"Stop!" the same creature snarled again.

Billy leaned in toward Bob. "You heard that, right?"

"Uhh, yeah..."

Billy regarded the creature. "You guys can talk now?"

The thing leapt forward, hitting Billy in a tackle before he could swing. The one with the bat swung it and hit Bob in the shoulder, Bob letting everyone know that it had hurt. Three more of the things burst from the shrubs just above the rock wall, hopped the railing and were on Billy in a moment. Bob tried to assist, but the one with the bat dropped it and threw a haymaker to the side of Bob's head. Bob crumpled to the ground.

Six of the demons fought Billy to the ground and disarmed him. They buffeted his head until he was unconscious and dragged him over the wall and out of sight. As an afterthought, the one who had knocked out Bob, grabbed the baseball bat and took it.

A lone undead stumbled toward the unconscious Bob. When it noticed him, it picked up its pace a bit and stretched one emaciated arm downward in front of it at an angle. When it got to within ten feet of its victim, the sprinting infected with the bat vaulted from the shrubs over the rail and thumped the dead woman in the head with the weapon. She fell to the ground and the Runner smashed the cranium of the thing until it was a splintered mess. The Runner made a quick glance toward the submarine, then disappeared back into the foliage. As an afterthought, a twitchy hand reached from the shrubs and pulled the soda off the rock wall and out of sight.

Several sailors raised their weapons toward Ship. They had helped save his life a few hours ago and he was now at the business end of their guns. The giant pointed furiously at Alcatraz, and made odd hand gestures, but none of the seamen could sign.

"What the hell is he saying?"

"I have no idea, but he stole my gun!"

The big man continued to point.

"Look at the damn island, you stupid squid jackasses!" croaked Remo from his spot on the deck.

221

Two of them spun to see one infected strike down another with a baseball bat, then disappear.

The ground was littered with bodies in varying states of decay, but Ship could make out Bob on the ground. Half a dozen undead rounded the bend and another four fell down the hill. All moved toward the hapless unconscious man.

Ship threw his hands up in frustration and moved to Remo. The men kept their rifle barrels on him. The CRRC pulled up to the sub and Seyfert threw a line to a sailor. "What the hell is going on here?" demanded the SEAL.

"Guy took my gun!" one of the sailors yelled petulantly.

Ship started signing frantically to Seyfert, but the SEAL had no idea what he was saying.

"There's a man down on the island in that pile of dead people," Remo told them.

Every sailor on the deck, Seyfert included, stared at Alcatraz.

Ship and Seyfert moved first. "Up and out!" he shouted at Donna, Steve, and Lynda. They climbed from the rigid inflatable up the cargo net and Ship yanked them onto the deck. Seyfert told Alvarez and the sailor piloting the small craft to stay and he and Ship climbed into the boat.

"Wait!"

All heads turned again to see the guy with the torn face thumping down the steel. He climbed down the cargo netting and into the boat.

"Where are we going?"

"We got a man down on the island," Seyfert told him. "We're going to get him."

"Great!" The guy narrowed his eyes and thumbed at the boat pilot, "Who's this guy?"

The guy pulled the line from Seyfert and dropped it in the boat, "Hooper."

"You're shitting me…"

The boat sped toward the island twenty feet away. "I'm not."

It took just a few seconds for the CRRC to make contact with the cut stone embankment. Seyfert, Ship, Alvarez, and the guy with the scratched face leapt from the boat and climbed up the stones. Ship sprinted toward three infected, swinging his machete when he had closed the gap. The head of the first one tumbled to the concrete walkway, as did the arm of the second one. Ship's machete had gone through the neck of the first and stuck in the side of the second after severing its arm. He gave a mighty kick and number two went flying backwards, the machete sliding out of its side. Number three reached for Ship, but a bullet from Alvarez' rifle dropped it.

Seyfert and Torn Face had made it to the unconscious man. "Shit, it's Bob," the SEAL blurted. "We could have left him here and he would have been fine! Cover me and I'll carry him."

"No! You're a better shot than me. You cover until I can get him to Ship."

In the end it didn't matter. Fifty or so infected were coming from the left and a dozen or so rolled down the hill to the right, but they were sixty feet away. Shots from the Florida dropped several as well. Ship sprinted back to the group and threw Bob into a fireman's carry.

Infected were now coming from the right as well, around the bend. Seyfert realized there were hundreds and that bullets would be half-measures in the long run. The group steadily made their way to the boat, covering Ship while he carried an unconscious Bob.

As Seyfert was pushing the boat away from the embankment, the pilot pointed back towards Alcatraz. The guy with the shredded face was running back toward where Bob had been picked up. A calico cat sat on the stone wall licking its paw. The dead were closing and the idiot either didn't see them or didn't care. He made it to the cat and the animal didn't move. He grabbed it and made to leave when an arm snaked out of the foliage and latched on to his wrist. It pulled him into the wrought iron railing hard where he smacked his head on one of the posts, stunning him. Two other infected leapt from the bushes and pummeled him until he was down. Two more ran headlong into the closest group of dead a mere twenty feet away. They fought and pushed the dead until the three Runners who had captured their quarry were able to manhandle him into the foliage. Rifle shots sounded, but it was too late, he was gone. The cat jumped back up on the stone wall and sat.

Ship gently placed Bob on the boat and with a triumphant smile. He glanced at Alvarez for reassurance, only to see the soldier aiming his rifle back at the island. Ship spun, not fully understanding what was happening.

Alvarez made to leap from the boat, but Seyfert grabbed him by his vest. "No!" You'll never make it, look!"

The dead were streaming toward this side of the island. Dozens milled about near the area where Ship's friend had been taken. Hundreds trudged from both sides of the hill or tumbled down it.

Ship snapped his fingers until he got Alvarez' attention.

"They took him," the soldier said, dejected.

Ship whipped his head back toward Alcatraz and immediately set his mind to calculations. All scenarios led to his death and if he were dead, he couldn't help his friend. More full of anger than sorrow, the big man lifted four fingers to his mouth. He ushered forth a whistle so loud that the rest of the boat covered their ears. Every dead head on the island focused on the CRRC and they all began their arduous trek toward fresh meat.

The cat leapt from the wall and sprinted toward the boat, quickly weaving through the shuffling feet of the dead. The animal deftly moved down the embankment and jumped into the boat, where Ship picked it up and looked into its eyes.

The giant man held the cat close, scratching the back of its head as the inflatable boat sped back toward the USS Florida.

This time, I'll find you, Ship thought.

AFTER

My head always seems to hurt in the friggin' apocalypse. Some entity has decided that my noggin is the world's punching bag, and I don't fucking like it.

I was moving, but not of my own volition. Someone was dragging me, but I must be on something because I could only feel the ground through a barrier. My plan was to flip out and kill whoever had me, but I was trussed up quite well. I opened my eyes and surveyed my surroundings, noting the sun had gone to bed.

I was on a sled, a kid's toboggin actually, being dragged up a dirt path away from the water. My captors were silent as they pulled me, but I could hear ragged breathing. I looked left and saw an equally ridiculous sled being towed right next to me. It also had an occupant. Billy lay on a piece of plywood, a trickle of blood escaping his hair line and left nostril. I couldn't help but be grateful to my abductors that I had warranted an actual sled and not just a piece of wood.

I was able to make out the shadow of a medium-sized rowboat twenty feet away in the moonlight behind us. I had never seen that boat before, but I had a sneaking suspicion I had just taken a ride in it. I lifted my gaze a bit higher, and I could just make out Alcatraz. It looked very far away.

Fighting these assholes was impossible as they had rolled me up in some type of plastic wrap, so I opted for conversation.

"Where are you taking me, shitheads?"

The dude on the left of me jumped like I had fired a shotgun next to him. The dragging stopped but I couldn't see the guy's face in the darkness.

"Yoo-hoo, anybody there?" I demanded sarcastically.

A figure stepped into view, and he leaned down to search my eyes. The guy was infected as fuck, his red eyes evident even in the low light. They darted all over my face looking for who knows what from three inches away. He had minty fresh breath and that freaked me out.

"Anybody else?" I pleaded, no longer wanting to look at this monster. It was the fucking infected, asshole, Runner-douche from the machinery room on Alcatraz.

"*Your* head is shit," it growled in an impossible voice that will haunt me forever.

Oh shit…

The thing stood and regarded one of his infected pals. He pointed at me and growled a command, "Sleep him."

The good-looking Asian kid from the boat who had helped me not get eaten was also there. He shrugged an apology and raised his fist.

"No! No no! Wait! No, nononono!"

His fist came crashing down and my headache went away.

The End

ACKNOWLEDGEMENTS

Seriously, writing a book takes a vast amount of time and patience. I'm a hobby writer so it takes me longer. I suck at it, so it takes me longer still. Thanking folks for helping during the process is the hardest part for me. It's the most difficult because of my poor record keeping. Firstly, as always, I must thank my family. Without them I'd be less than I am. To the folks who helped with this tome; Tim Ricketts, Kristi Cantor, the indomitable Allen Gamboa, and Janis Worrell: Thank you from the bottom of my heart for making this book suck less. Thanks to the folks at Horror Writer's Ink Facebook page. You're all crazy. Probably why we get along so well. Thank you to all our service members, here and not, for doing what you do. Your job is at once perilous and thankless. If you can accept a small measure of gratitude from me it would make my day, and hopefully yours too. Lastly, if you've made it this far, Thank you. Give me a shout out and chuck me a friend request on Horror Writer's Ink, or my personal Facebook page. I'd love to speak with you.

CHECK OUT OTHER GREAT ZOMBIE NOVELS

900 MILES
by S. Johnathan Davis

John is a killer, but that wasn't his day job before the Apocalypse.

In a harrowing 900 mile race against time to get to his wife just as the dead begin to rise, John, a business man trapped in New York, soon learns that the zombies are the least of his worries, as he sees first-hand the horror of what man is capable of with no rules, no consequences and death at every turn.

Teaming up with an ex-army pilot named Kyle, they escape New York only to stumble across a man who says that he has the key to a rumored underground stronghold called Avalon..... Will they find safety? Will they make it to Johns wife before it's too late?

Get ready to follow John and Kyle in this fast paced thriller that mixes zombie horror with gladiator style arena action!

WHITE FLAG OF THE DEAD
by Joseph Talluto

Millions died when the Enillo Virus swept the earth. Millions more were lost when the victims of the plague refused to stay dead, instead rising to slaughter and feed on those left alive. For survivors like John Talon and his son Jake, they are faced with a choice: Do they submit to the dead, raising the white flag of surrender? Or do they find the will to fight, to try and hang on to the last shreds or humanity?

CHECK OUT OTHER GREAT ZOMBIE NOVELS

DEAD PULSE RISING
by K. Michael Gibson

TOWER OF THE DEAD
by J.V. Roberts

CHECK OUT OTHER GREAT ZOMBIE NOVELS

VACCINATION
by Phillip Tomasso

What if the H7N9 vaccination wasn't just a preventative measure against swine flu?

It seemed like the flu came out of nowhere and yet, in no time at all the government manufactured a vaccination. Were lab workers diligent, or could the virus itself have been man-made? Chase McKinney works as a dispatcher at 9-1-1. Taking emergency calls, it becomes immediately obvious that the entire city is infected with the walking dead. His first goal is to reach and save his two children.

Could the walls built by the U.S.A. to keep out illegal aliens, and the fact the Mexican government could not afford to vaccinate their citizens against the flu, make the southern border the only plausible destination for safety?

ZOMBIE, INC
by Chris Dougherty

"WELCOME! To Zombie, Inc. The United Five State Republic's leading manufacturer of zombie defense systems! In business since 2027, Zombie, Inc. puts YOU first. YOUR safety is our MAIN GOAL! Our many home defense options - from Ze Fence® to Ze Popper® to Ze Shed® - fit every need and every budget. Use Scan Code "TELL ME MORE!" for your FREE, in-home*, no obligation consultation! *Schedule your appointment with the confidence that you will NEVER HAVE TO LEAVE YOUR HOME! It isn't safe out there and we know it better than most! Our sales staff is FULLY TRAINED to handle any and all adversarial encounters with the living and the undead". Twenty-five years after the deadly plague, the United Five State Republic's most successful company, Zombie, Inc., is in trouble. Will a simple case of dwindling supply and lessening demand be the end of them or will Zombie, Inc. find a way, however unpalatable, to survive?

Made in the USA
Middletown, DE
06 September 2022